OSCAR

SECRETS AND LIES BOOK 5

B J Alpha

Published by BJ Alpha

Edited by Zainab Heart Full of Reads Editing Services

Proofread by Anna at Potters Editing

Cover Model Alex Badia

Photographer RafaGCatala

Book Cover Design K.B. Designs

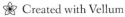 Created with Vellum

OSCAR

Secrets and Lies Series Book 5

BJALPHA

Dedication

To everyone who is hidden in the shadows.
I hope you find the strength to one day step into the light.
BJ Alpha

AUTHORS NOTE

WARNING: This book contains triggers. It has sensitive and explicit storylines such as graphic sexual scenes, violence, stalker tendencies, and strong language.

It is recommended for readers aged eighteen and over.

Prologue

Eight Years Old

   Oscar

Controlling my breathing, I close my eyes at the mention of my name. The man I hate spits it out like vitriol. "Face it. Oscar's a feckin pansy. Not cut out for this life." He flicks his cigar with the tip of his finger, sending the ash onto the floor—the floor my ma will have to clean.

Da takes a deep breath, then snaps with a cold voice, "I told ya before, Don. Don't come ere into my house and disrespect my family. There's a fine line, and you're crossing over it."

My uncle holds his hands up with a smirk before flicking more ash onto the floor.

The door quietly opens, and I shuffle my feet back further, the heels of my sneakers clipping the skirting board.

Ma walks into the office, and her gaze drifts over the

room before making eye contact with my da. She looks nervous, and I hate it. I despise them.

"Don is taking the boys away to the cabin next week," Da informs her as though he's in a business meeting.

Her shoulders sag in defeat, knowing she doesn't have a choice. Disappointed, I mimic her action, but then I remember what Bren told me. I'm mafia too. Tightening my posture, I watch through the netted curtain that's currently hiding me.

"Bren has a game on Friday. Maybe the boys could stay home this break?" Ma mumbles the words out, causing my father's jaw to clench tightly at her words... at her voicing an opinion. Women shouldn't have an opinion, not in our world. She's undermining him, in his house, in his office. My heart beats faster, my throat suddenly dry.

"The boys will go with Don." My Da's voice is low and deadly. My heart sinks. I hate the woods, all the flies, insects, and dirt. I hate the fact I'm the only one that doesn't like it. The fishing, the shooting, and everything. I hate it all. I clench my fists as I feel my body vibrate with anxiety.

Ma nods, her head dipping low.

"Oscar won't be joining them." When Da mentions my name, my head perks up, hope stirring inside me. Maybe I will get to stay home with Ma?

"He's going to a clinic."

Her eyes blaze with fire. "No." Her voice is sharp, determined, and strong. My ma should be none of those things; not to the naked eye, anyway.

Da flicks his eyes toward Don, and he takes it as his cue to leave the room.

He rises from his chair slowly, and just as his hand touches the door handle to leave, he turns his head to look over his shoulder at my ma. His dark black eyes drill into my ma's, his words cold and unsettling, an accusation in his voice. "Those boys are the closest thing I have to sons. I'll treat them like they're my own." A creepy smile paints his lips. My ma doesn't like it either; I can tell because her face is ghostly pale, and she turns her head away from him.

The door clicks shut, and my da starts his tirade, making me wince at his deep voice. "Do not feckin undermine me, woman!" His thick finger points in her direction, the veins on his neck protruding aggressively.

Ma stands still, fidgeting with her hands. I don't like it; I hate it when he talks to her like this. My knuckles turn white.

Ma raises her head. "You're not sending him away, Brennan. I won't have it." Her chest heaves as she knowingly goes against my da's demand. His jaw locks in annoyance; she shouldn't even try to change his mind, even I know that.

"Please." Her voice breaks into a whisper. She pulls a small blue teddy from her apron pocket, the one she always carries with her, and begins playing with the bear's ears as though it's a way to comfort her. Odd.

"Not another." She chokes on a sob but still doesn't shift her eyes from Da. And they say women aren't strong!

My da's eyes lock onto the small soft toy, and his

shoulders sag, a softness I've never seen passing over his face.

I can't believe it.

He's giving in.

"Fine." He stands, his tone clipped. "But ya need to sort him out, Cyn. He's weak. There's no room for weakness in the mafia."

Ma ducks her head in understanding. The moment the door closes, she relaxes and lets out a heavy sigh.

"You can come out now, Oscar." Her soft voice fills the room.

I don't know how she always knows where I am; the thought annoys me. I need to do better. Hide better.

I step out from behind the netting and the heavy curtain.

Her blue eyes soften on mine. I slowly approach her as she kneels down in front of me. Ma always does this; it's like her way of saying we're equal—leveled.

"You can't always hide in the shadows, Oscar. Sometimes you have to step out and be seen." I try to figure out what she means, and as if realizing my confusion, she simplifies it for me. "You're so much more than what you think you are, honey. You just have to see it." She brushes her hand down my face, and I revel in the fact I don't wince at her touch. A warmth spreads through me; it doesn't feel like something is crawling over my skin that I'm desperate to get rid of it.

I shuffle on my feet. She's wrong, though. My body coils tight. "I'm not like them. I'm different." I bite my bottom lip, clench, and unclench my hands, agitated because I can't make her see. Can't make her understand. Can't make her hear me.

"Remember what Doctor Yates told you about the breathing?" Ma looks at me pointedly, her voice low.

I nod and begin the process of doing the four, four, four technique, the one I prefer out of all the different ones Doctor Yates has taught me. I breathe in and count to four, hold my breath and count to four, then exhale through my mouth and count to four.

"Now, shall we try again?" Ma waits patiently for me to do another set of four, four, four.

"I'm different," I tell her, my irritation almost gone.

"You are."

She does understand, after all. She knows I'm not like them. I open my mouth to tell her so, but she puts her hand up. "You're different, but you're not less, Oscar. In fact, you can be so much more." She smiles softly at me before standing and leaving me with more questions whirling around in my mind.

What the heck does that mean?

Ducking my head out of Da's office door, I step out but come to a halt when I find Bren waiting for me in my bedroom. He's laid on my bed, and I hate it. That's my fucking bed. My hands ball into fists.

Bren notices the change in me and jumps up off the bed. "Shit. Sorry, little man." He laughs a weird laugh, one that shows he doesn't really find it funny. I tilt my head to the side, trying to figure him out.

Why would he laugh at something that's not funny?

"What did they say?" His eyes scan over my face as if looking for some sort of clue.

5

"You're all going to the cabin next week."

He swallows harshly at the news, his sulking body showing he's unhappy. He wanted to play at the football game next week because he's really good at it.

Out of all my brothers, I like Bren the best. He's the oldest, next in line to become the Don of the family, even though Da is horrible to him. Apparently, it makes you a man, but I'm pretty sure it makes Da an ass. My lip turns up at my own joke, but I choose not to voice it because it's mine, and I prefer not to share.

Walking over to my desk, I open the bottom drawer and pull out the sock I have stuffed at the back, then hand it over to Bren.

His face mars in confusion at the slight weight at the end. He opens the sock up and dips his finger in to see what it contains before pulling out a bunch of the pills.

"What are these?" His eyes dart to mine in worry.

I lift my shoulder. "My medication."

"You stopped taking them?" He stands there, mouth agape, but I just stare at him because why is he asking me questions when the evidence is right there in front of him? Agitation at his stupidity bubbles inside me, but I convince myself this is Bren. I like him.

I point toward the sock. "Just the red ones."

Bren glares down at the pills, then back at me. "You don't like the red ones?" Again with the dumb questions...

I shake my head.

Bren's eyes search my face as if waiting for an explanation.

I'm not about to tell him I hate red. Hate it because it

reminds me of the blood splatter on the crisp white sheets the first time I pulled the canula from my arm, the time they realized I'd have to be strapped down if they ever wanted to do that to me again.

"What are you giving me these for?"

Is he completely dumb? He's going to be the head of this family one day, and he doesn't even know why I gave them to him?

I sigh in annoyance. "Drug him, then you can go to your game."

His eyes almost bug out, then he shakes his head as though pulling himself together before swallowing thickly. "How many?"

My mind whizzes with answers. If Bren gives Da too many, it could kill him, then my da might not listen to all the horrible things Uncle Don says. But then Bren would be in trouble, and I like him. Since he recently got over a severe leg injury, he's been working hard to get back in shape for the game he loves so much. Da thinks he's going to the gym to get bigger muscles, but really, he's going to play football at school. I know because I saw him pack his kit bag; he put his finger over his lips and told me he trusted me.

Loyalty is everything in the mafia, especially to family.

I might not be strong, and I might not be able to fight like the others, but I can be loyal. Especially to Bren.

"Five. No more; otherwise, he might have a heart attack and die."

Bren's lip turns up at the side. "Thanks, brother."

7

My chest swells with pride at how inclusive Bren is with me.

"Ya know, Ma's right. Different doesn't mean less." He stares at me before straightening up and walking out of my room.

Her words play in my mind like a tape recorder.

You can't always hide in the shadows, Oscar. Sometimes you have to step out and be seen.

Chapter One

Thirty-three years old

Oscar

I straighten the cufflink on my shirt again. Why the hell does the damn thing keep facing the wrong fucking way? My jaw clenches in irritation.

The buzzing from my tablet on my nightstand alerts me that my eight o'clock appointment has just arrived. Perfect. I need to ease some of the pent-up aggression I feel, and tonight, I get to relieve it.

I take a deep breath and wait to hear the usual soft click of the bedroom door down the corridor.

Nothing.

That's odd.

Zara knows to shut the door behind her.

Perhaps I missed it.

No, I wouldn't have missed it. Come to think of it, I didn't hear the rhythmic click of her heels on the marble floor either.

Very odd.

I grab my tablet from the nightstand and ignore the alerts; I'll deal with those later after Zara receives her punishment.

Closing my door, I step out into the corridor.

Silence.

I tilt my head to listen for her.

Nothing.

I quicken my pace in annoyance until I come to a complete halt because there's a woman standing in my kitchen.

A woman I don't recognize.

A woman that is most definitely not Zara.

She gasps when she sees me, and the sound goes straight to my cock. I take the opportunity to take her in before I figure out what the hell she's doing in my kitchen, past security, for Christ's sake.

Taller than Zara, her long dark hair trails down her back in soft curls, and her figure is fuller than my normal, than Zara. She has red lipstick on that makes my jaw tick in annoyance, a short silver dress that shows off too much cleavage, making me ball my fists, and silver heels to match her dress.

I slowly trail my gaze back up her body; when my eyes latch onto her chest, she flushes pink around her neck and up into her cheeks. The thought of her being uncomfortable under my scrutiny makes me smile. Or at least quirk my lip; Bren said it's almost a smile.

Her face has a scattering of freckles she's tried to hide with make-up, and I don't like it. She shouldn't hide behind make-up.

On closer inspection, her hair has a red tinge to it,

10

close enough for her to be labeled as a redhead rather than a brunette.

"Are you done?" Her jaw clenches tight.

She stands stoically, still under my scrutiny. My eyes catch on to the manual sitting on the counter and then back to her.

"You're not Zara."

The woman scoffs. "Wow, you're observant. Nope, I'm not Zara. I'm Paige." She holds her hand out to greet me and smiles, her green eyes sparkling playfully.

Her mocking tone irks me; I don't like it. Not one bit. My hands ball into fists. I move toward her, and she steps back, making my eyebrows furrow in confusion. Her face pales, and it's then I notice that she's staring at my fisted hands.

My heart beats faster as I wonder how I can reassure her I'm not going to hurt her. Not like that, at least.

Ma always told me to use words. I do my breathing technique as quickly as possible, and when I open my eyes, Paige's have softened slightly, the concern almost gone.

Strange.

"I won't hurt you." I plead into her eyes.

She nods in understanding, swallowing heavily.

"Zara has gone on vacation with another client," Paige explains.

Lie.

There are no other clients.

Only me. I pay enough for them never to need another client. I don't share.

"Client?" I query, raising a disbelieving brow.

"Apparently so. Some rich guy she's screwing anyway." She waves her hand around my apartment as though making a point at my own wealth.

Slowly, I move around her, scanning her body from top to bottom. She fills the dress out perfectly, and although she is bigger than I normally would look for in a woman, I'm not deterred by her. No, if anything, I'm intrigued. I touch her hair. Normally red would put me off, but the tinge of red in her hair is so subtle I don't even dislike it.

"Your hair's red."

"Yeah." Her voice comes out breathy, and I wonder what it will sound like when I bring her to orgasm.

"I don't like red," I clip flatly.

She turns her face sideways. "Do you want me to change it?"

I think on the question for a minute. Do I? Do I want her to change it? Ma always tried to encourage me to try new things.

Maybe this is one of them.

"No, leave it." She breathes out as though relieved she doesn't have to change her hair. "For now." I tack on the end, causing her to bristle at my words.

I can't help but smile to myself. I like her reactions toward me.

Paige

Oscar toys with the strands of my hair, causing me to break out in goosebumps, then he lifts his finger and ever so slowly trails the tip down my arm as though memorizing the feeling of the bumps underneath his fingertip.

When I first locked eyes on him down the corridor, his cold, calculating eyes made me flush as his gaze roamed over my body as though taking in every inch of me, devouring me.

His sharp facial features make him appear serious and bemused. His crisp white shirt is buttoned up to the top, and I itch to open the top button for him and graze my hand over his sharp jawline.

He approaches me slowly, like an animal targeting its prey. His dark brown hair has a slight wave to it, making me want to drag my fingers through it and then smooth it out all over again.

When I took the job, I was informed Zara enjoyed working for Oscar O'Connell. She basically gets paid a lot of money to screw this hot, rich dude once or some-times twice a week.

Easy money, just what I desperately need.

"How long have you worked at Indulgence, Paige?" He's so close to my neck his breath ghosts through my hair all the way down to...

I swallow thickly, annoyed with my reaction to this man already. "This is my first job with them," I answer honestly, ignoring the tremor wracking through me.

Oscar moves his face toward my neck and sniffs deeply. "You smell of apples."

I nod tightly. "It's the moisturizer I use."

He steps back to analyze my face. "You don't use perfume?" His finger grazes over his lip as though deep in thought.

I shake my head, avoiding his assessing eyes.

"You're different." It's a statement, not a question, and with his scrutinizing eyes, I'm not sure whether it's a good thing or not. I decide to divert his attention because I really need this job.

"I filled out the paperwork." I tilt my head toward the file on the counter. "I got the door codes from the manager at Indulgence."

But Oscar just stands there stoically, still not even following my gaze. No, he's staring straight at me, and I'm pretty sure he's not even blinking.

Unease rests in my stomach, certain I've never done this before, but I really need this job. Like really need it. I mean, it's no different from a one-night stand, right?

I clear my throat again, "So, where do you want me?" I meet his piercing blue eyes, cold and assessing.

His body gives nothing away, a stone statue. "You didn't read the manual." Again with an observation.

I shake my head and laugh uncomfortably.

"Oscar, that thing"—I point toward the manual, the ridiculous bunch of heavy papers. I mean, if I'm honest, I gave up after the first fifty pages— "That thing is like a thousand pages long. You can't seriously expect me to read all that?" I chance a glance back up at him, and from the expression on his face... oh shit, he does expect me to.

His jaw ticks slightly, and he appears deep in thought, but I recognize he's doing a breathing technique.

"I do," he replies after what feels like a lifetime. The atmosphere between us is tense, cold, and unnerving.

"One thousand two hundred and twenty-four pages, to be precise."

I shrug nonchalantly. "I have a busy life. I have better things to do than read through that. Besides, I'm good with whatever."

His eyes sharpen, and he painstakingly slowly licks his bottom lip. My heart hammers watching his movement. Does he even realize how mesmerizing that is? How erotic. Jeez, I need to get laid.

"If you read the manual, you'd know the position in the bedroom down the hall." He tilts his head sideways toward the corridor he came from, but he still doesn't divert his eyes.

I breathe out a sigh. "Okay, well, I know now."

"And you'll read the manual." He glares at me pointedly.

The intensity of him makes me swallow again and fidget uncomfortably. "Sure. I'll give it a go."

15

He blinks once, twice, before repeating my words, almost dumbstruck. "Give it a go."

I nod in agreement. "So, what now?"

I roam my eyes over the expansive apartment. It's clinical, white, clean, boring, and cold. No personality and not a hint of color.

"Now, you leave." I jolt at his words. Oh shit, I screwed up. I should never have admitted I didn't read the damn manual; my mouth always runs away with me. Disappointment courses through my body, making me sag and for panic to crawl up my spine. I need this job so bad.

"You come back tomorrow." He stares at me with such intensity before he spits the words out. "Once you've given it a go." I ease at his words; my whole body relaxes. The tension leaves my body at his words.

I place a hand over my racing heart. "Oh god, thank you." I nod like an idiot in relief, and before he gets a chance to change his mind, I scurry toward the door.

"Paige." I freeze at his sharp voice, with my hand on the door handle.

This is it; this is where he tells me he's changed his mind already.

He sighs heavily as though disappointed in something. Movement forces me to turn to the side and face him. I cringe when I realize my mistake.

"You might need this." He hands me the manual, the thick, heavy fucking thing that is about to save my ass.

I meet his almost cocky stare, his lip quirked up at the side as though amused at my mistake. I flush as I take it from him before turning to make an exit. "Thank you."

"Oh, and Paige?"

"Mmm?"

"Don't wear red."

At that weird request, I walk through the threshold I had only crossed less than fifteen minutes ago, feeling far more nervous than when I entered.

There's no doubt Oscar O'Connell is an enigma I'm intrigued to unlock.

I only hope I can get close enough for him to let me.

Chapter Two

Oscar

I've had what was undoubtedly the most restless night's sleep in my entire life.

Paige. My tongue tries her name out again for the hundredth time.

As soon as she left, I was itching to find everything out about her, but I forced myself to stop. To not delve into her life. Indulgence would have done all the necessary checks into her, but still, I wanted more, needed more.

She's everything I shouldn't want, but there's something about her that I crave.

I want to own her, control her, but also allow her to be herself. Something I've never considered before with the other clients I used for my sexual needs.

She's testing me in every way possible, and the most annoying part is she doesn't even realize it.

The way she so blatantly disregarded the manual riles me. Does she not realize how important that information is? How it tells her everything she needs to know? Her nonchalance bugs me. I want to punish her, make her comply.

But then I like the fact that she doesn't comply at all. Odd.

I pace my room again, rubbing my finger over the top of my lip; I mull over her reactions toward me. She's unfazed by my odd behavior. I'm well aware I'm different, intense. I've been told that my entire life. But she took it in her stride, almost like... like she expected it? I freeze at the thought before shutting it down.

I need to be careful so I don't lose control of this situation, but there's nothing stopping me from indulging in the process.

That's why I named my business Indulgence, after all

Paige

I tried to read the manual, spending half the damn night flicking through it, but in all honesty, after reading for the hundredth time about safety warnings and possible reactions to certain products, I gave up.

In my line of work, there's always potentially a reaction, a risk—it's life.

I get that Oscar is trying to inform his client of every potential risk, but this was a little overkill. Okay, a lot overkill.

My mind runs back to some of the information in the manual that I was determined to memorize, ready for tonight.

On arrival at the apartment, you will leave your belongings, such as mobile phone and purse, on the kitchen counter.

Turn left and follow the corridor to the first room on the right. Upon entering, close the door. On the back of the door, a white robe will be hung up. All clothes should be removed and folded neatly onto the dresser, with under-

wear placed on top. Shoes are to be placed next to the dresser.

Wear the white robe.

You will kneel on the floor facing the mirrors, with your hands on your knees and your head bowed, until I enter the room five minutes after your arrival.

I squeeze my eyes closed at the noise in the next room. My niece and nephew are arguing again about who put the empty cereal box back into the cupboard. I cringe at the thought of another huge argument about something so trivial.

As much as I love my family, I miss the quiet of living by myself, having my own space, and not having to consider others all the time. Particularly kids.

I have to lock my bedroom door unless I want a rumbustious four-year-old little girl jumping up and down on my bed. Not to mention my six-year-old nephew who likes to come into my room and take over my bed at night, and let's not even get started on them using my bathroom when I least expect it.

Fastening my watch in place, I glance at the time. Ten-twenty. I have a late start this morning and am expected to be staying over at Oscar's tonight, so I opted for the eleven am shift.

I tie my hair up into a high ponytail, grab my purse, and make my way into the kitchen.

"Aunty Paige, Adam ate the last of the crunch balls." Casey pouts as soon as she sees me.

"I did not; it was you!" Adam screws up his face and practically screams back at Casey.

I hold my hands up and try to defuse the situation.

"Guys, I'm sure there's some other cereal you can choose from." Ebony, my sister, shakes her head solemnly.

Ever since her accident six months ago, things have been really difficult for her, for us all, really. So much so that I chose to give up my apartment and move in with her to help with the kids and bills.

I have student loan debts coming out of my ass, so when this job landed at my feet, I grabbed it with both hands and ran with it.

This is going to solve so many problems for me. For us.

"How about pancakes?" I suggest.

Ebony shakes her head again. Her leg is propped up on the table, still in a cast from her last operation. "Ebs, I'll pick some groceries up on my way home tonight, okay?"

"Sure." She stares at the wall, then moves her head toward me. "Wait. I thought you had a date last night? You said you wouldn't be home."

"Oh, I'm meeting him tonight. Things didn't go to plan, but it's all on for tonight." I smile at her and try to avoid her eyes by turning back toward the kids. Clapping my hands together, I ask them, "How about toast?"

They both eye me with disappointment, scrunching up their noses in disgust.

Yes, the sooner I start working for Oscar O'Connell, the better.

My day at work is long and busy. We had a cat that was choking on a ping-pong ball, a mouse that lost its foot, and a Doberman that needed emergency surgery to remove an abnormal lump from his leg.

Carl, the owner, and the lead vet, kept making eyes at me from across the examination table. I could feel myself flush every time he opened his mouth to speak, and once the room was empty. Each time he had a chance to speak, we were luckily interrupted with questions by the assistants or administrators that needed forms filled in.

The man has a bronze complexion, that Sun-kissed look that surfers have, and he's hot. He even has floppy blond hair that you want to run your fingers through. We've hooked up once before, but then my sister had her accident, and I had to put dating on the back burner.

I can't exactly date, not right now anyway, and certainly not while I'm doing this thing with Oscar.

Carl is on the evening shift tonight, so I don't have a chance to say goodbye to him before I call at the store to grab some essentials.

A knot of anxiety forms in my stomach at the thought of what's going to happen tonight, but it's mixed with excitement and anticipation. While I might not like the fact I'm essentially being paid to have sex, there's definitely an element of attraction at the thought of getting to know Oscar better. The man is surrounded by mystery. Throw in his sharp cheekbones and handsome face, and I'm pretty sure he's hiding a hot-as-sin body under his shirt and pants.

What better way to get over my current drought?

Chapter Three

Oscar

I couldn't help it; I had to find out more about her. Reece is tasked with performing a background check for me.

I'm eager to know everything about her, but then I like the thought of adding an element of uncertainty, allowing this arrangement to grow naturally.

Perhaps, this is how normal relationships work? After all, I've never had one.

Reece did what we call a level three check. Basically, I now know her home details, criminal record or lack of, job, finances, and a few other personal details.

Paige Summers, twenty-eight years old and in a mass of student debt while achieving her dream of becoming a vet. She's currently working as a veterinary technician at a small clinic twenty minutes from her home address. Orphaned at eighteen when her parents and younger brother died in a car accident.

She recently moved in with her sister Ebony and her

two young children after her sister had some sort of accident that meant she needed multiple surgeries. She lost
her job as an insurance administrator, so it appears Paige
has moved into the house and is currently struggling to
support them all.

Annoyance bubbles inside me.

This is why she's doing this—her first job as a paid
escort.

I should settle her finances and put a stop to all of
this.

But I won't. No, I won't because something tells me
Paige Summers is going to be my biggest challenge yet,
and I love nothing more than a challenge.

My alarm alerts me to her presence. I adjust the cufflink
in place. My balls tingle with excitement, eager to enter
her room.

I try to control my breathing; the excitement and
anticipation of having her here again, to breathe her in,
almost feels overwhelming.

The sooner I screw Paige Summers out of my system,
the better.

Forcing myself to slow my pace, I walk down the
corridor toward her room, then pause at the door and
breathe, exhale, repeat. I open the door—and her scent
fills my nostrils, and my cock throbs. Never before have I
experienced a reaction like this.

I'm elated to see she's read the manual.

She's kneeling on the floor, facing the mirrors just like

I instructed, her hair falling over her face like a curtain due to the way she's bowed.

Without warning, her head snaps up, and her eyes latch on to mine in the mirror. I clench my teeth together. Does she not do anything right?

"You're meant to have your head bowed down," I snipe the words out.

Her jaw ticks. "It says in the manual until you enter the room. You entered the room." I startle at her words because she's right; that's exactly what it says. Why has no one brought this to my attention before now? Before her.

Of course, she carries on, "If you want me to keep my head bowed when you're in the room, it should say so in the manual." She holds my eyes with a challenge. A challenge I don't quite think she realizes she's no chance of winning.

"It also states you're to be obedient and speak when instructed to do so, to be submissive." Her eyes narrow at me, and I decide to remind her of her place. "Maybe I should dock your pay accordingly, Miss Summers."

Her breath hitches, and a thrill courses through me. My cock throbs in my pants, eager to get a taste of her, to punish her.

She ducks her head, and I smirk at her compliance.

Slowly, I move over toward the armchair and sit, never taking my focus off of her. To calm myself, I study the way her hair shines red under the light and the way her hands have an ever so slight tremble to them as they rest on her knees. I wonder if they're as soft as they look; they seem delicate. Her fingernails aren't painted, and I wonder if it's because she's followed the manual or if she doesn't paint them at all. Maybe it's due to her line of work?

Did she wear it yesterday? I can't recall, and I don't understand why I missed important details like that.

Of course, I should understand. She threw me completely off guard by simply showing up at my apartment in place of Zara. So much so that my whole fucking night was plagued with thoughts of her.

I make myself wait longer, giving myself time to establish control.

"Rise. Take off the robe and drop it to the floor."

She does as I ask immediately, and I revel in it. My heart pounds as the robe slips from her milky body and falls to her feet. I slowly roam my eyes over her body, although she's sideways, which annoys the fuck out of me. I want to go over to her and force her to look at me.

I snap my eyes away to concentrate on my breathing. "Get on the fucking bed and open your legs." My words are deep and harsh, but I'm past caring. I need to assert my authority and let off some steam in the process.

I swipe up on the tablet and once again take note of her safe word, even though it's ingrained in my mind. *Orange*.

I don't let myself look at her body. I stand, towering over the bed, and keeping my eyes transfixed on the task at hand. I take hold of her delicate wrist and quickly clasp it into the leather cuff chained to the bed before I can take note of how her soft skin feels against mine. Then I take her ankle and do the same, repeating the process on the other side of the bed.

I'm aware she's watching my every movement. I can feel her eyes on me, so I don't rush. I stay smooth and in control. I keep my mask firmly in place when in reality, my cock is leaking, and I want nothing more than to fuck her hard and deep until she screams her throat raw.

Her breathing changes and I turn my head to see if she's okay with this.

Her green eyes stare back at me with intrigue. I watch, mesmerized, as she licks her plump pink lips coated in some sort of shiny balm. The motion of it draws me in, desperate for a taste.

I can't help myself, and before I know what I'm doing, I drag my finger over her bottom lip. Her tongue darts out and touches the tip of my finger, causing me to wince and pull back quickly at the contact, causing her face to almost crumble before she masks her reaction.

I stare at the tip of my finger, a light sheen of the balm on it but also the touch of her tongue, maybe the taste too, and I want to try it, to taste her. I bring my finger to my mouth and suck.

She tastes of apples. I glance toward her parted lips. Her eyes are heavy; apparently, she likes watching me suck her from my finger. My cock leaks as I imagine that balm on her lips around my cock.

Could I do that?

Could I feed her my cock?

For the first time in my life, I contemplate putting my cock inside a woman's mouth. I swallow hard, my heart thumping and my veins pulsating with need.

Paige's breath hitches, causing me to snap out of my trance, and I roam my eyes slowly over her body, her breasts. They're bigger than I normally ask for. They fall heavily to the side, and I have a strange desire to push them both together while I'm on top of her.

"Your tits are big." My words come out choked. "I'm not used to them being as big as that."

"I thought guys liked that?"

Her words cause my eyes to dart toward hers. "What fucking guys?" my spine straightens, on alert for hurting someone, causing damage somewhere. I squeeze my eyes closed, clench my fists, and then try my breathing technique.

Slowly, I open my eyes.

She flushes before tightening her jaw. "Guys in general, Oscar."

I relax slightly at her words, then continue my perusal. Her nipples are bigger than any woman I've been with before. Normally I desire smaller breasts that fit into my hand; their nipples are normally a lot smaller too.

Paige's skin has a light scattering of freckles, and I find myself following them in each direction they roam over her skin.

I move down the bed so I can see her pussy better.

A light dusting of short red hair covers her. She didn't read the fucking manual. I choke on my words, "You have hair." I snipe the words out in annoyance and point to the offending hair.

Paige lifts her head from the pillow to glare down at me. "Jesus, Oscar. Have you ever tried waxing?" I stare at her in disbelief. "Have you?" she snaps at me again. And I can't quite grasp what's happening because I should be the one mad at her right now. But she's the one mad at me, especially considering she's the one who didn't read the fucking manual!

"Oscar! Have you?"

Her eyes hold mine hostage, drilling holes into me, and I have no choice but to respond to her, so I shake my head.

"Right, so don't ask me to do something unless you've done it yourself." She raises her chin in defiance while mine drops open in shock. Is she serious? The glare she's throwing in my direction and the venom coming from her eyes should make me want to throttle her, but instead, I can't help but curl my lip on a tight smile. She's a spitfire, that's for sure.

My spitfire.

I've no intention of doing the things I intend to do to her, absolutely fucking not.

Still, she doesn't need to know that.

Not yet, anyway.

Chapter Four

Oscar

"Open your legs wide as far as the chains allow."

She complies instantly. "Put your feet flat on the bed." My fingers twitch to touch her and to feel her slickness on my fingers.

I suck in a sharp breath at the sight before me. Soft pink pussy lips are forced wide open; the scattering of red hair more prominent than the hair on her head, but I don't dislike it. Strange.

Her slit glistens, and I wonder if it's because she's aroused. I glance back up at her face to find her eyes studying me. We stare at each other before she swallows and averts her gaze.

My cock stands tall, the tip rubbing against my belt. I stroke a hand down it while watching Paige, but it doesn't take away any of my need; it only magnifies it.

"You ticked yes to all the questions."

That gets her attention, her eyes latching onto my bulging pants. "Yes."

"I can fuck you anyway I want." My cock leaks pre-cum at the thought, so I give it another slow stroke. My boxers are drenched, and my balls tingle already.

Her breath hitches, and my control snaps. I press the button on the bed that locks the chain in place. The jerk causes Paige to jolt with wide eyes. I move over to the panel hidden within the wall and scan my hand over it.

Once upon a time, this was also controlled by a button, but after finding my nephew, Reece, in here, I changed the settings, determined to keep his inquisitive mind out.

The panel doors slide open, giving way to an array of sexual paraphernalia—everything my cock desires. Cuffs, lubes, condoms, butt plugs, dildos, gags, whips, and paddles. The gasp that leaves Paige's mouth sends a shiver down my spine.

Fuck, this is going to be good. I try not to show my excitement. I've learned to keep what little emotions I have in check, never exposing them, not when people don't understand or, at the very least, try to understand me.

Taking out the condoms and lube and moving over to the dresser, I begin the process of opening my cufflinks and placing them side by side. Slowly, I roll my sleeves up to my elbow.

I remove my belt and fold it, placing it next to the cufflinks, then I unzip my pants, tug down my boxers and exhale in relief when my cock is finally freed.

Opening a condom, I roll it down my cock and check to make sure it's secure. Although all women that work for Indulgence are screened, and my doctor administers the contraceptive injection, I can't bring myself to come inside a woman, no matter how great the need may be.

I turn around to face Paige, her eyes transfixed on my movement. I press the button at the side of the bed, the one that extends her arms and allows the lower chain to pull her toward the end of the bed. She's now stretched with her arms above her head, and her lower body pushed up and open at the bottom of the mattress. The perfect angle for me to be able to stand and fuck her. Her green eyes widen when I pick up the lube, and part of me wants to ask what caused that reaction, but I couldn't give a shit because right now, I need her to relieve me. I flick the cap open and pour more than necessary down her pussy, so it drizzles into her opening.

Taking ahold of my cock, I slowly drag it up and down the lubrication, hissing through my teeth at the contact between us. Even through the rubber, I can feel her heat, her softness.

Paige's chest flushes, and my eyes latch on to the color spreading toward her tits. The thought of them bouncing... I like it.

I thrust inside her without warning, causing her to groan. I like that too. Fuck, how I like the sound escaping her lips.

I grip her thighs tightly, the touch of her skin sending electricity flowing through my veins. A determination to fuck her harder and faster surges inside me. For her to know it's me that's fucking her, fucking away anyone that's previously entered her.

I slam into her again, annoyance in my veins at the

thought of her previous partners experiencing what I am currently.

"Oh god," she pants loudly.

I want to hear more. I prefer silence when I fuck, but I want to hear her enjoying it as much as me.

Enjoying me.

Drawing my hips back, I snap them forward sharply, causing her to jolt and groan. The sensation is incredible, and for the first time in my life, I wonder what she would feel like without a condom, without a barrier between us. "Fucking take my cock."

I snap my hips again, my balls already tingling when normally I need a lot longer to unload myself.

"Oh god, Oscar." My name on her lips sends a bolt of pleasure to my balls, and I want to hear it again.

"Say it again!"

"Oscar, Jesus. More."

"Fuck yes." I work faster, watching the rhythmic bounce of her tits as I thrust in and out. "Fucking take it. Take my cock." My cock rubs against her soft walls.

I can feel her pussy gripping me as I push as deep as possible determined to be where no man has been before.

"Oh god." Her internal muscles clench, and I feel her wetness all the way to my balls. The sensation makes me bite the inside of my cheek to ward off my release.

I rail into her, slamming faster and faster. "Fuck. I'm going to..." I spill into the condom, reveling in the feel of her walls holding me in. My head drops forward on its own accord, sweat beading my forehead, my heart pounding against my chest at what was undoubtedly the best orgasm of my life.

My breathing finally settles, and I release my grip on her thighs. My eyes latch on to the marks left behind, causing my cock to jump. I peel myself out of her warm pussy, and watch, mesmerized, at her juices leaking from her swollen pussy. I lick my lips, unsure if I could actually taste her there.

I don't like uncertainty.

I take the condom off, the heavy tip filled with my cum. The cum I wish was inside her, marking her as my own. A reminder to her and anyone else that my spitfire belongs to me.

For now, anyway.

Paige

I can't help but stare at him. He has me splayed open for his pleasure, and I enjoyed it. Oscar watches with fascination as he pulls out of me and then peels the condom off himself. His cock is still hard and jerks slightly, making me wonder what caused the reaction. He tugs up his pants with one hand without much effort. Every movement he does is so precise, so calculated. From the way he placed his cufflinks and belt to the way he folded the sleeves of his shirt... it's all so planned.

Like a ritual.

I could tell from the first moment I laid eyes on him that he was different. His cold, closed off demeanor, the way he spoke as though he found me strange, and the way he analyzed me. But now, I know exactly what it is.

Oscar has autistic traits.

I'd recognize the signs anywhere since my brother had it too. I swallow thickly before the memories of my brother and parents assault me.

"Have you tasted a man before?"

When did he move to stand beside me?

I stare up at him and nod. A flash of something crosses his face, and it almost looks like hurt. Surely, he can't assume I've never had oral sex before, and why would that bother him anyway?

"You're going to taste me."

I nod at his instruction and open my mouth to accept him but watch in confusion as he dips his finger into the condom and withdraws it again. With his cum flowing down his finger, he holds his finger out. His voice gruff and heavy, "Taste."

I swallow heavily, my throat suddenly dry at the oddity behind his actions. "Taste," he repeats. His eyes are trained on my lips. I open my mouth and allow him to place his finger inside because something tells me that Oscar wouldn't appreciate me taking control.

No, he needs to choose what we do and how we do it. He strokes his finger over my tongue, wiping his essence on it. His taste is salty but with a hint of freshness.

He quickly withdraws his finger, scooping out more of his cum, clumsily this time, as though desperate to fill my mouth with his taste.

I flick my tongue over his digit, and he lets out a moan of appreciation. The sound causes me to hum in response. Oscar begins to fumble with his pants, pulling his hard cock free from his boxers once again. I watch in awe as he jerks his cock over me while I suck on his finger. His breathing becomes labored when he replaces one finger in my mouth with two.

His hips work in time to him thrusting his fingers in and out of my mouth in a desperate frenzy. The veins on his forearms coil tight at the grip he holds around his steel cock, and the head leaks strings of pre-cum, looking angry and desperate for release.

He grits his teeth, words spewing out of his mouth. "Fuck. Taste me. Fucking taste me." I watch, completely paralyzed, as this strong man before me comes undone. Streams of his warm cum flood over my body, causing my clit to throb and his mouth to drop open in awe.

I wait patiently for his hazy eyes to meet mine, but they don't.

They refuse to.

With a grimace, he withdraws his fingers and wipes my saliva from them onto the bedsheets as though he's ridding me from him completely. I swallow away the lump of disappointment.

He straightens up and tucks his cock back into his pants before slowly unfolding his sleeves, reattaching the cufflinks with precision, and weaving his belt back into place as though nothing has happened between us.

I'm still locked into position when he turns his head to the side. He presses the button on the bedpost, and the chains drop, and the cuffs open.

"You can use the facilities." He points toward a door I assume is the bathroom.

Then he walks out of the room.

Leaving me feeling completely used and aching for another release.

I bite my lip, annoyed as hell, because what the fuck was that?

Chapter Five

Oscar

I used her. There's no denying that. That's what I pay them for; that's what they're here for— for me to use as and when I like. As a purpose for my pleasure, not theirs.

Then why do I feel this gnawing feeling inside of my stomach, punching to get out?

Why couldn't I look at her after I fed her my cum?

I wonder if this is what embarrassment is like. I've never had a woman taste me before, and I got off on it. I don't do embarrassed, and if this is what it is, I don't like it either.

What's so difficult about putting my cock into her mouth, anyway? I could restrain her? I brush my finger over the top of my lip, liking the idea. But what if I can't do it? What if the sensation freaks me out and makes me feel like I have something crawling over my body? Something that I can't control makes me want to lash out.

I rub her black lace panties between my fingers again. I want to keep them as they smell of her.

I want to keep her.

For now.

Paige

I slept so damn well in this enormous bed. The sheets are like satin, not like the scratchy, shitty ones back home.

I stretch wide, feeling a little achy from the position Oscar had me in yesterday. As much as I didn't feel like moving, I forced myself to shower, then I got back into the luxurious sheets and slept all the way through the night until morning with no little bodies hogging the bedsheets. It was bliss. I take in the white room. Even the furniture is white. So clean, clinical looking, and boring. So bright.

I tug on my clothes, darting my eyes around the room, when I realize my panties are missing. They were definitely on top of my clothes last night. I know this for a fact because it's in the section of the damn manual I memorized.

Annoyed, I go in search of the panty thief himself.

Oscar's at the glass table, eating breakfast, but his eyes are trained on me, watching my every movement. His shirt is buttoned to the top again, and his sleeves are rolled up to his elbow. He's so in control and concise; it angers me. He cuts into the fruit with such precision, like he's done it a million times, using a knife and fork. Who the fuck uses a knife and fork for fruit?

"You took my panties."

He doesn't so much as blink, but his lip quirks up at the side.

"You're meant to leave the apartment by seven am." He points his knife over toward the clock that tells me it's almost nine.

Oops.

I shrug. "It's my day off. It doesn't matter." I pull out a chair and sit opposite him.

His eyes practically bug out of his head, and he stops the fork that's halfway to his mouth to glare at me. "What do you think you're doing?"

Leaning over and grabbing the muffin from beside his plate, I tear into the wrapper, then place a piece on my tongue before responding, "Eating breakfast." I practically moan when the juice of the orange hits my tongue.

"You weren't invited. You're meant to be gone before seven am." He repeats the time again as though I didn't hear him the first time. His hands tighten around his utensils, probably due to my lack of movement.

I roll my eyes at him, causing his pupils to dilate further. His lips part slightly in disbelief.

Wow, I don't think he's ever been challenged.

I place another piece of the muffin into my mouth and ignore him, then taking the cup that has orange juice in it, I help myself, all the while smirking at him.

"Do you not feed the women you fuck, Oscar?" I raise a brow in his direction.

His eyes scan over my face as though searching for an answer from me. "No."

"Well, I'm different. I need feeding in the morning before you kick me out."

His chest heaves, and he repeats my words low, almost to himself. "Different."

"That's right. Different. Also, is seven am necessary on my day off, Oscar? It's the only day I get to sleep in. Also, do you think you could grab some coffee for me? I seriously need a coffee to wake me up in the morning. Black is just fine."

He blinks once, twice, before he shakes his head. "No."

"No, what?"

"No to everything you just said."

I stop eating and cross my arms over my chest. The movement attracts his attention toward my breasts before he raises his eyes back toward mine in challenge.

"I want my panties back," I snipe out because his scrutiny is making me flush.

His lip curls up at the side. "No."

Our eyes drill into one another before I decide to test a theory. "Oscar, I have to leave the apartment with no panties on and catch a taxi with this short dress. The taxi driver that'll take me home could be anyone, like a pervert or something, and he'll be able to see me. Everything." I fake a pout, hoping he's as controlling outside of the bedroom as he is on the inside.

"You can have them back," he concedes easily, too easily.

I smile triumphantly. Oscar doesn't like the thought of people knowing I won't have panties on. He doesn't like the thought of men knowing in particular.

His lip quirks before he quickly stops himself; he withdraws the screwed-up panties from his trouser pocket and hands them over to me.

"Put them on here." He points to the space beside him, his eyes challenging mine, so I push back out of my chair and snatch the panties from him.

They're damp? What the? My head spins to face him accusingly. "Oscar, did you...?"

"Yes." He does the lip thing again. I can only describe it as a smirk, causing my face to flush profusely; he flicks a finger up my body, motioning for me to put the damp panties on, the ones with his cum all over. "Now."

I grind my teeth in annoyance but do it anyway. I pull them on, feeling the slickness between my thighs. His slickness. He jerked off in my panties, and I don't particularly hate the thought. In fact, I quite like the thought of his ownership of me.

More than I care to admit right now.

Chapter Six

Oscar

I listen around the table to my brothers discussing strategies for a new shipping container containing an arsenal of weapons that could invite trouble if we're caught.

But it's not so fucking difficult. I just explained my plan, and they're still arguing over it.

I zone out, my finger naturally finding the button that allows me to view Paige's cellphone conversations. Without giving it too much thought, I open it to find an array of conversations between her and her sister. I swipe downward and come across a male's name. Carl.

My stomach roils, and my muscles tighten; just who the fuck is Carl? I do my breathing technique to try to control my turmoil. I need to know who the fuck this prick is.

I scan over the last few messages sent yesterday.

Carl: Do you want to meet up for a drink sometime?

Paige: I'm struggling right now, Carl.

Carl: I can close the clinic early tomorrow if that helps? I only have one client booked in after six.

Paige: Can I let you know later?

Carl: Sure.

Paige: Text later

Carl: x

An X? A fucking X? This guy wants in her panties—my fucking panties.

Absolutely not.

I attempt my breathing technique to try and calm me down, but I know it won't help... not until I have her with me tonight, knowing she won't be with him.

I angrily swipe for her name and tap out a message.

Oscar: Six pm at my apartment.

Paige: How did you get my number?

Oscar: It was on your application.

Paige: Oh. Well, maybe I have plans later.

Oscar: I pay you to work for me when I say.

Paige: I'm not a fucking dog, Oscar, who comes when it's called.

I smirk at her response. She's so easy to rile.

Oscar: I pay you enough.

Paige: You're an ass!

Paige: A big fucking jackass.

Oscar: Don't be late, or I'll dock your pay.

Paige: Fuck you, Oscar.

Oscar: Yes, you will.

I smile inwardly at my own response. For some unknown reason, I enjoy toying with her. She's an alternative type of challenge, and I'm actually quite enjoying it.

Opening the bedroom door, I find her in position on the floor—her head bowed as per instructions, and I love it. I love her at my feet. For me. Only me.

I do something out of the ordinary. Instead of sitting in the armchair, I stand over her. Marveling as the sun streams through the blinds highlighting the red in her hair, my fingers twitch to touch it, and my breathing escalates at the prospect.

I play with the strands of her hair between my fingers, and a shiver passes over her, causing my cock to jump at her response, enjoying her reaction toward me.

My breathing intensifies at the thought of her out with Carl tonight instead of here with me. The prick she currently calls her boss. After excusing myself from the shitty meeting I was in, I looked into the smug little bastard. My finger hovered over the button to ruin his veterinary career, but something was holding me back... or someone. I decided to watch the blond wannabe model from the shadows, and when I've had enough, I'll ruin him simply for looking at her.

My breathing technique is no good now as I'm past that point. I need to sink my cock inside Paige and remind her that she's mine.

Chapter Seven

Oscar

Paige's eyes widen when the panel moves aside, revealing a small room. A room equipped for my needs.

A bench is situated in the middle of the room, and I tell her to go and lie on it face down.

Where possible, I try to have sex with my clothes on to avoid any unnecessary touching, but for some reason, I want to push myself and experience her flesh against mine. I take off my clothes and fold them neatly, placing them on the dresser, everything, including my boxers. My hands tremble as I undress, but I try my best to ignore it.

I can't count on one hand how many times I've been naked in front of a woman. Exposed.

I palm my hard cock when I turn around and see Paige bent over the bench. The position of the bench has her ass high in the air for the taking. I rub my arousal over the head of my cock and continue stroking as I move around her.

"I'm going to untie your hands, then I'll fasten you in."

She doesn't lift her head, and she can't see due to her hair acting as a blanket over her face. I don't like it; I want to see that she understands, so I tuck her hair behind her ear to find that she's biting on her lip.

"I understand." Her voice is breathy and full of need.

Paige's green eyes peruse my body, and I want to push my chest out with pride. Nobody sees my chiseled body, ever, but I'm proud to be showing it off to Paige right now.

She licks those lips again as I fasten the cuffs in place before working over her slender ankles.

I scan down her spine all the way to her ass; her hole is exposed to me for fucking, causing a sliver of jealousy in me at the thought of someone fucking it. "When was the last time your ass was fucked?" My voice is clipped and cold. Me.

Her breath hitches, and she takes longer than I like to respond. Annoyance bubbles inside me. "Answer!"

"I-I..." She attempts to lift her head over her shoulder, but the position she's in makes it difficult for her to achieve. Nervously, she licks her lips, and I can't antici-pate her answer when it finally comes. "I haven't." She shakes her head, causing her hair to drop like a curtain once again, hiding the truth behind her words.

"You ticked yes to all," I spit as I recall her answers on my tablet. I know her fucking answers; I studied them.

She fidgets against her restraints. "I wanted the job."

She wanted the job. Of course, she fucking wanted the job and was prepared to do anything to get it, even lie.

My fists tighten, and my veins boil at her deceit. I breathe my four, four, four before calming.

"And now?" I ask her to be sure she realizes what I'm asking of her.

"I said I'd do anything, Oscar. I meant it." Her words send a surge of lust and desire through me, but I know better than to trust her. *I'd do anything* echoes in my mind. Anything. Damn fucking right, she'll do anything.

I'll take her ass like I'll take everything else she's offered. I'll take everything, and only then will I set her free.

I turn and take a condom, vibrator, and bottle of lube from the cupboard behind me.

Striding toward her like a magnet, I settle down on my knees behind Paige and take in the sight before me. Her pink pussy glistens, making my throat go dry with a need to taste her. Again, it's something I've never done before, although I have considered trying it. I wasn't willing to force myself into doing something just because I'd seen it and heard how good it was. No, I stopped myself because I didn't crave it, not like this one, the pussy with the scattering of red hair. I breathe in her scent, not too close to touch but close enough for my breath to cause Paige's body to break out into a shiver. The feeling of euphoria knowing I caused that is surreal. My cock leaks with joy, and I find myself rubbing the pre-cum over the fat head.

Paige moans as though she can sense my movements, no doubt hearing the small grunt leaving my lips. Before I get too carried away, I withdraw my hand from my steel cock and coat the vibrator in the lube. My intentions were to fuck her with it, but after hearing the moan slip from her lips, I want nothing more than to feel her pussy clench around me.

I quickly slide on the condom, then set the vibrator to high speed, the buzzing noise filling the air.

I grip one of her ass cheeks firmly, pulling it apart more so I can see the position of the vibrator settling against her pussy lips and clit. She jolts at the contact with a moan. "Oh fuck."

Her words should aggravate me, annoy me, but I want them, need them to feed my craving for her.

My cock leaks in strings when she tries rubbing herself on the vibrator. "Oscar. Oh god."

"Is your pussy leaking on the cock, Paige?"

Her breath hitches, and she moans at my words. I love it; I fucking love it.

"Please."

"Please, what?"

"Oh god, please let me come."

I withdraw the toy. There's no fucking way I'm allowing her to come on that. I stand and position my cock over her entrance; I have to bend my legs slightly at the angle before I agonizingly slowly push my cock into her slick heat.

I close my eyes at the feeling as her pussy molds around my cock perfectly. Like it was made for me. Only me. I withdraw, then push back in, and Paige moans, her response spurring me on. "Yes... that's it, more," she moans, accepting every inch of my hard cock.

My legs are on either side of the bench, effectively straddling her ass but pumping into her pussy. I lean over her spine, licking the sheen of sweat gathering over her smooth milky skin.

"Oh... Oh god."

Her sweet voice fills my veins like a fuel, pushing me to continue my pursuit. I slam into her over and over. I grab her hair from her face, wrap it around my fist, and pull her head back, forcing our eyes to clash in the mirror directly in front of us.

Her mouth parts. I pound into her from behind, practically mounting her body.

Paige's pussy clenches, holding me in, forcing my balls to tingle when I want it to last... need it to last. I bite into my lip, fucking desperate to hold on.

"Oh fuck, Oscar." She clenches on a scream, and I can't hold it back any longer as she begins milking me.

I push through her tight muscles over and over. "Fuckkkk, yes." My cum shoots into the rubber, and again, I wish it was inside her. The thought makes me quickly withdraw and pull the condom off, throwing it to the floor. But I pump my cock over her back, draining it of every last bit until my head drops forward in relief.

I raise my eyes to find Paige staring directly at me.

I stare back at her before sniping the words out, "I'm going to fuck your ass raw."

Paige

Oscar made quick work of rearranging me—first unclipping the clasps, then changing the bench position, and now, I'm on my back, strapped in again. No doubt, all because he doesn't want me touching him.

He needs that control, the reassurance that allows him to partake in exploring his sexual needs. And boy, do I want to explore them with him.

"I want you to watch me when I fuck your tight virgin hole, Paige." His words cause me to clench my thighs, but that gives me little relief as I'm spread open like a turkey for him.

I should feel worried at his words, nervous even. I've never so much as had a finger graze over my ass, let alone his huge, angry cock stuffed inside it.

But right now, with the flare of desire within his eyes, I want to give him this. I want to give it all to him.

"Okay."

He takes the lube in his hand and coats two fingers.

Oh shit, is he putting them inside me? Two? I swallow away the trepidation.

Oscar gently strokes over my asshole with a finger. He talks low, almost to himself. "You're so wet I shouldn't even need lube." His eyes narrow in fascination as he prods one finger inside, past the tight muscle, and it's a little uncomfortable at first. I watch as his other hand goes to his solid cock, and he jerks himself in time with the intrusion in my ass. It sweeps around inside, exploring, and I so desperately want to move. I can feel my pussy leaking.

"Ah." My voice wavers when he withdraws, only to replace one finger with two, scissoring inside and out. The sensation of being stretched in my forbidden hole makes me excited for more. "Oh, Oscar," I pant heavily as my pussy demands his attention. "Please."

"Tell me you want my cock." His eyes draw away from my ass to latch on to my own. "Fucking tell me you want it in your ass, that you want my cum in your ass." His chest heaves, and the look on his face is a look of barely restrained lust. His eyes are heavy with a searing heat behind them and flicking back and forth from my face to his fingers.

"Please. Please, Oscar, I want you in my ass."

He gasps in delight before he shakes his head, a flicker of panic over his face. "I've never..." He swallows loudly before righting himself again. "I've never fucked without a condom on. I want to." He winces as though not happy about making that admittance.

"I want you to. Please, Oscar." He watches me closely, so I add on my own admittance. "I've never..."

My eyes move away from his as I feel my face flush more. "... done anything without a condom."

His lips part as though I've given him a gift, and he drops his gaze from mine toward my ass. He spits on my pussy, and it drips toward my hole—the one he withdraws his fingers from. He replaces them with the tip of his thick cock, and he jolts slightly when our skin meets before a tug pulls at his lips, and he pushes in bit by bit.

"Ow shit."

He stops instantly at my words. Then he moves his other hand to my clit and rubs circles on it.

Arousal floods my body as his cock spears my ass open with the head inside. His spit pooling around me, my clit throbs under his touch. He presses harder on my clit as he eases his cock inside me.

He turns his head away from us, biting into the side of his mouth. "Fuck, it's so tight, Paige."

"Please, I need more."

His eyes snap back to mine before rearing back and slamming into my hole. Fuck, a combination of a burning sensation and a feeling of being stuffed full of him makes my pussy clench. He slaps his hand down hard onto my waiting clit, earning a moan of appreciation.

"Fuck. This is my ass, Paige. My ass to fuck when I want." He clenches his teeth and spits out filthy words I want to drown in. "To come in when I want."

My orgasm builds from nowhere. "Oscar, oh godddddd." I throw my head back as a wave of euphoria passes over me, making me float so high I'm not sure I'll ever come down.

His eyes widen, and he pistons into me harder, so

hard it hurts but hurts so good. "Fuckkkkk." I feel his cock swell deep inside me, and it only heightens my experience. He smacks my clit again. "Gonna fuck this pussy raw too." His words slam into me, into my core, desperate for him to make it a reality.

"Yes. Please, yes," I scream into the room while Oscar empties himself in my ass.

Chapter Eight

Oscar

I fucked her into oblivion, and I fucking loved every second of it. The feeling of touching her raw without protection almost made me come on the spot. But I was desperate to wane off my release, hungry to feel the heat of her warm ass against my cock. The slickness inside and the tightness of her muscles were unlike anything I'd felt before. I felt every fucking thing. It was like an awakening, and now, I need more. I need her pussy raw. I just don't know if I can; annoyance rumbles inside me.

She didn't so much as wince when I pulled out. No, she was almost hollow, comatose. I unstrapped her cuffs and tended to the marks, but she barely even registered the care I gave her.

I scooped her up, her body draped in my arms, and then I gently deposited her on her bed, pulling the sheets over her flushed, spent body. My own body itched to stay with her, not to leave, not like usual. Different.

I stand and watch her shallow breaths. Her eyes had

grown heavy as soon as she was in my arms, giving me the opportunity to breathe her in fully, bask in her beauty, in her scent.

I take in all her details—the small scattering of freckles over her nose and the tinge of red to her eyelashes.

A fierce determination of protectiveness wraps around me and pulls me in with each breath she takes. Her lips flutter on an exhale, making my own lips quirk up at the soft snooze escaping those lips. The ones that will give me my first blow job, the ones that will give me my first kiss. I decide here, and now, I'm keeping her. She belongs to me.

Mine.

For now.

Paige

A shrill noise wakes me from my perfect sleep, my perfect fucking sleep. Instantly, I'm awake and ready to smash the noise into obliteration. My hand lands on the alarm clock beside the bed. A fucking alarm clock? He put an alarm clock in the room.

I slam my palm down on the button to stop the noise, six thirty am.

I scrub a hand down my face. Jesus, this man is the devil.

Pushing back the sheets, I wince when I shuffle my butt onto the edge of the bed, the tenderness of my ass now surfacing. Another thing to thank him for this morning. I have a shift this afternoon, and now I have to work in this condition.

My eyes latch on to the muffin at the side of the bed and the bottle of water. He's got to be kidding me. Water? Who the hell drinks water for breakfast? If he seriously thinks he can give me this for breakfast, he has another thing coming. I stomp into the bathroom and make quick work of freshening myself up before tugging on the robe, grabbing the water and muffin, and striding out the door toward the living area on a mission.

Of course, the man is on his tablet, working quietly while eating his melon with a knife and a fucking fork. His eyes lazily pull up toward my own as if it's a difficult task to pay me any attention at all.

"What the hell is this?" I hold the bottle up for emphasis.

His blue eyes narrow on the bottle before his lip tugs up at the side. "Water," he replies nonchalantly before moving his eyes toward his tablet once again.

"I know it's water, Oscar..."

I don't get a chance to continue before he butts in, "Then why ask?" He quirks a brow at me in question.

I move and slam the bottle on the table. "Oscar, I need coffee in the morning. Coffee. Not fucking water. This"—I wave my hand in the direction of the bottle—"doesn't cut it."

His eyes assess me for a few moments, and then he exhales in annoyance and turns his eyes back to his tablet.

Annoyed by his lack of response, I decide to push further, "You pumped and dumped in my ass, Oscar. The least you can do is give me a coffee for the trouble." I cross my arms over my chest in defiance.

This gets his attention. His eyes flare with rage, his fists clench and unclench, and he appears to be doing some kind of breathing exercise. "Pump and dump," he repeats lowly for his benefit, not mine.

I nod. "Exactly. I gave you my ass. The least you can do is hydrate it."

He jolts as though realizing something before he swallows away the thought. "Are you sore?" He watches me closely for a response, and like a damn idiot, I blush at his concern. I quickly dart my eyes away in embarrassment and wave my hand at him to distract him from my awkwardness, throwing over my shoulder, "I'm fine. I just need something other than water." making my way over to the kitchen area, hoping to ease the sudden tension, I wince as I hear him push his chair back.

I distract myself and open the refrigerator door. Holy. Fucking. Shit.

Stacks upon stacks of containers, each neatly labeled with their contents, along with a calorie amount. Each container has color-coordinated lids—black for meat, green for vegetables, blue for fruit, pink for sauce, and orange for cheeses.

The door stretches open further, and before I know what's happening, Oscar is standing between me and the fridge.

He tilts my chin up to look at him with his forefingers. "Do you need pain relief?" His simple touch causes a shiver to run through me, or maybe it's the cool air escaping the open refrigerator?

I search his face for answers. "For your ass?" he adds before I can think.

Oh shit, he thinks he hurt me. Well, I mean, I am tender. I gulp uncomfortably and shake my head. "No, I'm fine. Thank you."

His eyes don't leave mine, as though searching for a lie. His face is laced in concern before his face softens ever so slightly. Then he leans past me, takes a bottle from the refrigerator, and hands me a smoothie. "I'll order a coffee maker." Turning on his heel, he resumes his position to continue typing away.

I stand glued to the spot, gob-smacked. He's ordering me a coffee machine? Why exactly? Because he pumped and dumped in my ass? Because he hurt me? Didn't give me medication? No, I know exactly why Oscar is buying a coffee machine just for me. He likes me. I smile internally at the thought.

"Oh, and Paige?" He neither lifts his head nor acknowledges me in any way. "Clock's ticking." He points toward the clock behind me, and I narrow my eyes on the damn thing—six fifty-five.

I storm down the hallway.

"Fucking asshole!"

I swear I hear the prick laugh.

Chapter Nine

Oscar

I hurt her. I pride myself on aftercare, but I hurt her. Page three hundred and fifty-six states that sufficient care will be given to the submissive, yet I didn't provide that. I'm angry with myself, annoyed, fucking raging that I'm so distracted by her that even the simplest of things I fuck up. I never mess up. I ball my fists.

"Every fucker messes up once in a while." Con snaps me out of my thoughts, and I realize, glancing around the poker table, that I voiced my thoughts aloud. Again something I never do.

"You would know about that, wouldn't you?" I quip back.

My youngest brother, Con, seriously screwed up when he was younger, practically begging his then-girlfriend, Will, to have an abortion while finishing things with her in the process. It doesn't seem so long ago that I helped track her down. Thankfully, Will kept the baby. Keen, my nephew, and the couple are living together and planning their ridiculously elaborate wedding. Not before a pile of shit went down where Con tried to end his life, though. I inwardly shiver at the reminder.

A chip hits me in the face, bringing me out of my dark thoughts.

"You playing?" Finn, my younger brother, glares at me, so naturally, I stare back at the moron. He chokes on an awkward laugh before glancing away, ignoring our stare off.

I don't need to keep looking at my cards like my oldest brother, Bren does. He fidgets uncomfortably, giving away his hand. It's a good one; the guy is built like a tank but cannot, for the life of him, mask his excitement like a school child. I almost want to shake my head at him.

"How's Charlie settling in? Angel and the pregnancy going well?" Cal, my next oldest brother, asks Finn with concern in his voice.

Finn recently got reacquainted with his high school sweetheart, Angel. He left to join the Army to make a better life for them both away from the Mafia world we live in, only for her to disappear while he was gone. At the time, I was too young and far too busy to take much of an interest, but I saw how broken my brother was. The man has remained obsessed with her, so naturally, when the opportunity arose to have her back in his life, he took it. The only problem was she came with baggage. A lot of it. And not just her eight-year-old daughter, Charlie. No, Angel didn't disappear on Finn. The poor girl had been kidnapped to be sold to the highest bidder. Worse, our Uncle Don was the orchestrator, along with two other men. Finn finally managed to knock the girl up, so he's over the moon about that. A fact he throws in our faces constantly, he says he has super sperm. More like stupid sperm impregnating Angel so quickly.

I pump my fist under the table and breathe away the regret of not seeing through our Uncle's facade sooner. Even though I hated the control he seemed to hold over my father, I never looked into him sooner.

If I had? I'd have discovered that not only did he rape Angel, but he also attacked our ma, leaving her pregnant with her son, Teddy.

We recently discovered that Teddy had been killed along with his adoptive parents. For Ma, it was like losing him all over again. She's the strongest woman I know.

"Oscar! Fucking play your goddamn hand," Finn snaps from across the poker table.

I slam my cards down on the table without making eye contact with my brothers.

Obviously, I win.

Grumbles and groans erupt around me.

"Reece has a date tomorrow night," Cal throws out with a heavy sigh causing my eyes to dart toward his.

I know all about the obsession my nephew has with someone I know Cal would not approve of. Just how much does Cal know about her? I wait anxiously for him to ask me to do some sort of search on the poor girl, but it doesn't come. He just leans back in his chair, looking defeated.

He chokes a fake laugh, "Yeah, he asked me to show him how to shave his pubes off." He stares at the table. "Fucking pubes..." He shakes his head. "My kid had pubes before I even knew he existed." The sadness in his voice is understandable. Cal discovered he had a teenage son with Lily, a woman he fell for in Vegas. Stupidly, neither one of them thought to exchange details. Utter morons.

Cal suffers great regret with how things happened and therefore missed out on almost fifteen years with his son.

"When I was a teenager, I couldn't wait for pubes. Nowadays, they cut 'em off." Con attempts to lighten Cal's somber mood.

"You get them yet, brother?" Finn smirks in Con's direction.

"Got 'em and clipped 'em." Con's smile broadens. Before making a hand gesture showing how he shaves off his pubes, he even adds the noise for emphasis. "Zzzzzoom. Clip. Clip. Boom."

He thrusts his groin out on the boom, causing Finn to laugh. "You fucking dick, do you do your ass too?"

"Too much fucking information." Bren's deep voice makes my lips tug up. Always so blunt. Bren is so straight to the point with anything regarding sex. I can't imagine he takes much time in giving a woman pleasure, and how the hell his woman, Sky, puts up with him is beyond me.

My mind goes back to how stunning Paige looked spread out and spent on my white satin sheets, utterly mesmerizing.

As if she appears on command, my tablet pings with the tone I set just for her, alerting me that she's received a text message. I grind my teeth and open the app.

Carl: You fancy that new seafood restau-

rant tomorrow?

Paige: I'm not dating right now, Carl. I'm sorry.

Carl: We can go as friends? Work colleagues, discuss your opportunities within the clinic when you graduate?

The fucking ass is using her career as an excuse to meet outside of work. Anger boils inside me. Absolutely fucking not.

Before the chump can text her again, I block her number from reaching him.

There, fucker, try contacting her now. My anger dissipates slightly before my mind conjures up some sort of conversation they might have at work about meeting as opposed to texting, and then I wouldn't even know about their plans. I need to do something about that too. I muse over the thought while tapping out a message.

Oscar: Dinner tomorrow seven pm.

Paige: I might be busy.

Oscar: I might dock your pay.

Paige: You're a dick!

Oscar: And you need to suck it.

Paige: You need to be nice.

Oscar: You need to do what I pay you to do.

Oscar: My driver will collect you. Be ready.

I smirk at her responses, and my cock jumps in my pants, imagining her glossy lips around me again.

Tomorrow can't come soon enough.

Paige

"You never responded to my message," Carl states while handing me the empty needle he just used on the German Shepherd for pain relief.

My spine straightens. We had a fling a while ago, but that was before Ebony had her accident and before everything went to shit. I told him I had too much going on to date, and I hadn't failed to notice he appeared to be waiting for me to have time to date again. The only problem is I'm not so sure I want him to wait.

I can't avoid his eyes any longer, "My phone wouldn't let me message you back. It's really weird because I could text everyone else."

He eyes me skeptically. "I'm not lying to you, Carl. Here..." I storm over toward my purse and withdraw my phone before giving him an example of me trying to shoot a message over to him, only to be stopped with an error message.

He scratches his chin, clearly unsettled by his assumption, before meeting my eyes, minus an apology, making my own eyes roll internally. I need to stay on side with Carl. I need this job, this future.

"So, do you want to go out tonight? For that meal?" He gestures toward the phone.

I dart my eyes away once again. "I'm sorry. I have plans."

"With who?"

My spine straightens. I don't know whether he means to be intrusive, but I don't like it. "With a friend," I reply softly.

"Maybe another time, then?"

I turn my back on him and pay attention to the big furball on the table. "Maybe," I reply with little to no enthusiasm.

Chapter Ten

Paige

I'm well aware I'm late. But after the way, Oscar barreled into my life and took over without thought or even so much as asking pisses me off.

When I got home from work, Ebony greeted me with a wide smile. Apparently, a parcel had been delivered. Childish excitement bubbled inside me when I pushed open my bedroom door to see a white dress box on my bed with a big ribbon and bow on the top.

I ripped the box open to find the most beautiful royal blue fitted dress with matching heels. Of course, they were the correct size; I almost roll my eyes when I make the mistake of even considering checking them. Ebony and I spent the remaining of the evening preparing for the meal.

My hair looks effortless despite the time put into it, and my natural-looking make-up flawless.

I stride across the restaurant toward the man with piercing blue eyes, the very bane of my contempt. His head is raised high, his sharp jaw clenched, and his eyes boring into mine behind glasses? I wasn't aware Oscar wore glasses, but still, I noticed his blue eyes shining behind them.

That's what Oscar O'Connell does—he draws you in, so you only ever see him but still never really see him at all. Only the glimpses he allows, and that pisses me the hell off.

He stands out in the restaurant because his whole stance screams danger, money, and power. His face is a mirror of command and control, yet also indifference, like he doesn't care for anyone else's opinion or the fact that he's alone.

I drop my purse on the table with a huff and ignore his questioning look.

Eventually, he sighs heavily, glares at his watch, and then back at me. "You're late."

"You're very assertive, Oscar."

His lip curls slightly. "You're going to be punished for breaking the rules."

I scoff. "What rules?"

His jaw tightens, and his fists clench on his napkin before he leans toward me, "The rules in the fucking manual, Paige. Page four hundred and forty-five." His tone screams danger, *back the fuck up* kind of danger, but of course, I don't heed the warnings going off in my head because as dangerous as he may seem to everyone else, he's nothing more than a pussy cat to me. I smile at my own assertion.

"That manual is a nightmare. You really need to

scrap it and page whatever, and forty-five can go fuck itself." My serene smile is countered by his icy glare.

The tension is broken when a waiter arrives to fill our glasses with water and hands us our menus.

I almost choke at the prices. All for a bit of fish?

"Problem?" Oscar doesn't even lift his eyes to talk to me. No, the obnoxious prick keeps them trained on his menu like I'm so insignificant he doesn't want to waste precious time on me.

I lean forward and keep my voice low. "It's really expensive."

"It is."

"I can't afford these prices," I confess, shocked they can charge so much for something that effectively washes up on the beach.

He lifts his eyes to meet my own. "Page one hundred and twenty-two: all expenses incurred during time with employee will be paid for by said client."

I open my mouth with a comeback but find nothing comes out. I am rendered speechless at that. Traitorous mouth.

Oscar

She sits with her mouth agape, and it's not the first time tonight I imagine shoving my cock deep inside her sarcastic little throat.

Now I have the taste of a blow job; I want more; I want them fucking all.

From her lips. Only hers.

For now.

I dart my eyes around the room again, feeling like ants are creeping over my skin. I don't particularly like restaurants, and I sure as shit don't like ones I've never been to. They make me uncomfortable and angsty, and that's before you consider the element of danger that comes with being an integral part of the mafia family when leaving the house.

Not liking the noise, the hustle and bustle, and the uncertainty around me, I attempt to engage in my breathing technique. Not liking it at all.

"Oscar?" My eyes find Paige's face, concern marring her beauty. I narrow my eyes in confusion.

"You don't look very comfortable." She sees me. When I thought I'd masked my feelings well...

I tilt my head to study her. How does she do that? How am I so drawn to her when she could be so deadly to me?

"You're clenching your fists, doing your breathing thing. Your eyes are unsettled, and your shoulders are tense. Do you not like it here?"

"No," I answer honestly but give her nothing more.

"Then why bring me here?"

Her face softens as she speaks. She's like some sort of fucking therapist because I can't help but give her a reply when I really want to give her none at all.

"I thought you wanted to try out the new restaurant."

She searches my words and my face before her entire demeanor changes. "You have access to my messages?"

I stare back at her with force in my words, "Of course."

Paige pushes her chair back abruptly, making a scene before she grabs her purse and darts toward the door.

My own feet follow just as quick. If I gave myself time to analyze my reaction, I'm sure I'd find humor in the fact I've never chased after a female in my entire life.

Not even as a child.

I storm out of the restaurant to find her about to turn down the street into a crowd of people. Absolutely fucking not. I grab her arm forcefully and pull her into the alleyway. I cage her in below me with my arms on either side of her head, careful not to touch her, not yet, at least.

Her seething eyes glare up into my own.

"Page eight hundred and four: access to personal devices will be monitored under strict instruction by the client as he sees fit. Read. The. Fucking. Manual, Paige."

Eventually, the stiffness in her back eases, and she sulks against the wall in defeat, making jubilant triumph build inside me.

This woman is everything I never knew I needed—a sarcastic, fiery spitfire, a challenge.

Different.

Paige

The entire car ride was blanketed in silence. The apartment door clicks shut behind us, and I half expect Oscar to turn and shout at me, but of course, he's far more controlled than that.

"Go get into position in your room," he tosses the words over his shoulder as he makes his way down the corridor to what I can only imagine leads to his bedroom. "Your room." The thought that the room belongs to me fills me with elation, but of course, that's not true; I'm one of probably many other women he's screwed in there. My shoulders sag as I consider this, making my way to the room like a good submissive.

The door closes, and I hear Oscar take in a sharp intake of air before dropping down in the armchair.

"Stand and lose the robe." I do as he asks, my body heating at his perusal.

He points toward his feet for me to move and stand there. His eyes rake over my body, and a lump lodges in my throat when his eyes lock on to my breasts.

His sharp, commanding voice sends a shiver down my spine. "Turn."

I hear him moving around for something. "Hands behind your back."

The sharp tug of my wrists makes me wince as he binds them together with the rope from the robe. His palm then gently trails over the globe of my ass, making my heart thump out of my chest; even his simple touch arouses me. A smack hits my butt cheek, and I startle in shock. Before another rains down on the same spot. "Motherfucker, Oscar." I turn my head to glare over my shoulder at the man transfixed on my ass cheeks.

His eyes snap up to mine, and his jaw sharpens.

In a swift movement I don't see coming, he stands, roughly grabs the back of my neck, and throws me onto the bed.

Oscar kicks my feet apart and stands between them. He fumbles with his belt, and I've never been so turned on in my entire life. Wetness seeps from me at the expectation of his cock plunging into me. A sharp crack of his belt against my ass makes me seize up with shock, and then he repeats it. Another sharp slap on my ass causing pain to lance through me.

"Fuck. Oscar." I squirm on the sheets as the belt cuts through the air and cracks hard against my ass again and again. Each time, I scream both in pain and pleasure. Loving the fact he's taking his anger out on me, on my ass.

"You need to be punished, Paige. Fucking punished."

He hisses the words out. They should worry me, hurt me even, but in some sort of sick, screwed up way, I understand him. I should be punished. I haven't listened. I fought him at every turn, and I didn't read the damn manual.

Eight times, I scream into the sheets—four on each cheek, but I don't tell him to stop. I'm not sure why but I want him to punish me.

"Please. I need you, Oscar." I desperately want him to fill me to take away the ache between my legs.

I feel the rapid movement behind me, but when I try to look over my shoulder, he pins my head to the mattress, determined to keep my eyes away from his. My heart sinks.

His body jerks, the room filling with his scent. "Fuck, I'm going to come on you. All fucking over you." I virtually pant at his own admission.

"Fucckkkk." Warm ropes of cum hit my back and ass, leaving me more on edge than ever.

I feel him straighten behind me, then a tug on the rope as I drop fully against the mattress.

"Shower and dress. I've ordered food." Then he leaves the room.

Leaves the fucking room with me on edge.

I want to throat-punch the prick.

Chapter Eleven

Oscar

Of course, she walks down the corridor into the living area in just the robe. I'm not sure why I expected any different, but I thought she'd put the tight blue dress back on, the one I ordered her. Her chest is flushed, and I can't decide if it's from the shower she's just taken or from my blatant attention on her body. "I ordered." I snap my eyes over to the dining table, hers following my line of sight.

"Wow. Oscar, how many people are you planning on feeding exactly?" She stifles a giggle.

I fidget under her questioning, my hand brushing over my hair in discomfort. "I wasn't entirely sure what you'd like..." I leave the reply hanging, but it's a lie. I know exactly what she likes.

Exactly.

"Well, I don't know how you did it, but you managed to guess all my favorite types of food." She beams up at me, and my heart skips a beat. I can't help but smile back at her before I realize what I'm actually doing. The look in her eyes softens before she swallows thickly and glances away.

"Suppose we best make a start then, right?" Paige walks over to the table, picks up a plate, and begins loading food onto it. Two slices of pizza, a small burger, fries, and some chips—enough junk food to give your arteries a blockage. "Oscar, you're eating, right? You didn't order all of this for me?" She raises a brow at me in question.

I snap my eyes toward her. She doesn't need to know that's precisely what I did. "Of course not." I wince at my own flat tone but mask it by glancing away nonchalantly.

Paige walks over toward the couch, tucking her legs underneath her. It's the first time a female has ever sat on my couch, and I can't help but stare at her. Our fucking has left her hair disheveled, her cheeks tinged pink, no doubt aware of my scrutiny. Her luscious breasts peeking out from the dip in her robe. She looks like a vision of beauty sitting lazily on my white leather couch like she belongs there. Like she's always belonged there. My heart hammers at the thought... the thought that I quite like her there.

Here, close to me, in my home.

She leans over to the glass coffee table and takes the tv remote that has never been used. Flicking through some channels, she randomly stops on a nature show. I sneer in her direction. Her legs are now crossed like a child's. The plate nestled on her lap, and she nibbles away at the mountain of food.

Her eyes flit over toward mine, lighting up as she

speaks. "Are you coming to watch tv with me?" She tilts her head in my direction.

My eyebrows shoot up in response to her question. Am I? I've never sat on my own damn couch to watch tv before. Never. She must sense my apprehension because she sighs. "There's plenty of room." She even throws her arm out toward the space on the couches. Of course, there's plenty of room; I designed the damn thing.

She giggles, and the sound goes straight to my cock, making it twitch in my pants. It seems to be in constant need of her.

"Oscar, come sit on the freaking couch. I assure you it's comfortable." Her playful demeanor settles the tension I feel, so much so I add some food to my plate, grab a knife and fork, and head over toward Paige.

"I'm not watching fucking nature," I grumble as I drop down in the corner of the couch.

"Of course, you're not." She rolls her eyes at me, earning herself a glare.

She picks up the remote and leans over to hand it to me.

Paige

I watch him from the corner of my eye. Even his eating is methodical, but I pretend not to notice. The way he cuts into his salad, moving the cucumber away before pulling it back onto the fork, so the dressing doesn't touch it...

I suck the grease from the pizza off of my fingers. "You know what you need?"

Oscar quirks a brow at me. "I'm sure you're about to tell me."

I nod, casting my eyes over the clinical space yet again while throwing a chip into my mouth. "You're right, I am." I pick up a few more chips and pop in another. "You need a pet."

He scoffs before meeting my eyes. "I don't like animals."

My mouth drops open at his words because surely there's an animal he does like? Right? "What about a dog? They're loyal." I throw a chip in my mouth.

Oscar eyes my moving mouth, then glares down at the crumbs on the couch before visibly shaking his head.

No doubt trying to rid himself of my mess. "They make a mess, and I don't like fur. Con, my brother, has a hairless one, and I can barely look at it." He grimaces, causing me to laugh at his reaction.

"How about a small animal, one you can pet?"

His eyebrows knit together, and he stares at me in confusion. "What part of I fucking don't like touching things are we not getting?"

I stifle a laugh. "Okay, no touching. Gotcha."

"Finally," he deadpans with a quirk of his lips.

I rub a finger over my lips ."I got it..."

"Please don't." his tone deadpan.

I throw a chip at his sarcastic grimace. "Fish."

His face contorts in mortification. "Fish?"

"Yes, fish. Oscar, they're perfect. They're relaxing, you don't have to clean them, they can be colorful, and they're beautiful. And I love them." I smile sweetly at him.

"And you love them." He rolls his eyes.

"Yes, I do. So what do you think?"

"They smell."

I bite my lip, trying to hold in a laugh.

"Just fucking say it. What?"

"I'm just thinking I bet you've had a lot of fishy smells in this apartment." I can't help but snort at my own joke.

He appears blank, either not understanding my quip or not playing at all. "You know they're all tested, and any chance of impregnation is neutralized."

"Neutralized? So clinical, Oscar." I roll my own eyes this time.

"What I'm trying to say is..."

He doesn't get a chance to finish before I wave my hand at him. "I get it. They're all clean pussies you let in the apartment, right?"

He swallows thickly, then nods. "Right."

We're back to silence now. "Sort a fucking tank out, but if I don't like it, you can have it." I bounce my ass on the couch with excitement with a desperate need to throw my arms around him, but instead, I'm not sure what to do, so naturally, I can't help but throw a chip at his head. He stares at the tv screen, enthralled by a show about IT geeks of all things. He blinks, once, twice, before he seems to register what happened. I throw another at him for good measure and lift my eyebrows in jest.

"Are you wanting your ass spanked again? Is that it, Paige?" His lips move, but his face is stoically still. His blue eyes pierce into my own, causing me to swallow with uncertainty. Do I want my ass spanked again? I mean, it's still on fire from the last time.

I dig my hand into the bowl and draw out another large chip before I throw it at his face. He swiftly moves so quickly that I don't have a chance to think. Oscar's hand tightens in my hair, and he forces me face down on all fours on the couch. He pulls up the gown, the cool air hitting my exposed, delicate ass.

"Do you want a spanking, Paige?" His hand finds my pussy, dripping with the wetness he left me with earlier. "Or is it my cock you want?" His deep voice penetrates through my body down toward my clit. "Mmm?" he muses with a dark chuckle.

"Your... your cock."

"Louder." He slaps my pussy hard, causing me to moan at the pain. "Mmm, you love having your pussy smacked, don't you, dirty girl?"

He chuckles. "Fucking dripping on my couch." *Slap*.

"Oh shit, Oscar, please."

"Please, what, Paige?"

Slap. "Oh god. Your cock, Oscar. I want your cock. Please."

His zipper comes undone, tears a foil, and then he lodges the head of his hard cock at my pussy before he rams into me so hard I lunge further forward into the couch. "Oh god. Oscar."

The pressure builds quickly as one hand tightens on my hip while the other works between my legs, occasionally stroking over my entrance while his cock continuously enters me, quicker and quicker.

The heat builds inside me. He smacks my ass so hard it causes my mouth to part on a loud groan. "Oh god. I'm..." I scream my release as my pussy tightens around his throbbing length, holding him in and milking him all at the same time.

"Paige." He grits his teeth, and his stuttered movements let me know he's finished. My own orgasm is so powerful I zone out, squeezing my eyes close at the overwhelming sensation.

I feel him withdraw from behind me. "Wait a minute." I hear him move and a door open before he returns. I'm paralyzed from the incredible sex in a daze.

His soft hand soothes my ass as he applies a cold ointment to the lacerations. He chokes a little, his voice a soft whisper. "I almost forgot again. I lose my fucking mind around you, Paige. You make me lose my mind; all the rules don't seem to follow with you. I need the rules. Do you understand me?"

I nod against the cushion before finding my voice. "Yes."

"Good. Good girl." His palm tightens possessively on my ass. "I'm not sure how I'm ever going to let you go." His voice is lower now, so light I almost don't hear him.

Almost.

"Then don't. Don't let me go."

He chuckles mockingly. "We both know that's not an option now, don't we?"

My heart sinks, a wave of sickness taking over me at the thought of the inevitable, at the thought of hurting him.

I close my eyes, determined to keep the thoughts away.

Oscar

I watch her sleeping on the couch. After fucking her into near oblivion, I palmed her ass and gave her the aftercare she deserved.

The aftercare I promise in my rules.

My eyes track over every exposed part of her. She's nothing short of beauty personified. Her waves fall over the gown, the red onto the white, a clear contrast. Her coloring is growing on me, so much so that it may as well become my favorite. Her red, only hers.

Her breathing stutters, and I find myself holding my own breath until she breathes again. I've never had a woman that isn't family on my couch, let alone asleep on it, and the thought warms me.

My eyes flit over the mess of the living area, and it surprisingly doesn't repulse me, not as I'd expect. I kind of like the mess being there, the chaos of it all, her.

I stand and stretch my arms above my head, loosening up my constantly tense body. Paige's red hair blows against her face as air escapes those perfectly pouty lips.

How I long for those lips around my cock! My dick aches against my pants from just staring at her lips, for Christ's sake. I lean down and gently brush away the strands of hair from her lips. Her breath, a whisper against the tip of my finger, causes my heart to flutter for some unknown reason, and in this moment, I realize it's going to be difficult to let her go. Very difficult.

I might not be able to keep her like I want to, but I can keep her safe, and I'll do everything in my power to do so.

Chapter Twelve

Paige

I don't wake up to an alarm this morning. My eyes scan the room, and I realize that, at some point, Oscar must have put me in my bed. A pang of disappointment hits me—this bed, not his. I wonder if he ever had another woman in his bed or if he has always been so closed off and guarded. As much as I think the latter, I can't help but consider the other, and I don't like it at all.

My neck aches—it must be from the uncomfortable position I fell asleep on the couch, and I'm suddenly grateful that he must have moved me during the night. I stand with a groan and decide to wash up and dress before descending on him today. I nibble my lip at the thought of our ongoing banter. It excites me; he excites me.

Today, the closet door is open, and without thinking, I go to investigate why that might be; it's clearly been done on purpose.

Rows upon rows of clothes line the rails and shelves,

all in my size. I trail my fingers over the expensive items, the softness of the silk blouses, and the thickness of the designer jeans, unlike anything I've ever felt or been able to afford before. Tears spring to my eyes before I choke them down and decide to try something on.

When I finally enter the living area, his eyes are already trained on me. "You dressed?" he queries with a raised eyebrow. He's sitting at the table with a glass of orange juice beside him and his tablet in hand. My heart flutters at his instant perusal of my body, a flush creeping up my chest.

"I did." I continue walking toward him. "Thank you for the clothes."

He doesn't respond, and I don't expect him to.

"There's coffee in the machine." He tilts his head toward the kitchen area, and I break out into a smile, feeling like I've achieved something over him. A feeling of him caring about me warms my heart, and I want to grab it with both hands and run before he changes his mind.

Turning on the machine, I sniff the freshly ground coffee. I revel in the fact it's the good stuff and not like the instant, cheap shit we have back home. My mind stops when I consider home. A sinking feeling of guilt rises inside me. While I'm here with Oscar living the high life, my poor sister and her kids are struggling to pull together a measly meal.

"Oscar, what did you do with all the leftover food?"

"Got rid of it."

Panic builds inside of me. "You threw it out?"

He turns toward me with his ever-assessing eyes. "I did."

"Oscar, that's ridiculous. Half of that wasn't even touched." My shoulders sink. "I was going to ask if I could take it home. The kids would have loved it." I nibble on my lip, deep in thought. When was the last time they had treats like that?

"The kids don't have food?" He glares at me as though I'm the asshole.

I snap my eyes back up to his. "Don't be a dick. They have food, just not all that fancy shit you buy."

His eyebrows raise, "Fancy shit?"

I chew the inside of my mouth, pissed at his nonchalance. At his antagonizing manner when all I feel is disappointment and guilt inside.

"Pizza is fancy shit?"

I swallow thickly, overcome with emotion. He doesn't get it. People like him will never get it. It's the fact it's a treat; the kids would have loved it, Ebony would have loved it, and he threw it away without a thought. Then he tries to belittle me. I shake my head; well, screw him. My chest heaves with both hurt and anger.

"You know what? Screw your fancy-ass coffee, too." I push the scented coffee to one side and stomp down the corridor to gather my things.

"I didn't fucking say you could leave yet!" he shouts after me. I flip him the bird over my shoulder.

"I pay you to fucking stay when I tell you to!"

"I have a job to get to, Oscar. A real one. One I like," I

scream back at the ass, wincing at my own words as I stuff my belongings into my overnight bag.

The sound of glass smashing startles me, but I choose to ignore it. A lone tear falls down my face, landing on my hand. Jesus, what the hell is wrong with me? Crying over fucking pizza.

Of course, I know it's not that. It's his nonchalance toward his actions and his lack of empathy too. Is it even something that he's capable of? Will he ever be capable of something more? And why the hell should I care? It's just a job, right? A way to earn extra money to provide for treats like the ones he threw out.

I ignore his cold stare as I stroll past him toward the door. His knuckles tighten on his tablet, and the coffee machine is in pieces on the floor. I stride through the door and slam it after me, stopping when I hear his roar from behind the heavy wood. My head drops back against the door, tears staining my face, my heart thumping against my chest. My heart tells me to go inside, but my head tells me otherwise. I don't belong here. I have a job to do.

He's just a job.

Tears stream down my face. My head is lying.

Chapter Thirteen

Oscar

My mind wanders yet again to Paige, the way we left things I don't like. I can't handle her being mad at me. The disappointment in her eyes—I hate it there. I want to make everything better; I want her to believe in me and need me. Want me.

I avert my mind, pushing away the shit from yesterday, and concentrate on the here and now. And right now, my cock is rock hard and raging for release. All because of Paige, her red hair, her milky skin that flushes perfectly when I fuck her. I lick my lips, imagining tasting her. I want that. I want that so fucking bad it brings a pain to my chest. My fists tighten in annoyance with myself. Why can't I do it? Why the fuck can't I bring myself to touch her like I want to.

Let her touch me too.

My mind automatically darts back to my childhood, the place I never want to go.

"He's feral. Like an animal. We need to sedate him or

something, anything." The desperation behind the voice forces my eyes to flit from one doctor to the other. The white lab coats they wear are terrifying. I'm blocked in a corner with a scalpel in my hand. I'll use it too. As much as I hate blood, I'll use it on them if I have to.

Why can't they understand? I don't want them touching me. There's nothing wrong with me. Nothing. Ma said it's okay to be different. So why are they trying to find something inside of me that's not there to find? Why can't they leave me alone?

"Oscar, put the weapon down."

Scalpel. Weapon? A small laugh bubbles inside of me. Rocket guns are weapons, Glocks are weapons, and knives are weapons. A scalpel is not a fucking weapon.

"The kid's a fucking psychopath. Look at him." The doctor glances at me, waving his arm out toward me. His frantic eyes are coated in terror. I sneer back at him, making him take a step back at my response.

"Oscar, if you don't put the scalpel down, we're going to have to restrain you, son."

My heart races faster, my knuckles whitening on the scalpel.

I squeeze my eyes closed, preparing myself for the battle.

Bren always says I'm a fighter; I don't think he meant this kind of fight, though.

My eyes snap open, my heart hammering in my chest, and a sheen of sweat coating my skin. Fuck, I hate it when my mind goes back there. To being touched, and experimented on.

My throat is dry, and I know I need something to take

my mind off of the memories, off of the pain and torment.

I need her.

I lean over to my nightstand and take my phone off charge. Gripping it tightly in one hand, I tap out a message.

Oscar: I want you at my apartment. Now.

I wait patiently, going over in my head what I'm going to do to her. Bound. Maybe gagged. Perhaps I'll use a spreader bar on her legs? I bet she hasn't done that before.

The thought of her experiencing new things with me excites me. I want her firsts. All of them. They're mine.

I check my phone again. She hasn't even opened my fucking message yet.

Page one hundred and ninety-six says an immediate response is expected at all times.

I slowly drag my finger over my bottom lip. It does say to respond within thirty minutes of receiving the message.

I double check my timeframe—only twelve minutes since I sent the message. Fuck.

Jesus, I need something to take my mind off of the waiting. I also need to consider changing the response times since waiting is not my forte. Not when I want something. Now.

I skim through her social media again. This time, I take a more detailed note of where she is in the photos instead of what she's doing and what she's wearing, like the last six times I checked. She spends a lot of time outdoors with nature. That's not for me. I hate fucking bugs. I don't particularly like animals either, and she just so happens to love them. All of them, considering the images. She's smiling innocently at a horse as though the damn thing is a god. And in the next image, a dog is perched on her knee, while in another image, she's staring into a dog's eyes lovingly.

The little fucker makes her feel something I'm not sure I can ever make her feel. And I don't like it. Not at all.

I wince at the snake she's holding in her hands, and my grip tightens on the phone. Has she got a fucking death wish? A snake. I brush a hand through my hair anxiously. Maybe I need to add a clause into the manual about unnecessary activities that put you in harm's way.

I pay good money for her, and the last thing I want is a snake to harm her or worse.

I quickly swipe the image away and check the time— thirty-two minutes have gone by, and no response.

Paige, Paige, Paige. I shake my head, partly in frustration and partly in excitement. My cock jumps at the thought of punishing her ass red. Fucking it.

I stroke my hand over my tented joggers, determined not to take my cock out, not until I can have her again, no matter how desperately I'm for a release.

Oscar: Answer your fucking messages.

Strolling into the kitchen, I help myself to a cool water, hoping for some relief.

I tell myself not to look at my phone, but again, I can't help it. I'm like a magnet to her, yet I can't understand why.

Maybe it's the promise of a challenge? Maybe it's learning what's behind her eyes. Behind her motives?

Annoyance bubbles inside me. Is she with another man? Is this why she's choosing to ignore me?

I open the app to track her phone and its activities.

It's been dormant. It's still at the veterinary clinic, and there's been no activity on it for two hours and twenty-four minutes.

I don't like this. Not at all.

Is she fucking her boss, that prick Carl? Is that what she's doing? Fury bubbles inside me. They're fucking. She's mine, and they're fucking. I feel myself becoming unhinged.

Before I know what I'm doing, I throw the bottle of water across the room. My hands swipe at the kitchen counter, sending the contents clattering to the floor.

It isn't enough. I want to fucking kill him. Slaughter him. Draw the blood I despise.

My heart races so fast I can feel myself going into a panic.

I close my eyes and attempt my breathing technique. Over and over again. Desperately trying to regain some control.

After what feels like an hour, my heart slows, and my fingers ache from clenching them so tightly.

I open my eyes with a renewed sense of vigor. Lifting my phone from the counter, I'm grateful I didn't destroy that too.

A thought suddenly occurs to me. My irrational behavior could have clouded my judgment. I might be correct in my line of thought, and if I am, it might just have saved the jackass Carl's life.

For now.

Paige

I flick my pen in and out of my mouth, reading the same line repeatedly. I need this report to be perfect. I need to get at least ninety-five percent, and then I'll be flying and a step closer to my dream of becoming a fully qualified vet. But I can't get a single thing to stick in my mind. All it keeps doing is wandering back to Oscar. I know I over-reacted, and it wasn't fair that I lashed out at him without explaining. I should know better than anyone that some things need explaining. I just wanted him to under-stand... needed him to.

A knock on my bedroom door startles me, and I groan in annoyance. This must be the fourth time Adam has interrupted me. "Urgh, Adam, I really need to get this essay done, honey. Can you go to Mommy?"

I hear Ebony chuckle on the other side of the door. "Not Adam this time, hun. Can you open the door?"

I sigh in relief and pull myself from the bed, unlocking the door to find Ebony nibbling playfully on her lip. My eyebrows furrow as I scan over my sister, her hair in a high bun and a tangled mess on her head, her normally pretty face of defeat is now replaced with jest.

"Here, it's for you." She thrusts her phone into my hand before turning on her heel and walking away with a hobble in her step.

I look down at the phone and stare at it like it's alien before snapping back to reality and turning to enter my room. I hold the phone gingerly to my ear. "Hello?"

"Page one hundred and fifty-one says an immediate response is expected at all times." Oscar's deep voice sends a thrill down my spine and a stickiness to my panties.

I sigh heavily, trying to act unaffected by his rudeness. "I don't know what you're talking about."

He all but growls, "Page seventy-five, Paige. All forms of contact must be adhered to. Cell phones on at all times, iPads and tablets available at all times..." I don't pay any attention as his voice drones on about lots of forms of technology I never knew existed. Instead, I get comfortable on my bed, sitting back against the headboard and crossing my legs while flicking through the book about exotic diseases among reptiles.

"Paige, are you fucking listening to me?"

His cold voice snaps me back to the call. "Mmm, yes. Totally."

"Totally?" He rolls his tongue over the word as though it's foreign. "Then repeat what I just said."

I smirk into the phone, knowing I'm about to piss him off. "Totally."

He chokes, and I can't help but smile, imagining his mouth gaping open in disbelief. "What?"

"You asked what you last said, and I repeated it. Totally."

"Very fucking funny," he snaps back, and I grin, enjoying riling him far too much.

"Did you want something, Oscar? I'm busy right now." I feign boredom.

"What I want is for you to keep your goddamn phone with you at all times!"

"I was in a rush and left it at work. I've shit to do besides you." I clear my throat. "So what did you want?"

He's silent, and I'm not sure if he's doing that breathing technique of his or thinking of a quick-witted comeback.

"You."

I narrow my eyes in confusion. "I'm sorry, what?"

"You, Paige. I want you." My heart races at his admission, a swirl of butterflies taking flight in my stomach. He wants me. "I want sex; therefore, I want you. I pay you enough." The pompous prick had to ruin it by tacking those words on at the end. I grind my teeth in annoyance.

"I'm busy."

"Doing what?" he snaps back in equal annoyance.

"I have a school report to get in, Oscar. I need to pass this class." I rub at my forehead, feeling the pressure of the schooling, my work, the responsibilities of the house and kids, of Ebony.

He's silent for a while. "Do you have an iPad?" His voice is softer this time.

"Yes."

"Good. Now get it and follow my instructions."

Oscar

After instructing Paige on how to give me access to her iPad, I was able to set up her camera so it appeared on my television in front of me. I now have full frontal access to her bedroom, to her.

"Take off your little sleep shorts." I stroke my hand slowly up and down my cock, taking a little longer to smear my engorged head with the pre-cum leaking from it.

Paige flushes as she pushes down her sleep shorts, exposing her pussy to me. My nostrils flare at the thought of her being naked inside them. Any weirdo could sneak into her room through her window and see her pussy lips through them.

I pump my cock aggressively, biting on my lip as I imagine punishing her little ass, leaving a red print on her as evidence of my ownership.

"Stand in front of the iPad. Drag your top over your head slowly, then play with your nipples. Show me how much you like it."

Her chest rises and falls in anticipation as she slowly drags her camisole over her head and drops it to the floor, exposing those perfectly plump, juicy tits of hers. Paige's nipples are already hard. She's turned on, and I imagine her pussy dripping with her cream as she tugs on her peaked nipples.

She closes her eyes as she brings the tips of her finger to her mouth and languorously sucks on them before her eyes pop open, and she rubs the wetness over her hardened peaks.

"Fuck, Paige. You look incredible."

Her smile is blinding. My heart leaps in my chest and my cock jerks, virtually strangling it to ward off my orgasm.

"Get on the bed and spread your legs. Open your pussy up with your fingers. I want to see inside."

I stare at the screen. Paige is spread out on her bed, naked like a fucking goddess, begging for my cock.

I lick my lips when she follows through with my instructions and uses her forefingers to open herself up to me. Her lips part on a moan, and I know she wants this as much as I do. Fuck, I can feel her need from here.

"Please." Her eyes plead into the screen, into my skin, my fucking heart that doesn't feel.

I swallow thickly, giving her a nod, then realizing she can't see me.

"You can play with your clit now, Paige."

Her fingers circle her clit frantically, and I have to chastise her haste. "Nice and slow," I snap. I need to drag this out and make her crave me as much as I crave her.

She licks her plump lips, making my cock drip in the

process. Once again, I have the urge to fill her mouth with my thick cock. I pump myself in my hand at the thought, gripping it tightly to hold off my release.

"Oscar, I want to see you too." Her voice is breathy and needy, desperate and hungry. My balls ache at her sound alone.

"No."

"Please. Please, Oscar." The flush on her chest spreads to her breasts, and I want to shove her tits so far into my mouth I smother on it.

"Be good, Paige, and I'll reward you." Her pupils dilate at my words.

"Are you wet?"

"I want to see your face," she practically moans the words out.

Annoyance bubbles within me. I'm in charge, so why does she not understand that?

"Please." Her lips part on a seductive whimper. Her eyes plead with mine, making my heart skip a beat in apprehension.

"Fuck." I scrub a hand over my head and adjust the screen, giving her access to view my face.

Her lips curve up into a knowing smile, and I want to spank her for it. "Thank you."

I ignore her sweet voice and concentrate on the task quite literally in my hand—my throbbing cock.

"Are you wet?"

Her chest rises and falls and so do her tits. I wish I was there to sample her hardened nipples, to suck them into my mouth and flick my tongue over the peaks. "Fuck, show me how wet you are, Paige."

I watch as she pushes two fingers into her dripping pussy, and my mouth waters for a taste of her. I will do it; I will taste her one day.

"Push them in your fucking mouth and taste yourself." She does as I instruct. "Do you taste good?"

She moans, and the sound reverberates straight to my balls. The familiar tingle of my oncoming release in reach.

Her legs widen, giving me the perfect view of her hole, leaking with her arousal. For me.

I work my cock faster to the motion of her hand, playing with her clit.

"Faster, Paige. Fuck your little cunt faster." Her hand works quicker, and my hand matches her pace. Pre-cum drips from the end of my cock in long strings, and I imagine her lips there to catch it. "Oh, fuck. Yes."

"Oscar, please."

"Pull your nipples."

She tugs her nipples hard, one at a time, her back arching. Her neck elongates, and she screams her release, setting off my own. Thick ropes of warm cum coat my hands and abs. "Yes, Paige."

No sooner has my cum hit me than I end the call, not caring to deal with the awkward aftermath that is bound to follow.

That's a lie, even to myself.

Not knowing how to deal with the awkward aftermath is more like it.

Disappointment swirls in my stomach as I throw my head back on the pillow.

Disappointment in myself.

Chapter Fourteen

Oscar

I couldn't help but think back to the time I'd spent with Paige. Remembering the day she walked out of the apartment sits heavily in my stomach, almost curdling.

I don't like drama, most definitely not surrounding me. She wanted the food for her family, and like an ass, I spoke before thinking.

She's naturally a do-gooder, having given up her apartment and life to help care for her sister and her kids. Then there's the whole veterinary thing. But still, something about the whole situation doesn't sit well with me.

That's how I find myself here, outside her sister's house.

Ebony is currently at a physiotherapy appointment, the children are at school, and Paige is at work. My hands tighten on the steering wheel at the thought of her at work with that moron boss of hers. That needs to be resolved soon; I'm not sure how much more of the thoughts of them together I can take.

I exit my SUV and walk around the back of the small one-story property. It's quaint and tidy on the outside. The side gate is broken, and it pisses me off that I can access it so easily. Pushing it open, I sneer at the side window that is open for anyone to access.

I move around the back toward the door, and it only takes a small shove for the damn thing to swing open with a squeak. Absolutely. Fucking. Ridiculous.

What the hell are they thinking?

I need to resolve this; I can't possibly sleep knowing Paige lives like this.

Two doors flank the small corridor. I ignore them and wait until I've done what I came for.

I make my way toward the kitchen area, taking in the small space they have to cohabitate. It's neat and clean, but it would leave no doubts in anyone's mind that money is scarce. The furniture doesn't match, and the television is small and old. I wonder if some of it was brought from Paige's apartment.

I storm toward the refrigerator, pissed that my woman is living like this. Why the fuck doesn't she ask for an advance? Of course, I know the answer. She doesn't want handouts; that's why she's selling herself to me. My hand tightens on the fridge door, and I breathe slowly, realizing the dire state they're living in. I've heard of people living hand to mouth but have never witnessed it myself.

There're no luxuries, as Paige would call them, no Pizza. There's a family bowl of pre-made pasta. No doubt their evening meal for the four of them. A small carton of milk and a tub of butter.

Surely there's more? My eyes dart around the kitchen, and I open the cupboards frantically. I find half a box of cereal and a few slices of bread. What the fuck?

No wonder she insisted on breakfast before leaving my apartment. I tug on my hair; I can't fucking stand this. Pulling my phone from my pocket, I fix this shit before I venture further into the house.

I relax against the cupboard as my plan comes together before finally allowing myself to enjoy being in her space.

Walking down the small corridor, I open the first door to a neat bedroom with a double bed and white linen. I close the door, realizing this must be Ebony's room.

I try the door to my left, and the scent of apples fills my nostrils, causing my dick to bulge against my pants. It's hers.

All around me is her.

I step inside, closing the door behind me. My need for her is profound as her scent fills not only my nostrils but my veins too. I'm literally breathing her in.

There are boxes piled high in the corner of the room. They must be from her own apartment.

I open the wardrobe doors to find the contents pitiful, and my jaw tics in irritation. This is not how she should be living; she should have it all, and she deserves it all.

I go over to her dresser and pick up the photo of her with her family. Her parents, sister, and brother smile happily back at the camera, causing a sharp pain in my chest. I don't recall having a photo like this of my own family. I place it down, aggravated that something so beautiful has been destroyed.

I open the first drawer and find her underwear and my heart races with excitement. I stroke my fingers over the lace of her black panties, imagining her creamy cunt inside them. Without a thought, I unbuckle my pants and take out my throbbing cock. The tip oozes stringy pre-cum, and I swipe it away with her panties. Then I wrap them around my cock and begin to thrust into my palm rapidly, imagining her wearing these panties with my cum inside them. Me, coating her skin with my essence.

"Fuck." I tighten my palm and grip my balls. I imagine they're her hands touching me, but it's not the fucking same; irritation gathers inside me. I want her, need her.

Her touch, her scent. Her.

I place the lace over the tip of my cock, imagining myself thrusting against her wet heat. Her mouth opening and closing on a breathy moan as I force my cock against her panties. She'll take me... Fuck, she'll beg for me.

I roar as I cum in my hand, her panties still wrapped around my hardness.

I wipe my cock on her panties; they're covered in me now. I'm torn between taking them or leaving them for her as a surprise; I muse on the thought. Then decide against it, she might consider me some sort of creeper, and I don't want that, so I scrap that plan. No matter how much I protest my innocence. No, Paige needs to be treated carefully if I want to keep her.

For now.

I walk into her small en-suite and can barely move in the damn thing. Rinsing my hands with her apple-fragranced hand soap, I dry my hands on a towel and open her shower door, taking photos of the products she uses.

Next, I go back into her bedroom, taking out the small devices from inside my jacket pocket. I pick the perfect spot for the small cameras to hide.

Feeling a sense of accomplishment, I reward myself with a couple of her panties and shove them into my pant pockets.

Paige

Today has been a long ass day, my feet throb, and my head aches as I make my way toward the house after an exhausting day. Oscar and the video call have been on my mind all day. As hot as it was, the way it ended filled me with self-loathing. I know he's paying me to do this, but does he really have to make me feel so used?

I've never had video sex in my entire life, and in the past, just the idea of opening myself up to a man like that terrified me.

I trust him in a way I never knew was possible, but knowing what I know, I probably shouldn't...

After all, the man admits to not feeling, so why do I let myself feel when I'm around him?

Why can't I close down on him as he does me?

With the weight of my bag pulling me down, I'm just about to open the door when it swings open, and Adam squeals with delight. "See, Aunty Paige. Come, see."

Casey pushes past him, her eyes alight in delight. "Aunty Paige, we have so many treats."

125

My eyebrows furrow in confusion at the excitement of the kids. What the hell is all this about?

I step into the living area. Ebony is standing tall with a huge smile on her pretty face. "What's going on? The kids are all excited." I wave my hand toward the kids lingering in the doorway, their enormous smiles contagious.

"What did you do?" She raises an eyebrow at me. "Did you win money or something?"

Confusion must mar my face because she goes on to elaborate, "The food, Paige. The delivery." Her eyebrows shoot up at my shock. "You didn't do this?" She opens the cupboards hastily, one at a time, the excitement clearly buzzing through her. Then she tugs open the refrigerator. It's full to the brim—heaps of food stacked in the cupboards.

I stumble back a little, shocked.

"And the best part? We got a freaking coffee maker, Paige. A real one with actual coffee beans." My eyes dart toward the coffee maker she's referring to, the exact replica of Oscar's. I wince at the thought that the coffee maker is now obliterated to a thousand pieces after his outrage.

"So it wasn't you?" Her gaze flits over my face as though checking for a lie.

I swallow thickly, overcome with emotion at his thoughtfulness. I had him wrong; he does care. He does show empathy, just in different ways.

I choke as tears fill my eyes. Tears at his kindness and tears of guilt. "It wasn't me, but I know who it was," I admit on a whisper.

Ebony's smile encompasses her whole face. "Well, go tell him thank you." She waves her hand toward my bedroom door, and I nod, making my way down the corridor toward my room.

As soon as I step inside, something feels different, and I swear I can smell Oscar's cologne, but that can't be, right?

I shake my head at the silly thoughts. Clearly, I have him on my brain because of everything he's done for us.

Oscar

My phone rings right on cue, and I exhale sharply with anticipation.

"Thank you." Her voice is sweet and breathy. I can picture the smile on her face and her shining green eyes.

"For what?"

I imagine her rolling those eyes at me, and my cock twitches at the thought of spanking her for it.

"You know what for, Oscar." She sighs, and it causes my cock to throb. Every sound from her lips is erotic. "Everything."

"I'll send a car to pick you up."

"What?" The panic in her voice pisses me off. "No, I just got in from work, Oscar. I want a shower, food, and sleep."

I want her here with me. "You can do all that here." Besides, I have another surprise I want to show her, one I've been desperate for her to see all fucking day.

She exhales in annoyance. "Oscar, I can't just drop

everything and run to you when you say." Is she fucking serious? Of course, she can.

"I pay you enough."

She huffs. "Right. Of course, you do." The sharpness in her voice lets me know she's pissed, but I choose to ignore it.

"I'll send a car."

I end the call and smile, knowing I have her just where I want her.

Here with me.

Chapter Fifteen

Oscar

I wait anxiously for the door to open, hoping she's as eager to see me as I am her. "Oscar, you can't keep clicking your fingers and expect me to jump when you shout high. I'm not a fucking..." Her voice trails off when her eyes land on the tank.

The one I bought for me. And her. For us.

Her mouth opens and closes a few times, causing me to bite into my lip like a giddy child. I shuffle on the balls of my feet while looking down at her through my lashes. It takes everything in me to stop myself from laughing at her gob-smacked reaction.

Her eyes are bright and wide, and then they almost shimmer, filling with tears, confusing me.

"You don't like it?" I glance back at the tank. The aquatic technician assured me it was the best. He also said he could maintain it on my behalf. I mean, the guy was here all fucking day in my space setting the damn thing up, so she better like it.

"I love it."

"Then why are you sad?" My hand trembles to touch her, but I shove my fist into my pocket, annoyed at myself for not being able to fix her.

"I'm not sad, Oscar. I'm happy." She tilts her head toward me, staring straight into my eyes. My heart hammers against my chest. I want her.

"I want to fuck you right now."

She lets out a choked laugh and rolls those emerald eyes. "Of course you do."

"Really fucking bad," I admit while biting into my lip. I scan my eyes down her body, her tits pushing against her blouse. Fire flares in my veins at the thought of her working like this with him.

"Go to your room." Her breath stutters and her eyes fill with need. She licks those pouty lips before turning on her heels and swaying her hips as she walks away from me.

Paige

I don't have time to analyze how beautiful the tank is. No, instead, I'm thrust up for his pleasure in what I can only describe as a sex swing. My ankles each tied in and my wrists bound too; all so I'm unable to touch him, but he can touch me. I should be happy he insists on making me come too. I should be, but I can't help the disappointment whirling around inside me.

"You've no idea how hot you look, Paige." He strokes his cock again. "I'm going to shove my cock so fucking deep inside you, you'll struggle to work with that boss of yours without thinking of me."

My heart rate escalates. The unadulterated look he spears me with makes heat flush into my cheeks, over my body, even down to my throbbing clit.

His hair is a tussled mess, his forehead is dripping in sweat, and his shirt is open at the neck, giving a peek of his olive skin. Skin I'm desperate to touch. His pants are unopened, with his boxers underneath his cock. My gaze not missing a single movement of his when he palms his cock and tugs his balls. How I long to do that for him, if only... I lick my lips, and his nostrils flare at the action, clearly wanting me as much as I him.

His hand works faster and faster.

"Fuck, your tits are amazing." He moves toward me, standing between my legs, the heat from his body searing into me.

"Please, Oscar."

"Please, what? You want my cock, is that it? Little sex doll." I moan on his words, his dirty mouth forcing me to release arousal I'm desperate for him to touch.

"Yes. Yes, please."

He takes a deep breath. "Good, good girl. Little spitfire."

He takes another condom from his pocket, ripping it with his teeth, the action alone making me clench my thighs, but of course, it's impossible. How can a man look so seductive by ripping open a condom wrapper?

He sheathes himself quickly, then he leans forward, presses his large hand tightly around my neck like a collar, and slams inside.

"Fuck yes. You feel incredible, Paige."

"Oh fuck, Oscar."

"That's it, say my fucking name. I own you!"

"Yes, Oscar."

He palms my tit forcefully, pinching my nipple, sending a shockwave through my body and down my clit. I throw my head back in ecstasy. "Ohhhh."

"Fucking come all over my thick cock, Paige. Come."

I roar as he releases a guttural wail. "Fuckkk. Yes."

His head drops forward, and his chest heaves up and

down; then, as if remembering, he steps back, severing the connection. He pulls off the filled condom and tucks himself in. "Once I release you, you're to go to your room and leave before seven." He stares at me pointedly for me to agree. I nod at his words and bite my lip to contain my sob.

Oscar doesn't notice, and once my feet hit the floor, he leaves the room, leaving me feeling more alone than ever.

Alone and unwanted, only good enough for one thing.

His pleasure.

Not mine.

Chapter Sixteen

Oscar

I'm pissed, and my hand tightens on the steering wheel. She hasn't returned my messages again. She's not answering her phone, instead just freezing me out of her life as though I don't exist. As though she doesn't get paid to be at my beck and call. I grind my teeth in frustration while flicking open the app I have installed that tracks her phone. Just let her be with that prick Carl, and I swear to fuck, I'll finish him.

I wait while it loads, doing my breathing techniques.

When her location finally pings, my eyes narrow in confusion. She's at a fucking supermarket? Why the hell would she need a supermarket when I had food delivered to her? She shouldn't need any more food for at least a fucking week. I should know; I did the order and paid the goddamn bill.

Is she there with him?

I've never entered a supermarket in my entire life, but that's where I find myself.

I'm that pissed that I don't allow myself to think of all the germs, noise, or the sheer number of bodies crowding my inner space. No, I walk with my head down on a fucking mission following the illuminating ping on my phone.

I hear her giggle before I see her, and my heart fucking stills in my chest. She's laughing with him. I clench and unclench my hands.

Turning the corner, my eyes trail up her lean, milky legs, her jeans shorts tight on her hips, her top lifting as she's stretched to the upper shelf, exposing her stomach. My fucking stomach. I stride toward her, snatching the box from her reach.

She jumps back, startled, almost knocking out three kids in the process.

"Jesus, Oscar. What the hell are you doing here?"

I glance around the store, looking for the smug bastard, ignoring her question. Three more children run up to her, all with hands full of candy. What the hell is happening?

"Oscar?"

I glance down at a toothless kid, his beaming smile making me snarl in defense. I register his birthday badge, and then my eyes flit over toward the cart. Filled with birthday balloons, a cake, and candles.

"Oscar," Paige snaps at me. "What are you doing here?"

I stare into her emerald eyes, which are furious. I swallow back my mistake before glancing away, hoping she doesn't pick up on the lie. I'm good at hiding things; I've spent years doing it.

"Shopping. What the fuck does it look like?"

Her jaw tightens. "You weren't following me, then?"

I scoff, moving my mouth toward her ear. "I pay you enough to fill my bed when I want you. So what if I were?" Her chest flushes red, and my cock swells at the sight. But her eyes fill with disappointment at my words. She wants more; I know she does. I know this because so do I. I'm just not sure how to get it.

I gently tuck the strands of her hair behind her ear and soften my words. "I need you."

She steps away, her eyes moving over the bunch of kids. "I have a birthday party to arrange." She licks her lips as though in thought. Then she draws her eyes back up toward mine. "You could come?" Her eyes fill with hope, so much fucking hope I feel sick. I tuck my clenched fists into my pockets, fuck I'm such a loser. I want to shout; I want to smash up the fucking store. I just want her.

I take a step toward her. "I can't." My eyes roam over the noisy kids, the ones I want to scream shut the fuck up too.

Disappointment covers her features. I've never wanted to be someone else so much in my entire life right now. I just want to be... normal. I wince at my own assertion of myself. I'm not fucking normal.

"It's okay to be different, Oscar." I close my eyes at her words; it's so fucking not okay to be different. She steps toward me and brushes her hand against my arm, the hairs standing on edge at her touch. My fists ball painfully so, but I force myself to remain still, remain grounded.

"Can you come after?" I ask her, our eyes now locking. She knows I want her, need her right now. "Please?" My throat is dry, waiting for her response.

Her eyes roam over my face, and her shoulders sag in defeat. She's not coming over tonight. I should demand her to come; I should threaten to fire her. Tell her she owes me money. Blackmail her. Anything.

"Where will I sleep?" Her chest heaves as I blink, replaying her words. This is her making a stand. This is her wanting more. More than our arrangement. More from me.

"Where do you want to sleep?" If I tell her no, then what? I can't have her in my room.

She swallows deeply, my heart racing to hear her words, "Can you stay with me?"

My shoulders practically collapse in relief at her question.

"Yeah." I clear my throat and take a step back, breaking the tension between us. "Just don't be fucking late." I straighten my back and revert back to my usual asshole self. "And check your fucking phone. I shouldn't have to come looking for you when I want you."

She giggles at me, causing me to roll my own damn eyes.

Chapter Seventeen

Paige

I open the door to the apartment. It was later than I expected, but I didn't want to leave Ebony to tidy up the mess on her own. I got the kids to bed, helped clean up, took a quick shower, and came over here. I'm sure I'd have been a lot quicker if I wasn't replying to Oscar's one hundred and one messages asking where I am and wanting an explanation on what I'm actually doing as if my life revolves around him only.

"I didn't think you'd come." His voice comes from over at the couches. He's sitting staring at the fish tank, his eyes trained on them, not me.

"I had to tidy up, Oscar. Besides, you knew I was coming. I replied as per instruction." I hold my phone up, giving it a little wave in his direction. "Plus, I'm pretty sure you have a tracker on this thing, right? So you know my exact location." His lip quirks up at the side as I make my way over to him, neither confirming nor denying my thoughts. I drop down beside him, flicking off my flip-flops and propping my feet onto the table, the same as him. We both stare at the fish tank.

"It's my favorite part of the apartment," he admits. His words leave a pang in my chest, but I can understand why. It's beautiful—vibrant colors of all variations swim around the most magnificent display tank I've ever witnessed. Corals and caverns for the fish, beautiful lighting, and plants—it's a little marine heaven.

"Which one's your favorite?"

He's still for a moment, and when I think he's not going to answer me, he does. "The Angelfish. It hides in the cave and only comes out when it needs to. Out of the shadows." He points toward the small fish peeking out from the carefully constructed coral cavern.

"What about you?"

"The guppy," I answer instantly.

Oscar scoffs in disgust. "The guppy?"

I nudge him playfully and ignore his jolt at my touch. "Yes, the guppy. It's a strong, small, pretty to look at, low-maintenance fish. They're perfect."

"Well, if I had to pick a guppy, I'd pick the red one." He points to the single red fish currently swimming along the top of the tank.

"I didn't think you liked red?"

"Nor did I," he deadpans. My heart skips a beat at his admission. "Besides, I feel sorry for it. It doesn't seem to get much food compared to the other fish." I turn my head toward his face, his alight in a full-blown smile, blue eyes playfully sparkling, and I can't help but laugh at his terribly inappropriate joke.

I snort and then hide my face in my hands. His touch

142

sends a shiver down my spine as he tugs my hands away from my face. "Don't hide from me, Paige. I do enough of that for both of us, don't you think?"

"I wish you didn't." I hold his eyes, hoping he can see the sincerity behind my words.

"I wish so too." His Adam's apple bobs. "You know what else I wish for?"

I shake my head. "I wish I could do all the fucking things to you that I want to do."

My heart hammers forcefully against my chest. "Like what?"

"Like kiss you." His finger traces over my lips, then trail down my chest, grazing over my nipple. "Fuck these." He continues his carefully measured movement, cupping my pussy in his hand. "Taste this."

I swallow the lump in my throat. "You could try?"

His nostrils flare, his eyes close, and I recognize him counting in frustration with himself. Oscar's eyes snap open. "I could."

Oscar

Paige stands before me, bare, her whole body virtually glowing in the light of the room. Her milky skin torments me, begging me to mark her. My cock drips against my pants, eager for a release.

"Do you trust me?" My voice comes out rugged and deep, cold as usual.

"Yes."

"Good." I lick my lips eagerly. "I need to trust you too."

Her eyes stay trained on mine, and I wait for confirmation. The swallow in her throat makes me second-guess things, second-guess her. I force myself to clarify. "In here. I need to trust you in here, Paige."

She stands straighter, raising her chin. "You can trust me."

"Good girl. Now climb on the bed. I want to fuck your tits." Her eyes widen, and her chest flushes red with my candid words.

Jesus, she's hot when she's turned on.

She crawls onto the bed, giving me an openly perfect view of her ass.

I consider my workings. How am I going to do this exactly? It's not something I've done before, and I hate undressing or touching people unnecessarily, but it's her. I can allow myself to touch her like this, for her to touch me because the reward will be phenomenal. I can almost taste it.

She turns onto her back, and those gorgeous tits of hers drop to the sides. Fuck, I've never wanted to mark something so bad in my entire life. Maybe I should spank them first? Make them flush like the rest of her? Fuck yes.

I move over to the hand scanner, calmly placing my hand down while my veins pump rapidly with excitement.

When the door slides open, Paige releases a breathy gasp, forcing me to close my eyes and calm myself. The need to fuck her courses through me. But I'll savor every second of this. I take the paddle in my hand, gripping it tightly.

Turning to face her flushed face, I take in her body language. Her eyes widen, and she swallows past the lump in her throat. Clearly, she's nervous but also excited, considering her pupils are dilated; her breathing erratic.

"Grip the headboard. Don't move your hands from there."

She nods once, then does as asked. Her knuckles whiten as she holds the headboard. "Open your legs. I want to see your pussy cream when I spank your tits."

"Oh god, Oscar."

Excitement buzzes through my veins when she says my name; the sound is so fucking erotic I threaten to blow in my pants like a damn teenager.

I lift the leather paddle, raising it high before bringing it down on her tit with a smack. The jiggle of her breast makes my cock twitch and leak pre-cum. Fuck, I need her. I repeat the process before I think too much about fucking her, fucking them.

Smack. Her breast reddens almost instantly, and a moan escapes her plump lip as she bites into the bottom one. Her emerald eyes stay trained on me as I raise the paddle again and fucking again. Each smack better than the last, faster, harder, redder. Her back arches higher with each deliberate hit. Her nipples peak, so tight, so fucking perfect, urging me to bite them, to sink my teeth into them, while her hand encourages my head.

Fuck, I can't take it anymore. I make quick work of stripping out of my pants and boxers, my shirt hanging loosely. I look like a fucking idiot, and I know it. Can I do this? Be fully exposed to her.

"Os, please."

I quickly unbutton my shirt before I can think too much of it, determined to follow through with my plan.

"Hold your tits together. Real fucking tight."

"Oh my god, Oscar."

I grip her chin forcefully between my fingers, causing her eyes to widen. "Don't move your hands. Do you understand me? Don't fucking touch me."

I release her chin, and she nods earnestly. "Of course." I give her a sharp nod and wait for her to do as she's told.

My hard cock jumps when her hands grip her breasts, pushing them together. Fuck me, she looks sensational. A string of pre-cum oozes from my cock, but I ignore it. "Don't move them," I snap at her again as I climb over her waist, straddling her.

"I won't, I promise." Her voice is merely a whisper.

Her milky skin against her reddened tits is the most erotic sight I have ever seen; I could come just from staring at her.

I move up slightly, positioning the head of my dripping cock against her tits. "Fuck, Paige, you look incredible. Is your pussy wet?" I position my hands on either side of her head, so I can stare down at her.

"Ye-yes."

"Good, you want me to fuck these tits?"

I tweak her hardened nipple, causing her to moan. The vibrations go down her chest and over her breast. "Yes. Please, Os." That's the second time she's shortened my name, and fuck, I love it. It feels fucking intimate as if we're in a real relationship. I want that; I want her. I plough my cock through her soft flesh again and again. My eyes stay transfixed on the bounce of her tits. Working my cock through her tits, I revel in her hard nipples, begging to be sucked. "Oh god."

"Open your mouth, be ready for my cum. I want it everywhere, all fucking over you." My words come out cold and unfeeling, but I'm unraveling. On a fucking high. My balls tighten, and I pick up speed. My mouth drops open, and my eyes flare as I watch my cum hit her tits, her chest, and her lips. "Jesus. Fuck." I keep working my spent cock, determined to empty myself on her fully.

My chest heaves as I come to a complete stop, and sweat coats my skin. I slowly climb off her body. Staring down at her, she's the most beautiful, perfect thing I've ever encountered.

She still holds her tits tightly and watches me closely with panting breaths. Her attention doesn't affect me like I thought it would.

"You can release them. Hold on a minute. I need to get you..."

Paige

"You can release them. Hold on a minute. I need to get you..." Oscar turns from me, and I expect him to go into the bathroom and bring out a warm washcloth like in the romance novels I read. But no, he turns to his sex cupboard and pulls out a metal pole and a stretcher-bar.

I snort at my mistake, causing him to snap his head around to face me. He glares at me and lifts an eyebrow in question.

I nibble on my lip before I decide to share my thoughts with him. "I thought you were going to get me a warm washcloth like in the books I read."

His eyes narrow in confusion. "For what?"

I nod my head down toward his cum, coating my skin. "Your cum." His lip turns up at the side, and his half-mast cock seems to grow with a jump as his eyes roam over my body.

"I like it there," he simply says while moving between my legs. "By the look of your dripping pussy, it tells me you like it there too."

151

Oscar uses a finger to trail down my stomach and over my clit, dipping into my pussy hole. He then thrusts two fingers inside. The slick sounds of his fingers pumping inside of me make my back arch, and I release a breathy moan.

"Mmm, you like me finger-fucking your needy pussy, Paige?"

"Yes. Don't stop, please," I gasp, struggling for air against his intrusion.

He pulls his fingers out, and I swear I could stab him, and then he chuckles, earning himself a glare. The cold leather cuff snaps into place on each of my ankles. Oscar adjusts the spreader expertly with the simple click of a button. The way in which he does this leaves a bitter taste in my mouth.

I don't like it; he's no doubt done this with other women. He's treating me like one of them again. He's shutting me out, not trusting me. He's going to fuck me like I'm just another hole. I turn my head to look away, unable to control the emotion building behind my eyes.

"What's wrong?" He picks up on the change in my demeanor immediately. The thought should be startling; instead, it settles me.

"I-I'm just thinking about how many other women you've done this to." My admittance is there out in the open. My vulnerability is visible, but will he see it?

His Adam's apple bobs, and I know he has. He knows exactly what I mean. "A lot." His words hit like a dagger in my heart. I vaguely hear a crinkling of a wrapper. "It's what I pay you for, Paige."

Asshole! I turn my flaring eyes back to him just in

time for him to thrust inside me. I glare at him, and his eyes widen in panic as though he's suddenly aware of something. "Hold the fucking headboard!" I stare at him. "Paige." His panicked eyes penetrate my heart, leaving me no choice but to do as he says. I slowly raise my hands to the headboard, gripping it tightly.

He thrusts harder as though punishing me for his mistake. "Fuck, your pussy feels good."

My hips move involuntarily against his movements. As much as I don't want to feel good while he's fucking me, I can't help it. He's a machine. "I pay you so I can fuck you." *Thrust.* My hands tighten to the point of pain. "I fucking pay you to serve my cock." Harder, he snipes the words out like venom, like he's trying to convince himself of everything he's saying. "I fucking own you." He roars as he comes, still pounding into me.

Then he pulls out and angrily rips the condom off his cock. He's still between my stretched legs. He thrusts three fingers inside me, making me jolt, while his thumb strokes over my clit. "Oh shit, Os." His eyes soften at my words while his hand still works at a feverish pace.

I arch my back, my hips hurting from the position. I come hard, my mouth falling open and my neck stretching back as I scream up toward the ceiling. "Yessss."

He removes his hand slowly, as though he's reluctant, before wiping his hand on a small towel that seems to have appeared from nowhere.

My hands clench against the headboard as I watch him work to undo my ankle restraints. "Let go, Paige," he tells me without looking at me. Then he goes to the cupboard and removes a small bottle, placing it down beside me. "For your tits." He nods toward my marked breasts. A sliver of hurt hits me that he won't be using the lotion, but I quickly knock it away. Oscar watches me closely, his eyes locked on my face as though searching for something. With trembling fingers, he gently strokes my hair away from my cheek, his touch lingering. "You're different." His voice is merely a whisper. "Like me." Then he quickly withdraws his hand, turning from me; he clears his throat. "I'm going to my room to shower; I'll lie with you later." The door clicks shut, blocking me out again.

Lie with me? Is this his idea of being with me? Waiting until I fall asleep before he comes into my room? My jaw clenches with anger above the hurt.

Fuck him and fuck his money.

I pull myself up, covered in dry cum, and gather my belongings.

Chapter Eighteen

Oscar

Last night was a complete shitshow. Sure, my brothers managed to give Nico Garcia the information we have on his family but not before Cal started an all-out brawl that could have gotten them all killed. If it wasn't for Nico's love and guilt of how he treated Lily, Cal's wife, I'm sure the guy would have taken them all out.

They should have just listened to me and left him behind.

My eyes keep flicking over the dinner table.

Every Sunday, we all gather at our parents' estate for a family meal. So as per usual, I'm sitting at the bottom end of the table next to Ma and Reece, my nephew. We've developed a close bond together. He's eighteen now, and since my brother discovered he had a teenage son with similarities to my own, he has become an amazing father to both Reece and his daughter, Chloe. I didn't agree with how Cal tampered with Lily's birth control for him to get her pregnant, especially after the trauma she went through losing a baby she was expecting with Nico Garcia.

Then there's my youngest brother sitting opposite me; he's twenty-three going on eighteen; the guy is a man-child. How his fiancé Will, copes with him, I'll never understand. She must truly love him, that's for sure. Keen sits on the fucking table, stroking Reece's therapy cat. I spend half my meal trying not to consider the fur floating around me, landing in my fucking food. Finn chuckles beside Sky. He's almost twenty-seven and sits lazily stroking his wife's hair. Their daughter, Charlie, is smiling at Ma like she's the best Nana in the world. I have to admit she's pretty fucking amazing, considering how long she's been married to my bastard of a father.

Bren's jaw tightens, and his hand stops moving under the table. He might be close to forty, but the guy has only just found his forever with Sky. I take it she's come from the finger-fucking they think they've been discreet about. His hand moves again, and I'm forced to reconsider my analysis.

Taking notice of Reece, I watch him waiting for the perfect opening to ask him about the cat.

Finn's voice snaps me out of my thoughts. "So, Sky. What's it like living with Bren?" I notice Bren tense beside Sky.

"Oh, wonderful, thank you," she replies innocently. Fucking wonderful? He may be my favorite brother, but I've lived with him, and there's nothing wonderful about him. The man is a fucking pig, for a start.

Finn chokes on his beer at her words. Con starts

chuckling, causing his fiancée to elbow him swiftly in the ribs. I stare at Sky, watching her for a reaction. When she lifts her blue eyes to mine, I glance away and pull my attention toward Reece and my task at hand.

I clear my throat. "Reece, can I borrow the cat on Friday?"

Reece's fork stills before it reaches his mouth. He turns to face me, his eyes scanning over my face. He narrows his eyes. "Pussy?"

I nod in agreement before glancing around. Everyone's eyes around the table are on us, watching the interaction with intrigue. I hate the attention, as it makes me angsty and uncomfortable under their scrutiny. "Yes, the cat." I wave my hand toward the fluffy cat sitting on the dining table next to Con's so-called dog, Peppa. That thing looks like it's been attacked by fleas, but apparently, it's meant to be bald, and Con is actually pleased about it.

"Pussy?" Reece repeats again, acting like a complete dick and making me want to slam his smug face into the table.

I shuffle from side to side, my jaw now ticking and my temple pulsating in frustration. I do my four, four, four. "Yes, the fucking cat, Reece." I seethe.

"Say it." Reece leans back in his chair nonchalantly, not remotely taken aback by my unraveling state. A small smirk on his smug fucking face, he's struggling to hide his amusement.

"Say fucking what?" I snipe out.

"Say you want to borrow my Pussy." His eyes don't leave mine as if taunting me into an argument before adding, "Please." His smug little prickish lip curls up at the side slyly, and I want to rip it from his motherfucking face. I close my eyes and attempt my breathing technique. Then repeat the process while chanting not to murder the little fucktard.

"Reece," Bren clips out in warning across the table. His fist tightens around his fork. He hates people taking advantage of me; he's always been the protective one.

I exhale loudly, acting disinterested in Reece's antics when inside, I'm raging. "Reece, may I please borrow Pussy on Friday?"

His eyes narrow further. "What for?" The little shit already knows what for, and he's making a scene on purpose.

My jaw ticks once again so tight I feel it locking. I glance down at the table and mumble the words slowly, deliberately, and coldly, "She needs a check-up at the vet."

Reece scrutinizes my face before suddenly jolting with some sort of realization only he's aware of. Reece's mouth drops open. "Holy fuck, you're stalking the veterinary assistant, aren't you? You seedy motherfucker."

"Reece," Finn clips out and flits his eyes down on Charlie, giving him a warning about his language and conversation. I'm not sure why Finn does that because they all swear around the kids.

Of course, my nephew sits back with his arms crossed over his broad chest. He lowers his voice but not enough. "So she's a whore at night and an innocent veterinary assistant during the day? Fuck, I gotta see this. Does she dress up for you and shit?"

My eyes flare, my veins pulsate, and my chest heaves.

OSCAR

I AM GOING TO FUCKING KILL HIM.

"Reece, enough!" Cal snaps.

We stare at one another. Does he really want me to inform his father of his latest purchase? And he dares to query me over stalking?

How fucking dare he? Well, game fucking on. I curl my lip and open my mouth to start the ball rolling, but then he visibly gives in, no doubt realizing what I was about to do. What I was about to expose.

He exhales dramatically with a loud huff. "Fucking fine. You can borrow my Pussy, but I'm coming with you." He raises an eyebrow at me as if in warning.

"Fine." I push my chair away from the table and stand.

"Where the feck are you goin'?" Da snaps from the top of the table.

I stand still before raising my head to give Da my attention. "I have work to do. If you want answers, I mean..." I wave my hand around the table, gesturing at them all.

Da goes to open his mouth, no doubt to argue, but Bren holds his hand up and stops him before he has the chance to speak.

"Speak to you later." He nods toward me, then continues eating as if he hadn't just gone above our father's word.

I turn and leave the room without speaking to anyone.

I might have work to do, but first... first, I have to check on her.

My obsession.

Chapter Nineteen

Oscar

I'm beyond unhappy right now that Paige left without a fucking word the other night. If it wasn't for me checking my security app so often to make sure she was sleeping okay, I might never have known. Okay, that's a lie. The bedroom door slamming and the apartment door nearly ricocheting off the hinges would probably have been a dead giveaway, but other than that, I don't like not knowing what she's doing and when.

Anxiety ripples inside me when I think of her alone without me to protect her. I let her leave the apartment, knowing she wanted more from me, needed more.

I hurt her; I know that. I'm just not sure how to give her what she wants. So I let her leave the apartment and called my doorman to take her home, unbeknownst to Paige. I even watched her enter her room and fall into her bed with tears streaking her eyes. When all I wanted to do was wipe them clear and make everything all right, but I don't know how; I don't understand how. But I want to.

Today, I made a decision, one that will change both of our lives. Only she will never know about it. I stand from the armchair beside her bed. Each time I come in here, I have to move her shit out of the way for me to sit and watch her sleep peacefully.

When I paid to have her house made secure, I made sure I was able to access it at all times, but I also needed to have access to her location at all times. I take the needle from my pocket and feel of the object in my fingers. Knowing it's a necessity, one to keep her safe. I gently brush her hair back, like I do most nights when she doesn't sleep at my apartment, and I have to share her with her family. I take the needle, and in one swift motion, I inject the small tracking device into her neck, causing her to wince in her sleep and fidget. *Safe now, little spitfire.* Bending down, I leave a featherlight kiss at the mark on her flesh and breathe in her apple scent. Mine.

I settle back into the chair where I shall stay for a couple of hours to watch over her, enjoying the calm each breath she takes brings me, basking in her.

Tomorrow I'll put the next part of my plan in motion.

I need to protect her whenever I can't see her. I want to watch over her at all times to keep her safe, and short of killing that boss of hers, I can, at the very least, watch him too.

Chapter Twenty

Oscar

"What the fuck are they going to do to my Pussy?" Reece asks again while sticking his finger inside the cat's cage. I quirk my lip at his choice of name for his cat. The whole family assumes he innocently chose the name; they're all a bunch of utter morons. My nephew knows exactly what he's doing. Exactly.

I glance around the veterinary surgery, my skin crawling. I'd previously hacked into the system and canceled a bunch of appointments just so the clinic isn't as busy with all these god-awful animals. I sneer at the white puppy a little girl is holding, making her tighten her arms around it in defense. She damn near chokes the retched thing.

I force my mind to wander, and it automatically goes to the text messages I received from Reece last night.

Reece: Are you going to tell me why the fuck you need my Pussy?

Oscar: No.

Reece: It's my fucking cat. I have a right to know.

Reece: What the hell are they going to do anyway?

Oscar: It's a check-up. Nothing intrusive.

Reece: If they try shoving shit up my Pussy's ass, I swear to fuck, I'm going to kill them.

Oscar: I don't doubt it.

Reece: Hope she's fucking worth it.

Oscar: She is.

"Reece O'Connell," the blond behind the counter shouts, making Reece snap his head up in acknowledgment.

"I fucking hate you right now, Oscar. You owe me big fucking time." I nod in agreement as I stand to my feet and follow the sign for the jackass—Vet Carl Lithel. I don't bother knocking as I enter the room. I wave my hand toward the table for Reece to put the cage down.

He begins tugging on his hair, his stress levels rising. "What the hell are they going to do?" I should feel guilty for putting my nephew in this situation, but nobody asked him to come. Besides, it was a means to an end.

The end being her.

The door opposite us opens, and in walks the sly cunt with my woman following behind him. She fucking giggles at him. My blood boils, threatening to explode from my veins. I try my breathing technique as quickly as possible. The giggling stops instantly, and I know she's seen me without even having to open my eyes. I do so when my name escapes her pouty lips. "Oscar, what are you doing here?" Confusion mars her pretty face, and I revel in it.

"I'm here to have the cat examined." I point toward Reece and the cat that is now in his arms, him nuzzling into its fur.

Her eyes flit over toward Reece, softening at the scene. My fists tighten. She can soften toward a cat but not me?

The prick clears his throat. "So, who do we have here?" He smiles toward my nephew, a gleaming white, clean-cut smile that makes me want to send Finn after him. He'd soon pull out each of those sparkling teeth and turn the pompous prick into a bloody, dribbling mess. Reece pulls me from my thoughts when he practically spits his words in Carl's direction, "Pussy."

The douche sighs. "The cat, son. What's the cat's name?"

Reece scoffs, and his eyes flare with rage while nuzzling into the cat. "Not your fucking son. Goddamn prick. Fucking vet prick. Dick with a prick. Motherfucker. Fucktard." He doesn't ramble like this very often anymore, but it's always somewhat quite amusing when he does. I can't help but internally grin at my nephew's antics.

I watch Paige closely as her eyebrows shoot up before she realizes that Reece is very much like me. He's different.

She steps forward, pushing the moron with a mouth like a fish opening and closing out of the way. I mean, he clearly has no experience working with people. His social skills are shit. He should stick with animals, preferably ones that will maim his pretty appearance in some way. Yes, that would be perfect.

She lifts her hand, then stops herself. "Do you think I can stroke Pussy, Reece?"

Reece scowls at her, and then his eyes flick over toward mine. I give him a firm nod. "Fine. Just don't shove shit up my cat's ass. Pussy isn't into anal."

Paige chokes on a laugh before she quickly pulls herself together and gently pets Pussy. I find myself moving closer to her, close enough to breathe in her apple scent, close enough to touch her but not letting myself, not when the douche is in the room, too.

He claps his hands together. "Okay, so shall we get the cat checked over?" He earns a glare from all three of us. His eyes finally land on mine—deadly, cold and unfeeling. I broaden my shoulders and ball my fists, and my eyes must darken because the prick turns white.

I hear Paige swallow. "It's okay, Carl. I can handle this."

"Are you sure?" He fidgets on his feet, clearly uncomfortable about leaving the room and leaving her with me.

She turns her head slightly toward him, and I want to turn it back, force her eyes on me and not him.

"I'm sure."

"Do you know them?" he asks. His eyes flit around us.

"I'm her boyfriend," I snap in his direction but don't take my eyes off her. The intake of her sharp breath makes my cock stand proud, painfully pushing against my zipper. I've stunned her to silence, her mouth dropping open.

"I... I didn't realize..." the moron stutters.

I whip my head in his direction. "You do now. You can leave." I wave my hand toward the door. The prick pauses for a moment before he looks at Paige and, as if sensing defeat and truth behind my words, he leaves when she doesn't so much as acknowledge him.

"Reece, you too," I throw over my shoulder, giving him a knowing look. He knows he has some work to do in the clinic anyway, with the task I gave him.

"Fucking prick. Bringing me here just to fuck with my Pussy. God damn, owe me, Oscar." There's a fumble from behind me, then the click of the door.

I step toward her, and she takes a step back. We continue this until her back hits the wall. I brace my arms above her head, caging her in to look down on her.

"You're not my boyfriend." Her chin rises in defiance.

"No? What am I, then?"

Her chest rises and falls, making me want to pull her tits from her bulging top, exposing them for me to mark.

"Y-you are..." She swallows hard. "My employer, Oscar. You pay me." I wince at her words. The very words I throw at her regularly; only now they leave a sting behind.

He's her fucking employer. I'm more.

We're more.

I trail a hand down her cheek, and she nuzzles into it. The heat of her touch makes my heart hammers against my chest. I don't want to lose her. I can't lose her. She's mine.

167

"You haven't been answering your phone. You left."

My jaw ticks as the words leave my mouth, the hurt behind them evident. She left in the night and didn't come back. She's been ignoring me. She left.

"I had enough." Her voice is low. "I wanted more."

"More?"

"You. I want you, Oscar." Her admission causes my breath to stutter. She wants me.

"I... I..." I can't get the words out. How the fuck do I tell her I want it all too? I want more.

"I'll try." My fists tighten on the wall above her head.

Her lip wobbles; she's going to fucking reject me, I know it. Why have someone like me when she can have that prick who can give her everything she wants? Everything she needs.

My body trembles, desperation filling me. "Please, I'll try." Her hand moves toward my face, and I close my eyes, determined to let her touch me. I try not to pull away when her soft palm grazes over my cheek. "Open your eyes, Oscar. Let me see you."

My eyes flare open at her words, my throat clogging with emotion. "You're the only one that does see me, Paige," I admit gently.

"You see me too." She stares into my eyes, her words telling me a thousand truths, but her eyes tell me a million more.

I nod, "I do," My throat clogs with an emotion I don't recognize.

She drops her hand, and I miss the connection immediately—a loss of warmth, care, and love gone with a simple movement.

"I don't want you to pay me…"

"I can help—"

She holds her hand up and grinds her jaw. "I don't want it, Oscar. I won't have you constantly throwing that in my face."

She's too damn proud. I'll let it fly for now. "Of course."

"And I want to go on a date."

My eyes narrow, a date? I almost want to choke? Where the fuck am I meant to take her on a date?

"It's what couples do, Oscar. Can you try?"

I nod like a lovesick puppy. "I can. Tonight?"

Paige laughs. "No. Not tonight. I have to babysit. Tomorrow."

My fists clench, and I grind my jaw. "Paige, I need you."

She steps forward, forcing me to take a step back. "Then I suggest you think long and hard about this date of ours. Make it a good one, Oscar." She winks at me before turning toward the door.

Where the fuck am I meant to take her on a date when the last one turned out so badly?

Chapter Twenty-One

Oscar

"So, you want to take this girl you like out on a date?" Sky, Bren's woman, watches me closely, her eyes assessing my every move.

I nod, attempting to deflect the nervousness bubbling inside me.

"Well, what does she like doing?"

"Nature." I sneer, curling my lip for emphasis to show my complete distaste at her so-called hobby.

Sky giggles, then swiftly clears her throat at my lack of reaction. "How about taking her somewhere to eat?"

I sit forward, deep in thought; the last time I took her somewhere to eat, it didn't go down well. I shake my head.

Sky sighs, tapping her finger on her chin. "How about the beach? That's my favorite place."

The fucking beach? Hell no. "I don't like the sand."

She stifles a laugh between her lips. "Okay, well, what do you like doing?"

What do I like? I like my tablet. But I can't exactly make a date out of that. The only place I like to go... My lip quirks up at the side.

"See! You know exactly where to take her, Oscar. I knew you'd figure it out, and it's going to be beautiful; I'm sure of it." Sky's excited voice makes me choke on thin air. She leans her head in the palm of her hand, her elbow propped on her leg, staring into space as though imagining a sweet romantic scene. She needs to get into the real world.

If only she knew where I liked to go for pleasure.

Paige's wide eyes dart around the room, no doubt taking in the scantily clad women, some wearing chains. Some were kneeling at their owners' feet, waiting to be petted.

"Os-Oscar, what is this place exactly?"

Her silver sequin dress shimmers under the light. My eyes latch onto the slit, all the way up to the top of her thigh, making me swallow heavily, and my balls ache with need. I'm rock hard in my pants; I have been since the second I decided where to bring Paige for our date. I rest my hand at the base of her back, and she intuitively moves closer to me but not quite touching, as though she knows my limitations without even needing to be told. I turn my head slightly to face her side, my breath whispering over her ear. "It's a private club. Part of Indulgence."

She nods, glancing around the room once again. "A-and you like it here?" Her eyebrows raise, and her cheeks tinge adorably. When she shows innocence, it's something that feeds my appetite for her. My need.

"I do." I lift my chin toward Che, my club manager. Her eyes light up when she sees me. She puts an extra swing into her hips. The dress she is wearing is see-through. Her breasts a handful, her nipples pebbled, and panties missing. Che smiles adoringly, swaying her hips as she makes her way toward me. "Sir, I wasn't expecting you tonight."

"Room twenty," I clip, ignoring any form of conversation.

She dips her head in understanding before glancing toward Paige. Her eyes narrow slightly at the placement of my hand before she quickly masks it. Che turns on her heel, and I gently encourage Paige with my hand for us to follow. "Would you like one of the girls to accompany you?" Che throws over her shoulder as we follow her through the bar area toward my usual room.

I feel Paige stiffen beside me. Her jaw tightens. Something has pissed her off. My eyes quickly scan the room before landing back on Paige. Her eyes drilled into the sway of Che's ass. A thrill zaps up my spine. Is she jealous? Excitement causes somersaults in my stomach; I've never had a woman be jealous for me before. Until now, it seems.

Paige

We follow *little miss I can wear fuck all and make it sexy* past the bar and into a small corridor. She stops outside the room and gives Oscar another once-over.

The man seems oblivious at her blatant drooling. She even eyes the bulge in his pants. I swear I see red when she licks those lips. The tramp.

"Maybe I'll see you later?" She smiles at Oscar. I grind my teeth to stop myself from spewing unnecessary word vomit at her.

Oscar clears his throat, not even looking at her. Concern mars his handsome face. "Leave." His voice is cold with a sharp edge to it.

She sighs before clicking those trampy heels away.

He holds his arm out for me to enter the room. I step past him and into the room.

My eyes take in the room. Soft grays are everywhere and a beautiful crystal chandelier gives an elegant feel.

I notice a gray suede couch is turned, facing a black

wall, making me draw my eyebrows together in uncertainty.

"You seem..." His words hang in the air as though he's not really sure how to finish the sentence.

"Pissed?" I finish the sentence for him.

His lip turns up at the side, annoying me all the more. "Yes, pissed."

"Have you slept with her?"

Oscar watches me closely, licking his lips and smirking, making me want to launch myself at him and his smug face.

"What if I have?"

A sharp breath exhales from deep within me and hurt surges into my chest. He brought me to a sex club; he brought me around women he's slept with on a date?

"I want you. Only you." The sincerity in his voice makes my heart flutter. His bright blue eyes hold mine captive. His finger trails slowly down the side of my cheek, and I lean into his touch, desperate for more.

He clears his throat, taking a step back, breaking the short moment between us but leaving a longing void in his step. Longing for him to hold me, cherish me, and need me as much as I need him.

"Turn and face the glass." He unbuttons his shirt cuffs and sets the cufflinks down on the table one by one. Rolling his sleeves up to his elbows, he sighs in agitation at my unmoving body. "Paige, turn and face the glass." He tilts his head toward the black wall, and it's only then that I realize the wall is actually blackened glass.

I strut over as instructed, a swing in my hips to give

the tramp a run for her money. Flattening my palms against the glass, I glance over my shoulder seductively.

Oscar watches me with an intensity, and a thrill escapes me, traveling all the way from my toes up my spine and back down to my clit. I shuffle slightly, the wetness in my panties pooling from the sheer look in his hooded eyes. He licks his lips, causing my breath to hitch and my mind to run wild with visions of him on his knees licking me, licking away the throbbing ache between my legs. I wonder if he'd do that. Lick me. I wonder if he's done it with her? Jealousy and annoyance rumble inside me, threatening to explode.

He moves behind me, snapping me out of my thoughts.

His fingertips graze my skin, and I break out in goose-bumps at the sheer tenderness with which he unzips my dress, leaving it to pool at my feet. I hear him swallow and relish in the thought of me causing the reaction.

He takes a step back before positioning himself on the couch. I watch him from over my shoulder as he sits open-legged. He takes his time, his eyes traveling up my body, all the way from my silver heels to my black suspenders and lacy G-string. My bare breasts hang almost plush against the glass. Awaiting for something to happen.

What? I don't know.

Oscar

The anticipation of what is about to happen is absolutely awe-consuming. Paige fidgets uncertainly. I both want to soothe her trepidation and revel in it, loving the fact that she needs me to protect and provide for her.

She startles when the light in the room before her turns on. I glance at my watch, and right on time, the couple on the bed appears. A tall guy with dark hair, a curl to it much like my own, and a redhead woman, as close to Paige as I could get but not nearly as perfect. They're both bare as one another.

He's been ordered not to kiss her. I gave a complete rundown of my expectations for the scene I wanted to play out. He kisses around her neck and over her chest, tugging her hair over her shoulders gently before pressing delicate licks and nips on her exposed skin.

My cock presses against my pants, and I can't help but stroke it over and over, eager to take it out but determined to hold it in. My heart races with need. As if on cue, Paige turns her head over her shoulders and locks eyes with me. The flush in her cheeks evidence enough of her arousal.

"Are you enjoying the show?" I raise an eyebrow at her.

She nods once, enough for me to acknowledge both her need and my own. I stand and walk over to her. "Keep your hands on the glass," I whisper in her ear, and she nods in understanding, turning back around to face the glass.

I mimic the man, drawing her hair over her shoulder before working my lips down her neck and over her shoulders. Paige's breath stills, her shoulders tense at my touch, and I can't help but sniff at her skin, embracing her scent, her very being. My hard cock longs to be touched, and my balls ache to be released. I nip at her skin, marring her flesh with my teeth. She winces before I follow the action with a swift lick of my tongue to soothe the now-reddened mark. I leak in my pants. I've marked her, licked her. I want more. I'm greedy and desperate for more. I bite into her skin, tasting the copper on my tongue, and for the first time in my life, the thought of blood doesn't repulse me. No, I fucking ache for it. I lick away her pain and follow it up with a gentle kiss of my hungry lips.

"O-Os, please."

I close my eyes at her nickname for me, her need for me electrifying. She's both my salvation and damnation. How can this be? The sweet, innocent, fiery redhead. Mine. I bite again. "Shit, that hurt." I chuckle against her skin.

The man helps the woman from the bed, and they

move to stand in front of the glass, so close that if the panel wasn't there, you'd feel their every movement, every breath. "Oh god." Paige releases a needy moan as she watches, transfixed on the woman kneeling before him. "Os- Oscar, please."

"Please, what, Paige?" My tone is clipped, but I don't give a fuck. I'm pissed she is interrupting my enjoyment of her.

"I need... I need that." She nods her head toward the woman who is slowly kissing up the man's legs, caressing his calves, his thighs, all the way toward his balls.

I grimace at my own longing, desperate to feel her like that too, but knowing it's impossible. I nip again in aggravation, and she pulls back.

I'm pissed... pissed at her for wanting more and at me for not allowing more when I desperately need it as much as her. More than her.

I tug her hair tightly, exposing that beautiful neck of hers. Her throat stretches as I draw her head back. "On your knees." Her chest heaves, and I watch her swallow. Her eyes flare with eagerness, making me quirk my lip at her enthusiasm.

Paige drops to her knees, and I nod my head toward the glass. She follows my line of sight, watching the woman kneeling with her legs wide, her hand between her thighs, rubbing eagerly against her pussy. "Copy."

She licks her lips, her eyes flaring with understanding before she begins rubbing her needy little clit aggressively. Paige's eyes flit between mine and the couple. My own locked onto her. They close with the sound of her whimper.

I snap, unable to take it any longer. I rip my belt open and open my pants, tugging down my boxers aggressively; I relax in an instant. When my palm touches my aching cock, a hiss escapes my lips, making Paige's eyes dart toward mine. They widen as she watches me jerk my cock, rubbing my thumb over the sticky residue. I tighten my palm with the sensation. Feeling her eyes on me, I move faster, taking note of her own swift movements.

I glance my eyes over toward the couple, her taking him in her mouth. My eyes close with the desperation inside of me, the aching need building up inside me, painfully so.

"Please." My eyes snap back to Paige's breathy words. "I want it, Oscar. Please."

Fuck, I want it too. So fucking bad. My hand virtually strangles my cock in annoyance.

"Open." I'll try to fuck her mouth. Like him. He's moving inside her mouth at a feverish rate. Fuck, I hate him right now. Right now, when I want to be someone else, so bad, so bad, it fucking hurts. To feel her around my cock, her tongue moving, swirling over it, my balls drawing up. "Fuck, Paige. Fuck."

Her moans spur me on. I bring the tip of my cock toward her lips, not quite touching but almost. Almost fucking there, I can feel her breath. Surely, she can feel me too? I need it; need her so fucking bad.

Her mouth drops open wider, and she comes on a groan, her hand still working, her heavy tits bouncing and my come hitting her face, her lips, her tongue. I can't stop coming; the look on her face is amazing, covered in my cum, my essence. Me.

"Fuck." I drop my head forward and stumble slightly but manage to catch myself from falling onto her. My palm hits the glass, and my heart hits the fucking floor. I failed.

"I'm sorry." I choke the words out before stepping back, closing my eyes, and refusing to see the disappointment on her face. I quickly turn and buckle my pants back up.

"Oscar, hey. It's okay. It's fine." Her hand touches my arm, and I jump at the sensation. "I'm sorry. I didn't think." She winces at her natural reaction to reassure me.

"It's fine," I snap at her; too harsh, I realize. I tug on my normally perfect hair, annoyed with myself. Fucking hating myself.

I do my breathing technique while Paige takes a step back, waiting for what... I'm not sure.

"Get dressed. We're leaving," I spit the words out.

Her heavy sigh hangs in the air.

Along with the disappointment heavy in my heart.

Chapter Twenty-Two

Paige

I place my bag on the counter. "You're mad?"

He shakes his head. "Annoyed."

"At me?"

Again he shakes his head. "At myself."

"Because of the blow job thing?" His eyes dart to mine, his jaw ticking. "It's just a blow job, Oscar. It doesn't matter."

He lets out a disbelieving laugh. "Doesn't matter?"

I lift my chin. "It doesn't."

"Did you give that prick a blow job?" His eyes drill into mine with severity, making me shuffle on my feet.

"Oscar..."

He holds his hand up. "Don't try and placate me, Paige."

I swallow back the lump in my throat.

"Go get in position." He tilts his head toward the corridor. I thought we were past this. My stomach somer-

185

saults with trepidation. But his eyes scrutinize my face, so much so it's as though he can see into my mind. Waiting for me to make my decision. My choice—him or not.

I nod in defeat and make my way to the room.

My room, so it seems.

Oscar

I gather more of her hair into my palm and fist it, then tug her head back, making her neck strain.

Fuck me, that's hot. Her white neck is tight due to my hold, her pink lips slightly parted, a flush creeping into her cheeks, and her green eyes are latched on to mine.

Has he tasted her lips? Has she tasted him? The thought causes the veins in my neck to pulsate.

"Have you tasted him? Carl. Have you fucking tasted him?" I snipe the words out angrily.

Her eyes widen, and her face falls in shock at the realization I know the prick's name. "Os—"

I grip her hair tighter and tug.

"Fucking. Tell. Me."

She swallows thickly, and I watch in fascination at her throat bobbing.

"I'm not sure what you mean." Her cheeks pinken as she darts her eyes away from mine. She fucking knows exactly what I mean.

I choke, knowing the answer. She has. She's done that

to him. He's had that part of her. Something I'm not even sure I'm capable of. My breath hitches, and my hands tremble. I feel like I'm sinking, drowning in desperation to have something I can't quite achieve.

She licks her lips before talking. My eyes watch the motion with intrigue., "I can do it to you if that's what you want."

My eyes dart to hers, the sincerity in them settling me slightly, but the anxiety is still there, the knowledge of being different.

I turn my head to the side, frustrated with myself. Just fucking do it.

I hear her swallow but don't give her my attention. "Oscar, we can do it. Just differently." I wince at her choice of words. Fucking differently.

"Oscar, I want to taste you." My heart skips a beat at her words as I draw my gaze back to hers. Her eyes almost pleading. Is she as desperate for this as me?

"Do you think... do you think you could try it? For me?"

I swallow thickly before answering honestly. "I don't know."

Paige attempts to nod, but I still have her hair in a firm grip. "Okay, well, you don't like me to touch you, right?"

I scan her face, scrutinizing her. I fidget from one foot to the other while trying to figure her out. Her trail of thought.

As if hearing my thoughts, she adds, "I had a brother with similar traits to you." *Traits.* "I know it's not the same, but we worked around things to make him comfortable." I close my eyes. I don't want to work around things, for fuck' sake.

I hate that word, too. Any word that tries to give meaning to behavior that's not deemed normal. Fucking normal?

I mean, what the hell is normal, anyway?

I do my four, four, four breathing before opening my eyes.

Locking on to hers. "I want to try."

Paige

"I want to try." His words echo in my mind as he watches me drop the robe from his armchair before instructing me to turn around while he binds my hands tightly together with one of his ties, causing my wrists to instantly sting.

I kneel back on the floor, waiting for further instruction, my chest rising and falling, my insides eager to please him. Wetness gathers between my legs at the intensity of his stare.

I want to give him this.

But I also want him.

I selfishly want him. When I know, I shouldn't.

Not like this, anyway.

He stands towering above me. "Look at me." I raise my head to watch Oscar palming his cock; his eyes heavy and filled with lust. He's wearing a condom, and the thought of it disappoints me in a way I can't express.

I wanted to give him the whole experience. How am I meant to taste him without actually tasting him?

"Open your mouth." There's desperation in his tone as if he might change his mind at any second.

I open my mouth, and he shuffles his feet forward before coming to a complete halt with a jerk.

"How will you tap out if it's too much?" He worries his lip between his teeth, staring down at me for an answer.

"I won't need to tap out." His eyes scan over my face as though I'm a mystery to him, so I reassure him. "I want this, Oscar. Please give it to me. Let me taste your cock."

I barely finish my words before he takes hold of my head and pulls me forward, using the other hand to push his cock inside my mouth. He releases a hiss before thrusting out and thrusting back in deeper. His hips work in a quick motion. "Fuck. Oh fuck, that feels good."

My eyes lock on to his, and it's the most erotic sight I've ever seen. His deep blue eyes bear down on me in awe, and his mouth opens wide in disbelief. "Paige, I want..." I nod at him, eager to give him anything. I blink at him to give him permission to do whatever he likes.

He withdraws his cock out of my mouth before quickly pulling the condom off and discarding it on the floor. He quickly shoves his cock back inside my mouth. Worried we're going to stop, his hand tightens in my hair to hold me in place.

"Oh fuck."

Oscar's hips continue to propel forward, his mouth completely open and his eyes transfixed on me taking his cock.

I swirl my tongue around the head before he hits the

back of my throat again. The stutter in his movement alerts me he's close to coming undone.

"Fuck. I'm going to come in your mouth, Paige. Fuck, that's it." I moan at his words, the vibrations working around his cock.

His saltiness floods my mouth, pumping, and pumping until he stumbles slightly.

Slowly, Oscar pulls out, watching my mouth closely with a slight smirk on his handsome face.

I clear my throat. "Was it okay?"

He jolts at my words, and I'm unsure why. Before he swallows harshly, "Yes, it was okay."

Okay, well, I expected something a little more than okay, but judging by the look on his face, I'd say it was better than okay. I smile to myself.

"I'm going to fuck you now."

Oscar

I watch her sleeping, sitting in my chair in just my boxers. Sleeping peacefully. She's so damn beautiful I want to lock her away from the world so they don't even set eyes on her, shelter, and protect her. Keep her just for me. I want all of her.

She releases a small whimper in her sleep, making me lean forward on my elbows to make sure she's okay. I wonder what she's dreaming about. Is it about me? Or is it about more? Secrets maybe? Possibly lies?

I guess I'll find out eventually, but for now, I'll savor every damn minute with her until the inevitable happens and she realizes I'm not enough.

I'll never be enough.

We'll never be enough.

Chapter Twenty-Three

Paige

My eyes drift open, and I stretch. As much as I don't like being in this room, I must admit the sheets are incredible, and the size of the bed is a huge bonus.

I turn to face the alarm clock and almost fall out of bed. It's almost eleven. My clothes are neatly folded in the same position as they were before I fell asleep. I glance back at the pillow beside me. It's definitely been used this time. I can almost make the shape of his head out, the outline clearly visible. I smile, trailing a finger along the outline. He listened, and he's trying. What more can I ask?

I make quick work of washing and dressing before walking down the corridor toward the living space. Oscar's eyes draw up to meet mine from the couch, and I'm pleased to see him sitting there today, opposite the fish tank instead of his usual position at the dining table. He has his tablet in one hand and his phone in the other; his discarded glasses are forgotten beside him.

I nibble on my lip, unsure of what to say or do. It feels different this morning.

In a good way. He let me sleep in; he stayed with me.

Oscar's eyes never leave my face. "Are you working today?"

I roll my eyes. "I'm sure you know I'm not."

His lip quirks. "You're right, I do."

I drop down on the couch beside him. "I just have a little more work today, then I was thinking you could come to a BBQ at my brother's place." He glances at his tablet as though he didn't just ask to introduce me to his family. I notice his knuckles whitening on his tablet, his shirt stretching tightly over his tense shoulders. He's nervous—to take me or for the rejection? I guess there's only one way to find out.

"Sure."

He raises his head, his blue eyes locking with mine. A small smile plays on his lips. His shoulders relax, giving me my answer.

"Are you close with your family?"

He eyes me skeptically, but I try to ignore the knowing feeling that he doesn't want to overshare things with me. Before I have the chance to overanalyze his lack of response, he seems to shake the thought from his mind. "Yes. In my line of business, you have to trust your family. To trust them, you have to be close."

Interesting. "How many siblings do you have?"

"Four brothers. Bren is the oldest, then Cal, me, Finn, and the youngest is Con."

"And are they married?" I ask him, determined to keep him talking now that he's opening up to me.

He sighs at my question, "Con is the only one not married, but he will be in two months. Behave, and I might take you." His words both startle me and excite me. He might take me to his brother's wedding? "Now, be quiet, so I can finish up some work here, then we can go."

I sit back on the couch. "Okay, but shouldn't you be wearing these?" I pick up his glasses and can't help but put them on myself playfully.

Strange, I can see through them perfectly. "Oscar?"

He watches me closely as though searching for something. He tilts his head from side to side, waiting.

Oscar

"Okay. Shouldn't you be wearing these?" She picks up my glasses and grins at me, playfully putting them on.

Her eyebrows knit together in confusion. "Oscar?"

She's realizing that my glasses are different—a mask. Another thing to hide behind, in the shadows.

"The kid needs feckin' fixing. He stares at books all day. It's not feckin' normal. Fix it." Da glares and points his thick finger toward Doctor Yates. He's our family physician and the only doctor that seems to understand me. He never pushes me out of my comfort zone. Never.

"Sir, with all due respect, Oscar simply enjoys reading. All children are different."

"He's feckin' different, all right. He's not normal."

I watch the doctor closely, analyzingly so. His jaw works from side to side. He's annoyed at Da's analysis of me.

"Maybe he needs glasses?" Ma speaks up with hope in her voice. Does she think glasses will fix me? There's nothing wrong with my eyes. I open my mouth to tell her

201

so, but she shakes her head gently before darting her eyes over toward Da.

Dr. Yates seems to pick up on our silent conversation because he claps his hands together as though excited. I watch the scene play out before me, and it's almost comical as the doctor explains to Da I most likely concentrate on books so much because my eyesight is probably poor. The fool believes every word. As much as I don't like lying, Ma tells me sometimes we have to hide behind a mask to make things in life easier for us. I notice she does that a lot when Uncle Don comes to visit. I see the way she fakes her smile and moves away from him when he steps closer.

Sometimes it's okay to hide in the shadows.

Paige takes the glasses off. "Does your family know you don't even need them?"

I scoff at her words. "No."

"Do I want to know why?"

"Probably not."

She sighs, "You know you can talk to me, right?"

I consider her words for a minute. "Can I?"

She swallows and looks away, her eyes riddled with guilt. Changing the subject, I say, "Bren, his woman, Sky, is excited to meet you."

Her mouth transforms into a huge smile, and my heart swells at the thought that I put it there.

Chapter Twenty-Four

Oscar

She nervously nibbles on her lip, and I want to do something to take away her anxiety. I'm just not sure what. My grip tightens on the steering wheel. I flick my eyes back over to her. "Reece will be there. You've met him." My voice sounds snappy, not at all how I wanted it to come out. I wince at my own tone, pissed at myself.

"I know." She fidgets her hands together in her lap. "I'm just worried they won't like me."

My head snaps to face her. "Why the fuck wouldn't they like you?" I stare at her, my eyes traveling up and down her body before quickly glancing back at the road.

She blows out a breath, her voice low. "I don't know, Oscar. I'm just nervous." She turns and faces the window, and I don't like it. I want to do something. Why the fuck can't I know what I'm meant to do in situations like this?

What would my brothers do?

They'd probably have their hands all over their

woman; that's what they'd do. Comfort them, tell them everything is going to be okay and that our family will love them.

"You can put your hand on my thigh if you want?" I feel her eyes on me but make no move to recognize them.

She gently places her hand on my thigh, but the foreign action makes me flinch. She moves to withdraw her hand. "Leave it there." My tone is snappy again, and I cringe. "Please." I soften my words and turn my head toward her, hoping she can see that just because my body reacts that way, my mind doesn't agree; they're almost at war with one another. Paige nods, and her lips grace into a beautiful smile that helps my tense body relax when she places her hand on my thigh.

I concentrate on her touch, the warmth seeping through my pants, the feeling of being wanted and needed by her making me feel complete. Like she's the missing piece I've always searched for but never truly knew I needed.

My girlfriend.

She sits with a goofy look on her face, and my heart fucking soars at the thought that I put it there.

Me.

Paige

We pull into a huge, gated estate with security booths on either side of a cobbled wall. Flowers and trees line the paved driveway as we drive toward a mansion. My mouth drops open in amazement. Never in my life have I seen anything like this.

Oscar clears his throat. "This is Con's house. He's the youngest brother." He lets out a nervous chuckle. "He's always in competition with my brothers to have bigger and better, hence the ridiculous house." He waves a hand toward the mansion, and my eyes follow. He isn't kidding. It looks like it's had various extensions, and a whole forecourt worth of cars is lined outside multiple garages.

The car comes to a stop, and Oscar climbs out of the SUV and slams the door shut. A shiver of trepidation ripples down my spine. Am I doing right being here? I mean, the deal is off now, and I'm his girlfriend. Uncertainty travels through me.

Sensing Oscar's eyes on me, I turn toward my door. He's standing with his hands on his hips, glaring into the window before glancing at his watch. A laugh bubbles inside of me. He's so serious about everything, even a family BBQ.

I take a deep breath and steel myself, opening the door and exiting the SUV. The slam of the door feels ominous. I'm doing this. I'm going in there to meet his family as his girlfriend. Nothing else.

The door swings open before we even reach it, and a brunette pulls me into her chest. "Hi. I'm Will. Con's soon-to-be wife, and you must be Paige."

She's really pretty. A messy bun on her head, a beaming smile, and pretty hazel eyes that seem to sparkle as she assesses me up and down.

"That's me." Jeez, I sound like an idiot. Oscar stands behind me, his hand lingering above my hip. I wish he'd just touch me there. Will watches Oscar closely, her eyes lighting up.

"Mommy, Reece said there's going to be a tiger at the wedding, and it needs feeding while it's there. He said we can feed it a traitor."

My eyes widen at the curly-haired little boy. He's cute as hell, but his words cause my stomach to somersault.

"It's fine." Oscar's lips whisper breathlessly against my ear, and I lean into him. His hand grazes my hip as though holding me in place. He presses his chest to my back, and he rubs gently. "Can you feel that?"

A whimper escapes my mouth at the feel of his hard cock grinding against me. "You drive me to insanity, Paige. I want to change everything about me for you."

"I don't want you to change anything."

His blue eyes drill into mine as though looking for the truth. He clears his throat and takes a step back. "Good, I'm struggling as it is."

"I swear to fucking Christ, I'm going to kill him. Can you believe it? Telling our six-year-old, he's going to feed someone to a tiger? Keen isn't cut out for this life. He's gentle." Will appears to be having her own conversation with herself before turning on her heel and storming into the house.

I take the opportunity to look around. We're standing in a huge, white, marbled foyer with a grand spiral staircase to my right with black wrought-iron curved spindles. It's beautiful and elegant, beyond anything I've seen before.

"Come on, they'll be out back."

Oscar leads the way through the house, passing an enormous kitchen with every modern appliance you can imagine. Our whole home could fit into this space.

Large glass doors have been pulled open to expose the grounds, and my god, I've never seen anything like it. It looks like a vacation resort. There's a lagoon pool, and then there's a beautiful waterfall and a cave almost hidden at the back. My niece and nephew would love it here. A pang of guilt hits my chest that I'll never be able to provide anything like this for them. Hell, we're barely providing the essentials at the minute.

I glance over toward the dog barking on the grass. The lawned gardens have perfected lines in them, soccer nets, a ginormous pirate ship climbing structure, and a wooded area toward the back of the grounds that appear to hold a treehouse.

I cross my arms over my chest, feeling completely out of my element. This is not the world I live in. The luxury of it all... it's too much.

"Paige, what's wrong?" Oscar's voice is full of nervousness, and he moves from foot to foot, making me feel guilty as I let my own insecurities worry him.

I steel my spine and decide to deal with it for him. "Nothing. It's just a lot, that's all." His eyes roam over my face and then out toward where I was looking. He gives a sharp nod as though understanding, but I'm not sure he does.

"Come, meet my family."

He holds his arm out to his left, and my gaze follows, landing on a bunch of people who are watching our inter-action. I swallow back the nerves.

"Stop fucking staring at her; otherwise, we're leav-ing," Oscar snaps, his jaw tightening and his shoulders tensing in annoyance. He's protecting me, and I automat-ically want to jump to his defense and support him. I move around him and plaster on a smile to greet his family, who are all now looking everywhere but at us. They continue their chatter and drinks as though they weren't just frozen to the spot, all apart from one set of eyes.

His gaze drills into me, cold and calculating, his broad shoulders filling the large chair. A girl is seated in his lap; she's tiny in comparison to him. She has long, light blonde hair all the way down to her ass. She wears a cute summer dress. I wonder if she's his daughter. As if hearing my thoughts, he leans forward and kisses her neck affectionately. Brushing her hair behind her ear, he exposes a tattoo down her neck. The name 'Bren' is intricately placed as ownership. His eyes never leave mine. He stares at me as though I'm a threat when in reality, he's the big muscle head that looks like he belongs in some sort of a mafia film. The thought makes me chuckle, and the blonde's light blue eyes dart toward me. She breaks out into a sweet smile before practically leaping from the big guy's lap.

"Hi, Paige. I'm Sky. Oscar's sister-in-law." I instantly relax at her words. Sky's whole demeanor is sweet and innocent, and Oscar has spoken of her multiple times. She holds her hand out, and I take it without hesitation. "That's my husband, Bren. He acts all growly, but he's a pussycat, really." She throws the words over her shoulder, aiming them at the beefy muscle head who quirks his lip up at her words, much like Oscar does.

Oscar moves to talk to him. He's brought me here, and now he's leaving me without so much as an introduction?

"It's okay. He probably doesn't realize." I glance at Sky. How did she know what I was thinking? She points at Oscar. "I don't think it's an Oscar thing either. It's a man thing."

This girl might be young and innocent-looking, but

something tells me she's been through a lot and sees a lot more than she lets on. She certainly has a way of picking up on social cues.

"Come, meet the girls." She takes my arm and tugs me over toward a separate table with Will and two other women. They all turn to smile at me, and I can't help but smile back, my nerves receding slightly.

Sky begins the introductions. "You met Will. Right?" I nod. "So, this is Angel. She's married to Finn. He's the bad boy over there..." My eyes travel from the tattooed blonde, Angel, toward her man, Finn. He has his feet kicked up on the glass patio table, a leather jacket on, and his hair messy. His blue eyes latch on to mine, and he winks. A toothpick dangles from his mouth, and a cute toddler with replica hair bounces in his lap, determined to grab it from his lips. "That's their son, Prince. He's such a cutie."

Angel snorts. "He's something all right. Little demon is his father's double. Anyway, nice to meet you, Paige."

"Thanks, you too." She grins happily at me.

"This is Lily. She's Cal's wife and also Reece and Chloe's mom."

Lily waves toward me. She's a brunette with wavy hair down her back and bright green eyes. "Lovely to meet you, Paige."

"Thank you." I nervously nibble my lip at all the women's attention.

"Would you like a cocktail? Apparently, they're really good. I'm breastfeeding, so I can't touch a drop." I turn to face Sky. My eyes rove over her slender body. She had a baby in there?

Again, as though she knows what I'm thinking, she shrugs. "My tits grew. Bren loves them. More than the baby does, actually."

My eyes widen at her admission as I take a seat opposite Angel. She chokes on a swig of beer, then throws her head back, laughing. "Fucking hell, Sky. You're so open."

Sky's eyebrows furrow together. "What?" She clasps her hands onto her breasts. "It's true. He says he's going to keep me pregnant because he loves my tits so much."

"You had a baby? You said baby, right?" I ask as Lily pours me what appears to be a fruity cocktail from a jug.

"Oh yes, and I'm pregnant again. I had Sebastian first, who's almost nine months now, and I'm expecting another." My eyes bug out. This girl has a baby and another on the way, but she looks incredible. I can see a small bump now, but only because I'm looking for it. I wonder how far along she is, but I don't get a chance to ask before Sky starts talking again.

"Bren told me that all the milk makes my tits look epic." She grins down at herself while holding her boobs in her hand, jiggling them.

"Sky, what the fuck are you saying?" Bren barks from across the patio, making me jump in the process.

She turns her neck, once again exposing the tattoo. "I'm just explaining how having the babies have made my tits look incredible."

"Pretty fucking sure Paige is more than happy with hers." Finn chuckles, earning him a slap behind the head from what I can only presume is another brother.

Jesus, these guys are hot. They all have blue eyes in one shade or another, dark hair, and olive skin, and their shirts all tug along their muscled shoulders. I feel like I need to fan myself and stop myself from building a harem in my head.

"That's Cal, my husband." Lily smiles lovingly toward the brother that whipped Finn's head.

"And that's Con, my dipshit fiancée." Will points toward a guy in a white t-shirt playing ball with who I realize must be their son, Keen.

"He tried to kill himself. He's so in love with her and can't live without her," Sky shares. My eyes bug out at her words as I spin my head toward Will, who pinches the bridge of her nose. Angel bursts out laughing. "Shit, we really need to work on your social skills, Sky."

Sky's eyebrows knit together. "Why?"

"Because you don't just drop shit out like that around the table, and no offense"—Will holds her hands up— "but we barely know Paige. You don't disclose personal details to people you don't know."

Sky looks deep in thought at Will's words. "Reece does it all the time."

"Yep, I think she needs to get tested," Angel throws in while munching on chips. I try not to choke on the fruit in the punch because did she just say out loud that Sky needs testing for autism?

"I already did." Oscar's shadow looms over me. "Apparently, she's fine. Just needs to mix more. Socially."

Lily crosses her arms over her chest and narrows her eyes at Oscar. "When was this?"

He doesn't take his eyes off me. "A while ago. She's fine."

Lily's face reddens, her chest rising. "Oscar, that's not..." She doesn't get to finish her sentence because he rudely interrupts her.

"I need to show you something." He pulls my chair out, giving me no choice but to do as he demands.

Oscar

Seeing Paige with my family is something I never even dreamed would be remotely possible in my life.

She laughs awkwardly, probably unsure of the shit that comes out of Angel's mouth and Sky's blatant lack of filter.

"You sure you know what you're doing?" Bren's voice cuts into my thoughts.

"Of course," I answer him honestly with a glare for him to try to argue.

"And you have everything under control, right?" Cal asks.

My glare shuts him up effectively.

"Well, you know you got us, right?" I nod at Bren's words.

"Detective Anderson has taken over Flemming's Chief of Police role perfectly." I almost want to smile at how perfectly it's coming together. When I took off Flemming's daughter's head for trying to hurt Sky and Bren, we realized we needed to take the opportunity to use

Anderson and replace the grieving father's place as Chief of Police.

"And Flemming?" Bren asks.

"He's a wreck. Staying at a holiday home in New York."

Bren nods, pleased with my response.

My eyes catch on to Paige's milky, slender neck, the nibble of her lip as she listens to my family talk. Fuck, that lip felt good around my cock. I imagine holding my cock at her pouty lips before I thrust into her greedy mouth. She wets her lower lip, and I can't take it anymore. I push my chair back and storm toward her.

I listen in on the conversation as I near her table. "He tried to kill himself. He's so in love with her and can't live without her," Sky offers, her words making me wince at the truth behind them.

Angel bursts out laughing. "Shit, we really need to work on your social skills, Sky."

Sky stares back at Angel in confusion. "Why?"

"Because you don't just drop shit out like that around the table, and no offence..." Will holds her hands up in defense of her words. But we barely know Paige. You don't disclose personal details to people you don't know."

Sky glances in my direction as though I'm going to help. "Reece does it all the time."

"Yep, I think she needs to get tested," Angel suggests making me quirk my lip at her bluntness.

"I already did," I admit as I stand over my woman. "Apparently, she's fine. Just needs to mix more. Socially." I tack on at the end as I wave my arms toward the women.

Lily crosses her arms over her chest and narrows her eyes at me. "When was this?"

I stare at Paige, not prepared to listen to Lily a moment longer than necessary. "A while ago. She's fine."

Lily's face reddens, her chest rising. "Oscar, that's not..." I sigh and ignore her, instead choosing to concentrate on what I originally came over here for.

Her.

"I need to show you something." I pull Paige's chair out, leaving no room for argument.

Chapter Twenty-Five

Paige

My feet can barely keep up with Oscar as he moves through Con and Will's home. He opens a door and holds his arm out for me to enter before closing it behind us, locking it, and flicking on the light.

It's a game room, complete with a pool table, leather reclining chairs, a cinema-sized screen on the wall, a bar, and even arcade machines. All very cliché. I almost want to roll my eyes at the men's toy room. A man cave.

I spin on my heels when I realize Oscar hasn't moved from leaning against the locked door, his eyes trained on me.

"This is what you wanted to show me?"

He unfastens his cufflinks, slowly, methodically, one at a time, before folding the sleeves of his shirt up, exposing the bulging veins on his forearms.

Can a girl come from the look of someone's forearms? I'm pretty sure I could. Arm porn at its best.

My gaze travels up his body, his neck muscles protrude slightly, and his darkened eyes never leave my own, the blue almost black now. I lick my lips approvingly. I love this side of him—the mysteriousness about him. I fidget as my panties become uncomfortably wet at the thought of what exactly he has to show me.

"I wanted to show you this." He unbuckles his belt, zips down his pants, and puts his hands inside his boxers. My throat dries, watching him. He withdraws himself, his palm grasping his solid cock. He jerks it a few times before a hiss leaves his perfect lips.

"I want you on your knees, Paige."

I walk toward him, unable to remove my eyes from his. I drop to my knees, obeying his instruction.

He gently trails a finger down my face to my mouth, over my lip, and into my mouth. I don't think about what I'm doing. I flick my tongue over his digit, reveling in the groan rumbling from his chest.

"You've been tormenting me with this tongue." My eyes widen at his words. Have I? I certainly hadn't realized.

"Licking those pouty lips. All I can think about is fucking them. I couldn't stand it any longer." I love how I make him unwind—his inability to control his sexual urges around me.

"Put your hands behind your back, and don't move them."

"Open your mouth." I follow his instructions, opening my mouth wide for him.

His instructions come out forcefully, breathless, and eager. "Roll your tongue over the head; make sure you

OSCAR

can taste me." Pre-cum oozes out at his own words, making me dart my tongue over the swollen head of his cock, moaning when the saltiness hits my senses. "Oh fuck. That's good. Again." I do it again and again until he seems to have lost all control. He grasps my head in his hands and rams his cock into my mouth, thrusting his hips forward repetitively. I choke, tears filling my eyes. "Fuck. Like that. Fuck..." The sting on my scalp only spurs me on, determined to make him unwind. To please him.

"Oh fuck. I'm going to come. I'm going to come down your throat. You love it. Fuck yes, you do." I stare up at him as he throws his head back. He pumps his cock over and over into my mouth, not stopping when I splutter on his cum, his grip still holding my head like a vice. I wait for him to come down from his high.

He withdraws his cock, taking a step back. His chest heaves as he fumbles with something in his pocket. "The table... the pool table. Go over to it. Turn around and lean over. Hold the sides." His words come out rushed and sharp, as though he's angry.

I stand to my feet and do as he asks, leaning over the pool table with my hands stretched on either side; I can hear the wrapper and feel him tug my panties down. I move my head to look over my shoulder, but he holds it roughly against the table before plunging his cock into my pussy without warning, making me shift up onto the tips of my toes with the force. "Oh god, Oscar."

"Fuck..." He pulls back before ramming back in. "I can't get enough of you." He grits the words out between

221

his teeth as though it pains him to admit it. "You're my obsession, my fiery fucking obsession."

He leans over me, so his words are low against my ear. "You're the only one with the power to bring me into the light." His words are barely a whisper that I'm convinced I'm not meant to hear. "I'm just not sure I'm ready for it."

He rams into me continuously, the ferociousness of it startling, but still, I'm desperate for more. I'm desperate for him and his touch.

Just him.

"Oscar, I need..."

"Fuck." He moves his hand between my legs, then slaps at my engorged clit, taking my breath away with the sensation. He does it again, and I go off like a rocket. I clench my teeth so as not to scream too loud in someone's home.

Oscar's other hand still forces my head down as he moves to my shoulder and nips at the flesh before choking on the force of his release.

He falls on top of me before quickly righting himself. Even that action hurts my heart. The thought of him not liking to be too close to me. I swallow away the pain as tears spring to my eyes.

I wanted him. His touch.

Him.

He doesn't look at me as he unfolds his shirt sleeves. "Paige, you need to hurry. Dinner will be getting cold; I don't like being late."

A coldness settles in my body as I feel used and vulnerable.

"Paige," he snaps at me like I'm a petulant child, making me jump. "I..." My eyes draw up toward his face. He's staring at my feet. "Your panties, pull them up." I realize I haven't made a move to leave the room, and judging by the twitch in Oscar's jaw, he's pissed at me.

Chapter Twenty-Six

Oscar

She's pissed, and I'm not sure why. She's been quiet through dinner. Even the animals and kids haven't put a genuine smile on her face.

I can't recall what went wrong; I don't fucking get it. I clench my fists and breathe.

"When I grow up, I want to be just like you," Charlie muses from across the table toward my woman.

Paige's face lights up, a genuine smile tugging at the corner of her lips at my niece's sweet words. She's almost ten now, and her nickname, Princess, fits her perfectly. She may not be Finn's biological daughter, but in every other sense, she most certainly is.

"You do?"

"Yeah. I'm going to be a vet whore."

Paige's mouth drops open, and the fork in her hand stills before it reaches her mouth. Anger boils inside me, instantly knowing where Charlie got that from.

All eyes turn toward Reece accusingly. He continues

eating as though Charlie didn't just drop a big bomb at the dinner table. Nonchalantly, he shrugs. "Kinda true. Besides, I said that shit ages ago." He continues eating, but the roar from across the table makes the table clatter. Finn's chair falls to the floor as all-out chaos ensues when he throws himself across the table toward Reece.

"Here we fucking go again," Angel mumbles to herself but makes no move to dispel the drama.

Reece just sits there with a smug look on his face, like this is a regular occurrence that isn't worth his attention.

Even my breathing technique is in vain. My voice cuts through the chaos, dark and deadly. "Apologize." My tightened fists ache with the need to punch that motherfucker for calling my woman a 'whore.'

Reece swallows heavily, and for the first time throughout the meal, I see a flicker of emotion cross over his face—panic. He hates to disappoint me.

"I'm fucking sorry, Paige." He pushes his chair back as Paige goes to speak, no doubt to tell him it's all fine, but he stomps off toward the house before any words leave her stunned lips.

"You need to get a fucking handle on your kid, Cal," Finn snides out.

"Says you whose kid is eating fucking Pussy right now." Cal grins smugly while staring down at Prince. He's sitting on the table, pushing lumps of cat fur into his open mouth.

"He's a fucking toddler. They do shit." Finn shrugs. "He"—Finn points toward the house where Reece stormed off—"goes too far, and you fucking know it."

"Whatever. I'm done with this conversation," Cal

replies while uncapping another beer and sitting back down as though nothing happened.

"I think you should go check on Reece," Paige whispers to me, causing me to study her. Even though she's pissed for some unknown reason and my nephew essentially called her a whore, she's still concerned about his well-being. She's nothing short of amazing.

"Just go make sure he's okay," she repeats, giving me the perfect opportunity of not having to deal with these alien feelings.

I hesitate slightly, feeling the sudden need to kiss her. Where the fuck did that come from?

I stumble as I get up before quickly righting myself and walking away from her, my chest constricting.

I open Reece's bedroom door. He's lying on his bed, throwing a ball toward the ceiling, then catching it. He doesn't even like sports, so I don't know where the hell the ball came from.

"You didn't fucking knock!" His eyes latch on to mine before they soften. I'm the only person apart from his little sister who can enter his room without knocking.

"I said I was fucking sorry. Jesus." He goes to staring back at the ceiling.

I sigh, tucking my hands into my pants. "I know. Paige insisted I come check on you."

His lip quirks up at the side. "Yeah?"

I nod.

He turns his blue eyes on to me. "You like her, don't you? Like really fucking like her."

I nod.

He throws his head back against the pillow. "Jesus, Oscar. What the fuck are we going to do?"

I shrug. "Let it play out, I guess."

His head darts up as though suddenly remembering something. "She likes you too. I watched her. All her body language, everything. I think she loves you, man."

My heart soars, feeling like it's in my throat before it dips back down, then beats at a rapid pace at his words, my chest suddenly feeling painful at the foreign feeling.

I decide to change the subject, not wanting to discuss feelings with my nephew.

Not wanting to discuss them at all.

"You bought a club?"

Reece sits up, narrowing his eyes at me. His own interest is suddenly piqued. He probably thought he'd done a good job of covering his tracks. He had, but just not good enough to cover them from me.

"And?"

"You're eighteen," I spit the words out.

"And?" he challenges back with a smug smile before rolling his eyes. "Please. Don't try and get all law-abiding on me now..."

I cross my arms over my chest. "If your dad finds out..."

"He won't." He grins, thinking he's won.

I shake my head. We might have a good relationship, but I don't want my nephew getting involved in shit he's not capable of handling. Mentally, at least.

"I don't want you hanging out there."

He scoffs as though it's the most ludicrous thing I could say. "It's a strip club, Oscar. Who buys a fucking strip club and doesn't hang out there?"

I drag a hand through my hair. How the hell did I suddenly become a therapist for a teenager? "Reece, listen."

He sits up. "No. Fuck you." He points at me with a glare and his words dripping in venom. I raise my eyebrows at his outburst. "You're not keeping me from her."

Oh, Jesus, this is over a girl? Of course, it fucking is. They're the only thing that have power over us. So, it seems.

I stare up toward the ceiling as though the answer belongs up there somewhere. I try my four, four, four, but nope, I can't deal with this shit.

"What. The. Fuck. Ever. Just don't say I didn't warn you."

"You should come check it out!" he shouts as I turn to leave the room.

"Very fucking funny." He knows full well I'm not capable of something like that.

I can't even let my own girlfriend touch me. My heart drops. She deserves more... so much more than me.

Maybe I should let her go.

A memory assaults me out of nowhere, making me freeze in the doorway, my mind wandering back to a conversation in my childhood.

So many doctors, therapists, and consultants tarnish

any memories worth enjoying. The hospital stays ones even worse.

"Oscar, how do you feel about your father?" My therapist taps a pen on her mouth. The way she watches me makes me want to throw a book at her intrusive head, allowing me enough time to escape this godforsaken place.

"I hate him," I answer truthfully.

She nods and makes a sound in the back of her throat that leads me to believe she understands.

"And your mother?"

"She looks out for me."

"But how do you feel about her?"

I shrug a shoulder, unsure of what she wants me to say.

She leans forward on her elbows. "Do you love her?"

"No."

She raises an eyebrow. "Why do you say that, Oscar?"

"I'm not capable of love. I'm not capable of any emotion; I'm not normal."

Her eyes flare. "Who told you that?"

"Da. He said I don't feel a feckin' thing. I'm not normal, not one of them."

"You do feel, Oscar."

I shake my head violently, annoyance rumbling inside me. She's wrong. She doesn't know what she's talking about. Why the fuck does everyone tell me different things? "Liar!" I snap, balling my hands into fists.

Her voice is controlled and soothing. "If you didn't feel anything, honey, you wouldn't feel hate. Does that make sense to you?"

My mind plays over what she's trying to tell me.

230

Maybe I do feel. Just not in the way others do. Maybe I only feel hate?

"Whatever you're thinking, Oscar, fuck it off. You deserve her."

I glance back over my shoulder at my nephew, giving him a nod in acknowledgment.

Reece gets me. He understands.

———

Paige is silent and staring out of the window. "You're pissed."

She doesn't look at me, so I glance back at the road, but my heart hammers to make things right between us. "I'm sorry."

She turns her head to face me. "For what?"

"For whatever it is that made you mad."

She sighs, annoyed at my answer. I know, but that's all I've got. "I don't want to lose you," I admit softly to her before staring back at the road.

"I wanted more." Her voice is low, almost broken, and I fucking hate it. She wanted more from me. Of course, she fucking did. She wanted to touch me, kiss me. Every. Fucking. Thing. I'm incapable of all that's perfectly normal in a relationship.

I slam my hands onto the steering wheel in frustration and scream out at the top of my lungs. "Fuuuuuccck-kk." My chest heaves and my heart feels like it's coming out of my chest. I swerve the car to the side of the road and quickly unbuckle my seatbelt, needing to get the hell out of the fucking car before I kill us both in a fit of rage.

I breathe, and fucking breathe, but it makes no goddamn difference. I pace up and down, unable to clear my head, unable to stop my chest from hurting, unable to think of anything but losing her. I feel unhinged and desperate.

I don't register the door shutting, but her legs come into view, and automatically as though we're entwined, my heart settles ever so slightly.

"Oscar, it's okay." I glance up at her, standing taller from the position of being bent over.

"It's not okay."

I bite my lip, my chest heaving at seeing her perfect face marred with tear tracks. Tears I put there. "I'm... I'm trying, Paige, really fucking trying." I bite into my lip. I stare at her, hoping she can see the truth in my eyes. Hoping she can see how much I need her.

"I know." She crosses her arms over her shoulders, hugging herself. Is that what she wants from me?

"I'm sorry," I tell her again, hoping it fixes things but knowing it won't.

"It's okay."

"Stop fucking saying that," I snap the words out, then immediately regret it. I breathe my four, four, four, and then soften my tone. "It's not okay. I get it. You want normal, and I'm not normal." I shake my head in disappointment.

"Oscar. Don't you dare say that..." She throws her hand out, pissed at me.

"Well, I said it. We both know it. I'm not normal."

"You're different." Her words are soft.

I scoff at her analogy, hating it as much as being

labeled not normal. "That's not what you want, though, right? You want normal—hugs and kisses. I can't do those things, Paige." I grind my teeth, my jaw tensing with the force.

"You can try." Tears stream down her face. "Please." Her lip quivers, and I want nothing more than to hug her, take away her pain, and be normal.

"I want to. I just... I don't know if I can, and I'm scared of hurting you if I can't." *Breathe.*

She nods in understanding, her eyes never leaving mine. "I can't bear you hurting, Oscar. It hurts me in here." She points to her heart, and I wonder if Reece is right. Does she love me? I quickly reject the thought; I'll only fucking worry more about hurting her further when I tell her I'm incapable of loving her back.

"I just want you." She bites her lip to stop it from trembling further.

"Will you come back to my place? Please." I stare at her. Surely, she can see the hope in my eyes. "Please?" I shuffle on my feet.

"Can you lie with me?" She blinks away the tears that are pooling in her hopeful eyes.

I nod like an excitable fucking puppy. "Of course."

"Okay." One word and I feel like I'm floating, my heart soaring once again.

"Okay."

Chapter Twenty-Seven

Paige

I turn on my side to face him, his eyes studying my every movement. He swallows thickly. "I know it's not what you meant."

"It's fine." I bite into my lip precariously. When I said I wanted him to lie with me, I envisioned myself lying on his chest, preferably naked. Of course, that would be too much, too soon, but I'm hopeful we can get there one day. Oscar is fully clothed while I wear the white gown provided, and we're lying on the bed in my room. Urgh, I hate that I call it my room when so many others have come before me.

I clear my throat. "So what exactly do you do for work again?"

His eyes narrow ever so slightly before he just as quickly masks it. "We own businesses."

"Like Indulgence?"

"Yes." His eyes search my face as though looking for something before he seems to deflate. His hand has a slight tremble to it as he tucks a stray curl behind my ear. His tenderness elicits a shiver down my spine. "I don't want to lose you," he admits with worry in his eyes.

I sit up, suddenly feeling concerned at his words. "Why would you lose me?"

"We have other businesses, too."

My heart pounds. I'm not stupid. I've seen the security the brothers have. Their homes are like fortresses; their wealth is beyond my wildest dreams.

"Illegal?" Just how serious is this business?

He attempts his breathing technique before giving me a single nod.

"The mafia." His words echo in my mind. Mafia? My throat suddenly dries at the possibilities that I've gotten myself into.

He's letting me in. It may not be how I wanted or planned, but he's letting me in. Even though he's burrowed so deep inside me, there's no escaping him. Oscar seems to think I could dispose of him so easily without hesitation. He's wrong. When I told him I wanted him, that's exactly what I meant. Him.

"Have you... have you hurt people?"

He stares at me before glancing at the door. "I've killed if that's what you're asking me."

I drag a hand through my hair, exasperated. "Jesus, Oscar, you killed someone?" My body goes into a panic while he sits there without a care in the world. I'm not sure if this is normal behavior in the mafia world or if this is just Oscar. I climb off the bed and begin to pace beside it.

"When?"

"What?"

"When was the last time you killed someone, Oscar?"

He sighs heavily and throws his head against the pillow. "I don't like to think about it."

No shit, he doesn't like to think about it. I'd be concerned if he did.

"It didn't go the way I had hoped." His cold eyes meet mine.

"Meaning?"

"Meaning it was fucking messy." He grimaces, disgust oozing from his face.

My mouth drops open. "Oscar, you're scaring me."

His eyebrows furrow. "Don't be dramatic. You know I'd never hurt you." His voice drops low. "Not physically, anyway." We both know exactly what he's talking about. I'm sure as emotionally detached as he is, we both know he's capable of hurting my heart. I rub over my beating heart; I can only hope he won't.

"She deserved it."

"She?" I suck in air, my body shaking.

He simply sits up, staring at my reaction. "Yes. She."

He elaborates, taking in my panic, "She shot Sky and was going to hurt Sebastian."

Oh my god, someone was going to hurt a baby. My body shakes as I consider his words. He's a killer? But *she* was going to hurt a baby. "What?"

He drags his finger over his lip. "Mmm, I don't like to get my hands dirty. But I had no other choice."

"She shot Sky?" For some crazy reason, my voice comes out hopeful, like I'm desperate to hear he was left with no other option than saving an innocent woman and her baby. They must have been through hell.

"Yes. Sky was pregnant when the woman did it." My legs feel like they're going to collapse, so I sit on the edge of the bed, trying to regulate my breathing. How can someone hurt such innocent people? Babies? Sky?

Oscar moves slowly toward me as though I'm a caged animal. He's unsure of my reaction, but the shock of his words leave me stilling, and when the warmth of the palm of his hand strokes lovingly over my cheek, I melt against him. "We're not bad people, Paige. We'd never hurt anyone who is innocent. You realize that, right? You trust me?"

I feel like he's trying to tell me something more, trying to force me to see the bigger picture. And I do see it. I see that life isn't black and white. My man, my different mafia man, is the gray, the bit in the middle, the part of a much bigger jigsaw puzzle.

I nod against his hand. "I trust you."

"Good girl." He cradles my head in the palms of his hands, and for the first time ever, he brings his lips to my forehead, pressing a tender kiss there. "And I trust you, too."

His words wash over me like cold water. Sickness roils in my stomach as I replay his words.

Because, in truth, he shouldn't.

He really shouldn't.

Oscar

"The little shit needs forcing to be a man. We don't want no pansy-asses in the mafia, ain't that right, Brennan?"

"Aye," Da replies to my uncle. His cold eyes never leave mine. I hate the thought of what forcing me to be a man means. I feel like I'm going to pee my pants. I know Bren had to shoot someone when he became a teenager. I heard him tell Cal. But I have a feeling it's worse than that. My uncle wants to make me suffer. He hates me. He says I'm a stain on the family name. A weirdo.

He grabs me by the arm, and where I'd normally freak out, I'm frozen in shock. He grabs a rope from the toolbox and pushes my wobbly body toward the chair. I fall easily into it. As my body trembles, I stare at Da. Does he not see my pleading?

He watches from the chair in the corner of the room. Unblinking. Desperation seeps from every part of my body. Why can't he see it? Please, someone help. I want Bren. I want my big brother who comes to my rescue when I need him the most.

My body shakes as though going into shock, causing my uncle to laugh. It's menacing, sickening, and terrifying —all rolled into one. "Bring 'em in."

The door opens just in time for my uncle to take a step back. A young man gets thrown to the floor, his eyes filled with tears. He crawls toward me as though coming to help. I tug on my restraints, eager to help both him and me.

"Make him suffer." My father's deep voice booms toward my uncle, but his words catch in my heart. Does he mean the man? Or me?

I take one last glance in his direction, his eyes trained on me. Leaving no doubt in my mind my Da wants me to suffer.

"Oscar. Oscar, wake up. You're having a nightmare. Os, please wake up." Her soothing voice penetrates through my dream. The memories of when I was coated in blood in order to prove myself as a man. Little did I know that was the first of my many lessons.

Sweat coats my skin, pooling down my face and forcing my eyes to open. "Oscar?" Her soft hand touches my forehead.

My words come out gruffly. "Os."

"Huh?"

"Os. I like it when you call me Os."

She breaks out into a breathtaking smile, making my heart skip a beat. She has the capability of being my light, even in the darkness, and she's unaware of it.

"I like it, too."

I sit up, forcing her to shuffle back. "Good. Call me that from now on."

"Do you need me to do something?" She nibbles her lip while looking around the room for answers.

My cock twitches when I roam my eyes over her delectable body. Her gown falls off one shoulder, exposing her milky skin to me. The sudden urge to mark her becomes a necessity.

"Yes. I need to fuck you. Really bad. And to mark this pretty skin of yours." I touch her neck gently. The need to suddenly squeeze it excites me. Paige's pupils dilate, and I can't help but quirk my lip at the realization that she's turned on by my dominance. Maybe she likes a little pain with her pleasure. My cock weeps at the thought.

Chapter Twenty-Eight

Paige

The metal handcuffs cut into the skin on my wrists as I writhe in ecstasy. Oscar's pupils are blown as he slaps the paddle down hard against my swollen nub. My spine arches, my mouth parting on a scream. "Os."

He slams his sheathed cock inside me. "Fuck yes. I can feel your pussy pulling my cock inside. You want my cum, don't you, greedy girl?"

He slaps my clit again—with his palm this time.

"Yes."

"Fucking beg for it." He grits the words as he slams into me again.

"Please, please, I want your cum, Os."

"Fuck." He slams into me harder, deeper. A bite of pain hits me inside at the force.

"Fucking desperate for it."

"Yes. Oh god, yes."

He swoops down and takes ahold of my breast.

Squeezing it tightly in his large palm, he brings his mouth toward my nipple and bites down on it. I scream in pain, but the stroke of his tongue takes away the bite and replaces it with pleasure. I arch into him, meeting his hips, thrust for thrust.

"I need to taste you, Oscar. I want to taste your cum, please."

His hands collar my throat. Pressing on either side of my neck, he fucks me with vigor. The headboard slams against the wall, and my airway is constricted by his thick fingers, pressing tighter, but the feeling of ecstasy in reach. His grip tightens, and I feel him shudder from somewhere in the distance. Blackness clouds my eyes as I float.

"Open." My eyes snap open to find Oscar climbing over my chest on his knees, now on either side of me with his hard cock in hand. "Open your mouth and let me feed you my cum, Paige." His voice has a sinister edge to it, but the thought only heightens my already delirious body.

The taste of his cum from his cock has me moaning. "Fuck, you're so greedy. My greedy little sex doll." His eyes drill down on me as he watches his cock ramming in and out of my mouth. "All." *Thrust.* "Fucking." *Thrust.* "Mine."

His filthy words and actions are like nothing I've experienced before.

I've no doubt Oscar is a master in manipulation, my body being no exception.

He floods my mouth. His pace is relentless as his cum flows from my lips, and all I can do is try to keep up with him.

Eager to please.
Eager to keep him.

Oscar

I stare down at my woman, stroking a finger over her jawline. "You're perfect, you know that?"

She rolls her eyes. My gaze roams over her naked body as I trail a finger from her face all the way down toward her toes. "Eager and compliant, my perfect little sex doll." Desire leaks from her hooded gaze. She likes me talking dirty to her, and I fucking love it.

"You're courageous and fiery, a perfect combination. You'll need all those assets in this life, Paige."

Paige scoffs. "Compliant? I don't mind being compliant in the bedroom, Os, but in case you haven't noticed, I'm not compliant." She shakes her head at me as though my words are absurd.

My eyes snap back up and roam over her face. "You'll need to be when you meet my father." Her eyes widen slightly in panic, and I can't help but smile internally. Truth is that I was past giving a shit what that old bastard thought of me years ago. I'll be damned if I ever let him say a bad word about Paige, but she might have something to say to him when she realizes just how much he hates me. Something that will be deemed disrespectful if she voices her opinion; it is, of course, completely unacceptable.

"When will this be?" Her voice has a slight tremble to it. I unclasp her hands, wincing at the marks from the bite of the cuffs. "It's fine. I enjoyed it." She pulls her hand away from my inspection, but I quickly tug it back to examine it further. Without thinking, I bring her reddened wrist to my lips and press a gentle kiss there. My own action makes me jolt in surprise.

Her pretty eyes shine with hope as I open my mouth. "I like stuffing your mouth with my cock." She drops her mouth open further in shock. "Keep your mouth open, Paige, and I might just add my fingers in there, too, next time."

I spring up from the bed, leaving her to mull over my words.

"You're an ass, Oscar. We were having a moment there."

I shake my head with a smile as I leave the room.

"A jackass!"

Chapter Twenty-Nine

Paige

I bite into my apple as I go over the text messages I received from Oscar before lunch.

Oscar: Do you miss me?

Paige: It's been two hours.

Oscar: Is that a no?

Paige: I miss you.

Paige: Do you miss me?

Oscar: I miss your pussy.

Paige: Of course you do.

Oscar: I have to work late tonight at the warehouse. I want you there when I get back. I'll send a car.

Paige: I can't make tonight anyway. I have to study.

Oscar: Bring your books to mine, you can study there.

Paige: Not tonight, Oscar. Besides, I want to spend time with Ebony.

I haven't had a response from him since then. He didn't reply; that means he's pissed.

"Hey." Carl breaks through my train of thought. "The black terrier in the third cage is Mrs. Bethels', right?" His shirt sleeves are rolled up, and his sun-kissed arms bulge as he leans against the door of the lunchroom.

"It is." Every other week, Mrs. Bethel brings her terrier here, claiming she's eaten something she shouldn't have and needs to be under observation without treatment. It's only when our receptionist, Mollie, pointed out seeing her at a local twenty-four-hour bingo hall that we realized she uses us as a pet-sitting service.

Carl sighs heavily. "Did we pass on the information about pet-sitting?"

"We did." I take another bite of my apple. His eyes zone in on my lips, forcing me to shuffle uncomfortably at his attention.

"Are you joining us tomorrow night?" He raises a hopeful eyebrow before his shoulders seem to sag at the realization.

"To celebrate you signing the contract on the extension?" Carl has finally managed to wear the local planning department down, and he can now extend the premises, almost doubling the size of the current building. This is perfect, not only for the number of animals we can both house and treat, but I'm really hoping he keeps me on when I graduate. He'll certainly need the extra hands.

"Yeah, we're all going to be there." Discomforted, his gaze shifts to the side. "Partners are welcome too."

I swallow back the lump in my throat, guilt coursing through me. I've gone from telling him that I don't have time to even go on a date to actually having a boyfriend.

I tuck my hair behind my ear. "I'm sorry you found out about Oscar the way you did."

Carl brushes a hand through his blond locks. He really is handsome, but he's nothing compared to my dark devil. I smile inwardly to myself.

"He's a lucky guy, Paige." He nods his head toward me, then turns to leave.

I can't help but mull over his parted words. But the thought leaves a sour taste in my mouth because he couldn't be further from the truth, and when the truth finally comes out... It's going to destroy us both.

Oscar

My grip tightens on my phone as I read the words over again for the hundredth fucking time. *Not tonight. I want to spend time with Ebony?* What the fuck? I get she's close to her sister, but is it necessary she spends time with her when I need her waiting for me?

"Dude. Who pissed in your cheerios?"

My eyes snap up at my Finn's childish words. A huge grin blankets his sarcastic face. "I don't eat cheerios," I deadpan.

He rolls his eyes. "Of course, you fucking don't."

"You eat pussy, though, right?" Con's eyebrows dance.

I shift my palms under the table so they can't see my tense fists. Not only am I pissed at the fact I want to eat her pussy but haven't yet; I don't like them talking about her like that, either.

"You want me to talk about Will's pussy?" Bren throws out at Con. "How 'bout you? Angel's good?" His words have the desired effect, and both my brothers' mouths clamp shut. Finn looks like he's about to fly across the table toward Bren. "Yeah, thought fucking so. Show Oscar's woman some goddamn respect." Bren points his thick finger in their direction, the veins in his temples pulsating.

He winks at me before ducking his head back down to the plans on the table.

"Is she, though?" Finn queries, never afraid to back down from a fight.

Bren's head snaps up so fast that I realize it's good that his neck is so thick; otherwise, it would be rolling on the floor.

The thought of a head rolling on the floor makes me internally shiver. The last time I saw that it was at my own hand when I took an axe to the psycho bitch.

"Oscar?" Cal prompts.

I turn to face him. "Paige, is she your woman?"

I give him a firm nod and only one word because, truthfully, that's all they need. "Obviously."

Their eyes flit to one another like I've lost my damn mind, but they should know me well enough by now to know everything is under control.

Everything is as it should be.

Apart from the fiery little redhead in my bed tonight.

I stare down at my phone and send her another message.

Oscar: I wanted to fuck you tonight.

Paige: Tonight's not an option.

Paige: Choose another night, Os.

Of course, she had to add the *O*s to soften my raging mood. As though she knew it would, too; I don't know whether to be impressed or worried at her attempts at manipulation.

Oscar: Tomorrow.

Paige: I'm meeting friends at Diego's tomorrow.

My blood boils, and my teeth grind.

"Brother, everything okay?"

I turn to face Bren, my heaving chest settling slightly at the concern in his voice. "Fine."

"So we're good for tonight, then?"

I glance back down at the tablet, realizing they've been discussing the job for tonight. We have a new shipment of guns coming in, and with Detective Anderson suddenly taking over as Chief of Police, it's left us feeling angsty. We need this deal to run smoothly. It's almost like a test run to make sure Anderson keeps to his end of the deal. We help him into the position, and he leaves us the hell alone.

"Yes, security is in hand. It's all in hand. Just stick to the plan." I grind the words out, pissed they're even questioning me.

"We all have kids, Oscar; we just want an easy fucking life without the risk." Cal's words cut me deep, making me rub over my heart. Not because I don't have kids, and they do, no. Because I've no intention of having them and knowing how caring Paige is. I'm guessing she's going to want them too.

I decide to put that to the back of my mind. Maybe I could buy her a rabbit or something that can stay outside, and she'll be happy with that. I rub a finger over my lip. I could try to negotiate and let it have most of the balcony.

"So, the meeting with De-Luco went well, and you have the contract from Kozlov?" Cal asks Bren. Sergio De-Luco is a Mafia lawyer and one of the best, so it makes sense we'd use him to make sure the latest deal with the Russians isn't a scam.

"Yeah, De-Luco has taken it to check it over."

"How the fuck does he get away with dealing with so many Mafia families?" Con asks. The boy has so much to learn I want to roll my eyes.

"He's good. Knows people in high places. His daughter is promised to one of the Varros, and his main source of business is that family. They trust him, so we can. I mean, can you imagine if he ever went against one of them?"

"I get that, but he's got us dealing with the Russians," Finn spits out.

"It's a good deal," I point out.

"I'm the fucking Don. Let me worry about it." Bren slams his fist on the table.

We all know Finn is against any business with the Russians. Since discovering Angel was attacked by one, he now has them all pegged as corrupt. Completely unfair, but that's just his way of dealing with the aftermath.

My phone buzzes on the table, and I instantly pick it up to see the text.

Paige: You could come?

I scoff. She knows I can't fucking go there.

Anywhere.

Looks like I will be seeing her tonight, after all.

Chapter Thirty

Oscar

The break in the curtains gives way for the light of the moon to shine onto her chest, emphasizing her milky skin.

When normally, she brings me calm and settles my storm. Tonight, she only fuels my raging inferno. The chaos in my mind is at risk of reaching a boiling point, a tsunami of uncontrollable feelings determined to break out.

I don't like her rejecting me.

Not being with me.

I think it's time Paige learns who's the boss of this relationship. I may not like most things associated with the Mafia, but when you're forced into this world, there really is no choice but to live and breathe the harsh realities of it, and every mafia man knows the key to this life is strength.

Dominance.

And I just so happen to have that in abundance.

Paige

A soft rustling sound buzzes me awake. My breathing escalates with an awareness of someone watching me, someone being in my room. I move to sit up, but my ankles are tied to each end of the bedposts. Panic takes over. I open my mouth to scream, to let Ebony know she needs to get out of here with the kids.

A hand clamps over my mouth, and my eyes widen in fear. "Shhh, my little spitfire; otherwise, I'll have to tape that pretty mouth shut." My heart throbs at the sound of his voice. Relief is quickly replaced by anger. I purse my lips, a thousand things racing through my mind. Just what in the hell is he playing at? He makes quick work of tying my hands together above my head, and then to the head-board. My body is frozen in shock.

He settles over my body, straddling me. "I want you." He grinds his hard cock against me. "You're mine," he spits the words out like vitriol.

"I... Oscar..." My mouth races at what to say, confusion swirling in my hazy mind. Where the fuck did all this come from?

"I wanted you tonight. I just wanted to come home to you waiting for me." My heart stutters at the vulnerability in his tone. As much as I know Oscar hasn't had a relationship before, now it's becoming clearer to me that when Oscar desires something, he needs it. There's no room for negotiation; there's simply no other option in his mind. It's an obsession, and that obsession is me.

The glint of a knife appears, making me jolt in awareness; just how fucking far is he going to go? Is his plan to scare me into submission? It's not the first time I have had doubts about us. About him, and as if sensing those doubts, Oscar's fingers trail down my face. His eyes latch on to mine, seeing the terror behind them.

"You trust me, my little spitfire?"

I lick my dry lips and can only nod slightly in shock at how my night has turned out. "Good girl." His praise goes between my legs, causing a dull ache to appear.

Oscar bends down to the side of my neck and takes a deep breath, taking in my scent. "You smell so fucking edible." He pulls back and stares at me. "You were keeping yourself from me." It's a statement, not a question, one I quickly deny with a shake of my head.

"You. Were. Keeping. Yourself. From. Me." He punctuates each word, his unhinged behavior unraveling by the second.

In the blink of an eye, he leans back on his heels between my legs. His cold eyes travel over my body, the bulge in his pants straining for release.

He holds the knife up before moving toward me so

fast I barely register what's happening. The tear of my nightshirt sends a chill over my body, my nipples pebbling in the coolness of the air. He trails the knife along my chest. It travels over my stomach and down to my pussy, swirling in the small hairs there. "You deny me at every turn, Paige." I shake my head. "Oh, but you do. Even down to the fucking manual you do." He's referring to the hair still between my legs.

I raise my chin in defiance. "You like the challenge, Oscar."

Oscar's eyes soften slightly. "You're right, I do. I love the challenge." His words penetrate my heart. Is he telling me he loves me? That's what he meant, right?

A sharp sting pulls my eyes down to my chest. He cut me? His eyes bore into mine, watching for a reaction before he lowers his head and drags his tongue over the sting, licking it away. I close my eyes at the sensation, an overwhelming urge to cry at the gentleness of his lapping tongue over the sharp sting. His thick hand palms my breast roughly, and then he pinches my nipple between his fingers, causing me to arch off the bed.

"I love how you react to me." The sharp sting of his knife causes me to hiss, but his gentle tongue soothes away the sting once again. I want to run my fingers through his hair, and hold his head in place as he licks away the wound, the blood he hates so much.

"Oscar. Os, I need you."

His head snaps up with understanding. I need more. His jaw locks, annoyed, enraged at both himself and me.

"And I needed you, Paige." He spits the words out cruelly. But it's not the same, is it?

He withdraws from me to stand at the end of the bed. Pulling his belt from his pants, he folds it meticulously in two before raising it. The crack penetrates the air; the force of the slap against my thigh is both a violent sting of pain and a rush of pleasure at his dominance. He's punishing me, and I should be pissed. I should be scared, but instead, I'm turned on and eager for more.

The slap of the belt against my leg makes me dig my heels into the mattress, my skin feeling like it's on fire. "Fuck yes," he groans in awe.

Oscar fumbles with his pants. He pulls a condom from his pocket and rolls it on expertly. A pang hits my chest at the thought that he doesn't trust me enough not to use them by now, even after the tests I endured as part of becoming an Indulgence member and the contraceptive his doctor gives.

He slams into me so hard my mouth drops open in a silent scream.

Oscar

Her pussy clenches around me, her walls squeezing me in tight as though determined not to let go. Never let me go. I love it. I revel in the feeling of always being in this tight pussy. Hers.

She hisses when I run my hands over her thighs, digging my fingers into her flesh roughly, no doubt red, swollen, and sore from my belt. I press harder as she writhes beneath me. "Fuck, your pussy feels good."

I grind my hips, the force hitting the perfect spot inside her. Her slick, warm wetness fills my cock, and not for the first time, I wish I went inside her raw. The thought makes me wild. I quicken my pace, my balls tingling, the need to own her completely overwhelming me. I grab at her breast, pinching her nipple, and trail my tongue over the small cuts on her chest. I grip her throat; I fuck her so hard the headboard clatters against the wall, and her eyes bulge in fear. Her walls tighten around me, pulling me in, holding me in. She shudders and bites into her bottom lip to stop her from screaming out her orgasm.

I fucking come... so hard, so violent, I see stars. "I fucking own you!" I grit the word out into her neck.

My body involuntarily drops beside her. We both stare up at the ceiling, our chests heaving up and down.

My cock is spent from the most intense orgasm of my life. Each one with her better than the last. How is that possible?

"I'm never letting you leave me." I turn my head to face her to make sure she heard my words.

"I know."

I simply nod and pull myself up to my feet, but I hear the whisper of her words only meant for her. "That's what I'm afraid of."

I jolt. Does she not see? That these feelings terrify me too?

I pick up my belt and thread it back through my pants. My shirt sleeves already in place, the routine of having to take off my cufflinks long forgotten. This is what she does to me—breaks down my carefully constructed walls, unravels the chaos in my mind, and settles the trepidation in my veins. She's the half of me that's missing, the part I should have had. She's the part that makes me feel.

Feel normal.

She's simply mine.

I ignore her stare as I untie her. Not wanting to discuss what occurred before tonight because none of that matters now—she knows she's mine. I own her.

"Oscar..."

"What?" I snap.

She shakes her head, slightly disappointed at my

reaction. "Are you... are you not staying?" She meets my eyes as I pull on my suit jacket.

"No."

"So, why all this? Why come over?" She waves her hand around her and the bed.

I cast a look over my shoulder. "You needed a punishment and a reminder."

She chokes at my words, her mouth falling open. The sight makes my cock twitch, and for a second, I reconsider staying, but I'd already decided, and I won't have her disrupting my plans. She crosses her arms over her glorious tits, her nipples peaked in the light of the moon shining through the curtains. I turn my back, slipping my shoes on.

"I'm going to Diego's, Oscar."

My jaw clenches. I attempt my breathing technique, all the while refusing to turn and face her fully. "No, you're not."

I hear a rustle behind me, and then a pillow hits my head, forcing me to face her. Her eyes alight with anger, she tugs the sheets from the bed and stands, raising her chin. "You're welcome to join us, Oscar. But I will be going."

I clench my teeth as I glare down at her. She's going there with him; I fucking know it. I've seen the goddamn messages she's sent her friends. I know exactly who's going, and that pompous prick is going to try and put moves on my woman, and I won't be there to do anything about it. I won't be there to stop her from realizing she can have the normal with him.

"Paige," I bite out in warning.

"I'm going, Oscar. You're just going to have to trust me."

I smirk mockingly. Trust her? She must know that's a joke. She wavers at her own words, nibbling at her bottom lip. "I'm going."

"You're mine. I pay you to listen to me!" I regret it as soon as I fucking say it. Her face crumples. I don't know what to do; I don't know what to say. She stares hopelessly past me.

I don't think I just act. The storm inside me builds. The hate, the anger, the lack of control. I swipe the contents of her dresser onto the floor, the noise ricocheting through the small house. I stare down at her belongings on the floor, the photo frame of her family smashed. Disappointment settles inside me, already eating away at me at a furious pace. I panic, my eyes flicking up at her, hers locked on to the smashed photo; they glisten, and a tremble works through her body.

"Please leave." Her voice is soft and broken, and I want to fucking fix it. I step toward her, but she holds her hand up. "Now, Oscar." She forces through determination, strength, and unhinged rage. I fucked up. Shit, I fucked up.

"Now."

A noise in the corridor makes us both turn. "Paige, is everything okay?"

"Mommy, what was that noise?"

She turns back toward me. "Please?" Her desperation seeps into my own as I shuffle on my feet, reluctant to leave her like this in the aftermath of my destruction.

"Please." Her pleading tugs on my heart.

Defeat builds inside me when I hear the hushed whispers of the children in the corridor. Knowing I don't have any other option but to grant her request. I nod my head reluctantly before turning toward both my entrance and exit—her open window.

Chapter Thirty-One

Paige

The music is so loud I can barely hear Mollie speak. She takes another sip of her champagne. "I said, you don't look happy," she yells.

I plaster on a fake smile. "I'm fine." Truth be told, I'm anything but fine. I spent my day between being mad at Oscar, and then the wallowing feeling of sadness would tamper the raging fire inside me.

Mollie raises one of her perfectly constructed eyebrows. "Girl, you have bite marks on your neck, fingerprints too, and you're walking as though you rode a horse to Texas and back." I choke at her analogy, the bubbles of the champagne coming out of my nostrils. She quickly hands me a napkin from the table.

"Please tell me it was your dark and mysterious man that gave them to you. And it was consensual, right?"

My hand goes to my throat, my fingers drifting over his marks, a flutter in my stomach at the reminder. "Don't worry, you can't see them, not fully anyway. I know

271

they're there because I live that life." She smiles proudly. My eyes bug out. The innocent, normally quiet receptionist seems to have quite an active sex life.

"They are." I use my hair to try and cover the marks on my neck. "Consensual, I mean." She nods and graces me with a knowing smile and a dance of her eyebrows.

"He's too bland for you, vanilla." She peers over her shoulder toward Carl.

I shrug a shoulder. If I'm being completely honest with myself, I spent the entire morning talking myself out of a relationship with Oscar and into one with someone like Carl. Someone with less baggage, someone with a normal life and job.

But each time, my heart constricted so much that it felt like it was breaking. I'm in too deep now, and there's no way out. I think we were destined to be together because, quite quickly, Oscar O'Connell has become my everything, and I wouldn't have it any other way.

"Come on, let's go dance." Mollie takes my hand and pulls me up from the table. The guys watch us as we pass, making a thrill race up my spine. Oscar doesn't know what he's missing out on, and with that thought, for the first time tonight, I feel like having a good time.

Screw Oscar.

Tonight is about me. I'll deal with him tomorrow.

Oscar

Quite possibly, I've tugged all my hair out. I'm going, In. Fucking. Sane watching her. I don't know how much more I can take.

After spending the entire day locked in my apartment, going over and over how I fucked everything up, I'm now torturing myself, watching her dance with her friends.

She looks magnificent, a tight blue dress molding to her perfect curves, my fucking curves. I roar with frustration; my fists hurt through clenching them so tightly.

My heart hammers against my chest so hard it hurts, and I rub at it.

I breathe; I abandoned my four, four, fours this morning. I breathe some more, but when that dick touches her hip and she smiles at him, I see red. I throw my tablet against the wall, not caring it's shattered to a thousand pieces. What was once my lifeline is now worthless because she is the only thing that matters to me. She's the only thing I see, the only thing I want, and the only thing I will ever need.

My hands shake uncontrollably as I pick up my phone, knowing she's going to be pissed as hell and hate me further, but feeling so out of my element, I don't see I have any other choice.

"Do it," I snap into the phone before slamming it onto the counter.

I stand with my hands clasped tightly on the countertop, determined to keep a distance between her and myself as I wait for the door to open. The loud grumbles of my men, along with her voice, make my head snap up. "Don't fucking hurt her," I snap at the two security guards holding my woman roughly, one on either side of her. "Leave us."

They release their hold on her, and her shoulders drop in defeat.

She waits until the door clicks shut. "What the fuck, Oscar?" I duck my head and wince at her tone. I know I've gone too far; I knew that last night. "I can't keep doing this. This is insane." She walks toward me, but I refuse to lift my head. "I didn't sign up for this shit. I deserve better. I'm going to have better." I eye her from under my lashes. Her lip trembles as she tries to hold herself together.

She turns on her heel to leave, but my hand snaps out and grasps her wrist roughly. "Please." I lift my head, and her eyes take me in; jolting when she sees me, pity seeps through her eyes at my clearly unraveled state. The fact I'm in a t-shirt and sweatpants is an indication of how low I feel.

"Oscar, I'm sorry." She shakes her head, her voice a sorry whisper.

My heart sinks, but I refuse to release her hand. I pull her toward me, bending to place my forehead against hers, hoping she can see inside me—my sorrow, desperation, my fears of losing her. I beg her to see something, licking my dry lips. "Please."

She goes to pull back, but I clasp my hand on her hip, holding her in place, my throat constricting and my heart hammering heavily, my veins pumping with desperation. I can't help the shake in my hand with the knowledge of what I'm going to do. My last-ditch attempt to keep her. I'm going to give her my everything. I lean back slightly, tugging my t-shirt over my head and dropping it to the floor.

Paige's emerald eyes hold mine as I turn her hand over and place her palm on my heart. The action makes my body want to withdraw. I hold it there, hoping she can feel the strong beat of it, the beat for her. "Please." I open my eyes to find hers shimmering with tears streaming down her face.

I move my lips toward hers, her scent filling my nostrils, driving me insane. The scent that dick Carl would have been smelling. My woman.

My lips crash down on hers aggressively, my tongue plundering her mouth, sweeping all around. Her arms band around my neck, pulling me in further; my whole body alights at her touch. I lift her onto the counter. Her legs wrap around my waist. Fuck, she tastes incredible... every fucking inch of her is incredible.

I kiss down her neck, over her jawline, and back to her mouth as she grinds against my hard cock. "Please don't stop." Her heady voice causes my cock to spurt in my pants.

I devour her mouth, holding her head in place with one hand. We kiss frantically with so much fucking passion I threaten to combust. It's aggressive and rough. A clash of teeth and tongues and a bite of her bottom lip fills my mouth with her coppery tastes. My cock jumps, desperate to join in on the action.

She tugs on my waistband, and I help her slide them down. Her soft, silky palm grips my cock, and my eyes roll to the back of my head at her simple touch. "Fuck, Paige. You feel incredible." I choke out the words, completely unprepared for the emotions she's brought to the surface of me.

She rocks against me, her voice trembling. "I need you, please." I swiftly move her panties aside as she pushes the head of my bare cock toward her hole. I grit my teeth at the sensation. In. Fucking. Credible. She strokes my cock over her slick folds, and I use this as lubricant when I take my cock from her and drag it back and forth over her slit. An incoherent moan escapes her, forcing a growl from me. I can't help but push inside. This feeling is like nothing I've ever experienced before.

This is life-altering.

It's everything.

She throws her head back. Her mouth opens wide as I work myself in and out, in and fucking out at a frantic pace. "Take it. Take my bare cock, Paige." My balls clench already, eager to empty inside her.

"So good," she pants against me.

I draw my fingers to her mouth, the ones with her moisture coating, before forcing them inside. "Taste your pussy." She moans around my fingers, her pussy clenching at my filthy words. I grind against her; the power of her hold on my cock is incredible. My balls tingle, forcing me to work faster. "Yes... that's it, more," Paige screams out her release, causing me to stumble forward, gripping the cupboard above her head as my cock erupts inside her. My cum surges deep in her womb, flooding her tight pussy with my essence.

Our chests heave together, our foreheads meeting once again. Paige's eyes search mine as though waiting for me to withdraw into myself once again. I refuse to let that happen. Determination seeps into my veins. I want to be her everything like she is mine. Her mouth parts to speak, but I shake my head. Her gentle fingers move the wayward curl from my forehead, the tender action making my determination stronger. I'm keeping her. I'm going to be the man she deserves.

I'm going to be her everything, too.

"Hold on to my neck." Her eyes search my own as I lift her ass from the counter. Her hands clasp around my neck.

I pull up my sweatpants and stride down the corridor, her giggles filling the air. "What the hell, Os?" Her shock and playful tone make me nuzzle into her apple-scented neckline, leaving a gentle kiss. I want to kiss her everywhere, taste her everywhere, leaving nothing untouched, and I'm going to.

I bypass her bedroom door and stride toward my own. She clings to me harder. "Os?" She pulls back and searches my face.

I launch her into the air, her body bouncing off my silk sheets.

I take down my sweatpants. Kicking them to the side, leaving my cock standing proud.

Paige makes quick work of her dress, her milky tits bouncing at her action. My cock oozes pre-cum, but I pay it no attention because there's something much more important to do. I need to taste my girl.

Chapter Thirty-Two

Oscar

I drop down on the bed further, having to grind my cock against the mattress like a teenager to warden off the need to fill her again. Is it always like this? The need to consume every part of your woman?

I stare up from between her milky thighs, the red lashes of my belt prominent on her skin. Kissing the redness, I realize I've never shown her the care she deserved. That stops now. She's my everything, and it's time she believed it. Time she knew about it.

I press my face into her pussy and inhale, an arousing scent filling my nostrils. I close my eyes, embracing it. Embracing her.

I've wanted to do this for so long now but never allowed myself to actually indulge. She's broken down my walls, and I won't ever construct them again. No, we'll build new ones together. We'll set out our own foundation and build on it together. The realization and strength give me the confidence to swipe my tongue through her slit, making me groan into her pussy when her taste explodes on my tongue. I stroke my finger over her hood, flicking at her nub, then drag my tongue down her slit again.

She arches her back and clutches the sheets; her reaction to me is an aphrodisiac. "Oh god, Os."

"Fuck yes. Say my name while I lick your pussy."

She raises her head slightly, looking down at me as I drag my tongue over her slit once again. "Os, you came in me." We hold one another's eyes. Did she think this would stop me from tasting her sweet pussy?

I swipe again and flick my tongue over the bud of nerves. "Mmm, our cum tastes so good together, so fucking good." And it's true. As her musky taste mingles with my own saltiness, it only seems right that I experience this moment tasting us both. How we should be.

I curl my tongue, shoving it deep into her hole, eager to fuck her with it while my finger draws circles on her clit.

Her hand moves to touch my head before she stops with the realization she is about to touch me without permission. Annoyance rumbles inside me. "Fucking do it, Paige. Grab my hair and fuck my face!" Her eyes startle, but she licks her lips and moans when my tongue plays with her clit, toying with it as I kiss and caress it.

She moves her hand to my hair, holding me in place as she pushes herself into me. "Oh fuck." She thrusts against my face, holding me where she wants me. I'm in awe at my sexual spitfire. She's fucking incredible, and

I've been holding her back. She knows what she wants, and she's using me to get it. I fucking love it. My cock rubs against the sheets as I hump them to the motion of her fucking my face.

She's on her elbows now, so she can watch. Sweat coats her milky skin. As her lips part on a moan and whimpers drop from those bruised lips, she looks fucking incredible. She grips my hair to the point of stinging, but I love it. I groan against her pussy, flicking my tongue over and over her clit, pushing inside her, tasting us both. I finally use two fingers to push inside, the wetness of our cum running down my wrist. In. Fucking. Credible.

"I'm going to come. Oh god, I'm going to come!" And she does. Her pussy squeezes my fingers as I rub her perfect spot deep inside. Her ass lifts off the bed as she fucks my face. My tongue, lips, and nose being used as her personal fucktoys.

Her pussy finally releases my fingers as she drops to the bed, seemingly exhausted. But I'm far from being done with her, not when I've broken down my walls, not when I've opened the cage and released the animal trapped inside.

"You're going to lick your pussy juice from my face, Paige. Then you're going to fuck my cock and bounce those tits in my face for me to suck on."

Her eyes widen, her pupils dilate, and I can't help but smirk at her as I crawl over her delectable body with her juices dripping from my chin. I watch her face for a reaction. Will she shy away from my words? Will she play coy when I know how desperately she wants it, wants me?

Determined, her eyes lock on to my chin, wet with our arousal. Our faces only inches apart now. I raise an eyebrow in question, and in a split second, she grabs my neck, her fingernails digging into the flesh as her tongue laps against my face, up my jaw, and finally into my mouth, tasting us both on her tongue. Fuck me, she's incredible. My little spitfire gives me as good as she's gotten. She moans at the taste of us, and I spear her with my aching cock, ramming into her as her hold on me tightens.

"I need..." Her breathy words make me stutter my pace.

"I need to be on top."

My body tenses. She wants to be in control. As if sensing my thoughts, my anxieties creeping inside me, she tugs on her tits, rolling her nipples between her forefingers, and a thrill zaps up my spine. "I need to feed you them." How I don't come on the spot at her words is beyond me.

I roll us so quick we almost fall out the bed. I grip her and shuffle us to the middle. All the while, Paige is stifling a giggle between her bottom lip with her teeth. She grinds down on me, the feeling foreign and exciting. She looks like a vision as her red hair sways with each action of her hips. Her tits heave, begging to be marked and sucked. We moan in unison as she bends over me and hand-feeds me one. I close my eyes at the feeling of her tit in my hand as my lips latch on to her hard peak. I flick my tongue over it, nibble, and devour it before moving on to the next.

"Paige, fuck, you're incredible. Fuck me, baby, so incredible."

Her flush chest heaves. "Mmm, I love it when you suck my tits, Os. Hard, do it hard."

I suck her flesh into my mouth, feeling her pussy clench around me as I sink my teeth into her skin, sucking and pulling to leave an everlasting mark on her as she has me.

I feel her pussy clench, her muscles drawing me in. "Ohhh god."

I push up into her, deeper and deeper, harder and harder, determined to get my cum in her as far as possible.

"Fuck. Fuck, I'm coming, Paige." My hand tightens on her hip; the other squeezes her tit as I suck on the other. She releases a scream, her body tensing with her release. I finally allow myself to go fully; a shudder wracks through my body, "Fuckkkkk."

She drops on top of me heavily, my arm automatically banding around her in a protective stance. My spent cock stays inside her, our releases oozing out of her and down my balls, but I couldn't give a shit right now. Because right now, in my arms is the only thing that matters. She may have pulled down my walls, but in my arms, I've carefully constructed new ones with her burrowed inside with me.

We lie with one another—Paige with her head on my chest, the moon shining into the room, exposing the marks on her milky body. I swirl a finger over her skin, and a chill spreads over her body.

She raises her head. "Oscar?" Her lips part and nothing comes out before she tries again. "I'm scared." My eyebrows narrow, and my body freezes.

"Of what? You know I'll keep you safe, right?"

She nibbles on her lip. "I do. But..."

I cut her off and take her chin in my fingers. "I care about you, Paige. You realize that?" It's as close to a declaration of love as she's ever going to get. Someone like me is incapable of giving more.

She shakes her head. "Oscar, I need to talk to you about something." Worry mars her beautiful face. My body tenses at her words, and my muscles tighten. I don't want her words to ruin the night. Not tonight.

"Tomorrow."

She searches my face and finally settles her own as though defeated. "Tomorrow?" I nod but doubt myself because whatever Paige has to say, I don't want to hear it. Not when I'm creating our own walls with us both safe inside.

She sighs and drops her head against my chest, her finger now mimicking my own, drawing lazy swirls over my chest. "I care about you, too." Her voice is soft, and the rumble from my chest surprises even me.

"I know."

I practically feel her roll her eyes.

"Now, tell me about this fucking charity event I have to go to."

She giggles into me, the sound lightening the mood

and air because if I can have this night with her, without the mafia world tainting her, tainting us, then I will.

I clutch her tighter, silently telling her I'll keep her within our walls, safe and secure from the outside world.

Safe and secure from our enemies.

Chapter Thirty-Three

Paige

I flit my eyes over toward Oscar. His leg bounces nervously, and his hands tighten on the steering wheel. He's anxious. I can understand that. I am, too, for him. We're going to a charity barbeque at the clinic today. It's an event to help raise funds for owners that can't afford their pets' treatments.

It's going to be a busy day with a lot of people, but I assured Oscar we only had to show our faces and I'd stay by his side. I know he doesn't want to come, and I wouldn't have dreamed of pushing something like this on him, but after last night, he seems more determined than ever to live, to push his boundaries.

Although I'm completely in awe of him, I can't help but worry he's doing too much, too soon, and it's all going to come crashing down on him, on both of us.

He looks drop-dead gorgeous as always and smells edible. I nibble into my lip, imagining tasting him.

His white shirt is pulled across his chest tightly, and I

feel privileged to be the only woman to ever touch him there. His black pants are so tight I can see the outline of his cock, and it makes me squirm in my seat, thinking of it stretching me.

His knee jumps again, and I feel a need to protect him consume me. "I promise to stay with you." I place my hand on his thigh, and butterflies flutter inside when he doesn't so much as flinch from my touch.

His eyes dart to mine, a small smile playing on his lips. "I know, it's not that." I get it. The crowd, the noise, the uncertainty... too much for him. I nod in understanding.

"We won't stay long," I reassure him once again.

He takes my hand from his thigh, and my spine straightens, steeling itself with the rejection, but he moves my hand to his lips, pressing a tender kiss on my palm.

"I want to do this, Paige. For both of us." Our eyes meet once again, and I give him a smile. His own follows. "Besides, I want to fuck you while I'm there."

I choke, raising a brow. "Really?"

"Fuck yes, you think just because I fucked you all night and again this morning, I want to risk my cum drying up inside you? I want you permanently wet, Paige. Wet from being filled by me."

I squirm at his words, his wetness still evident right now in my panties. As if knowing my thoughts, he smirks, causing me to playfully tap him, earning me a rare, throaty laugh.

Oscar turns into the busy parking lot with a heavy sigh. He bends forward and reaches for his glasses in the center console, his hand shaking slightly. He pauses and meets my eyes as if questioning what I might think of him wearing the glasses, knowing he doesn't need them. "I like you in them. You look like a super sexy nerd."

He chokes on a chuckle as though trying his best to suppress the laughter. "I just want you to be comfortable."

He nods slightly, giving his head a small shake before putting the glasses back in the console. I can't help but lean toward him, pecking his lips. A moan emanates from his throat when I open my mouth and allow him to sweep inside with his tongue. I can't help but whimper into his mouth. His hand finds the back of my head and tugs on my hair, holding me in place. He pulls back, our chests heaving, our heavy eyes locked, and the car filled with a sexual promise. He quickly begins to unbuckle his belt. "I need your lips around my cock, Paige." His hooded, lustful eyes are transfixed on my face. "Now," he snaps as though at the end of his tether. I jump at the sound of his voice and lower my head to his oozing, solid cock in the fist of his hand. It looks angry and desperate. Desperate for me.

Oscar

I grip her hair tightly in my hand. "You need to hurry and make me come, baby. We're in a parking lot." She groans around my cock, and the vibration goes all the way to my heavy balls.

Never in my life have I been so goddamn reckless... never have I so much as considered emptying my balls in a public place like this. But she does this to me; the raging inferno inside me needs to be let out.

All the built-up anxieties, the nervousness, the sexual tension. All of it.

My head falls back against the headrest, and my eyes fucking roll when she goes as far down as my shaft. She gags when I hold her head in place and thrust up into her, hitting the back of her throat. "Fuck yes. Fucking take it." I tighten my hold. She whimpers when I use my other hand to grip the back of her neck forcefully, fucking up into her mouth.

My cock swells, and my balls draw up. "Fuck. Choke on my goddamn cum." I thrust again, my cum flooding her mouth, but I'm determined to make her take me all, my full load, at whatever cost. "Take it." *Thrust.* "Fucking all of it." Spent, my hand releases her neck while the other strokes over her hair lovingly.

The tension in my body is erased, and her mouth is still wrapped around my softening cock. "Clean me up," I snipe the words but love the filth and dominance behind them, especially when Paige flicks her tongue up and down and moans against my hardening cock.

A loud knock against the window startles me. My hand covers a frozen Paige. Staring back at me are my brother's eyes, dancing with mirth. Con the little shite. "Hurry the fuck up, man; Keen wants Paige to show him the puppies." He wiggles his eyebrows at his own low joke, and I narrow mine further, my fists tightening once again. "See you out here. When you're done." He winks and turns his back.

Paige's head pops up from my crotch, her reddened cheeks and plump lips things of natural beauty. I graze a thumb over her bottom lip as she stares at me in panic.

"Shhh, it's okay. Finish me off, and we can go." Her eyes flit over toward my window, then back at me. I give her a sharp nod, letting her know how serious I actually am. Her shoulders slacken, and she returns to licking me... licking me so damn much my cock needs relief. Again.

Paige

After Oscar came in my mouth a second time, we finally exit the car.

For the first time, he takes my hand in his, and my heart swells. I smile so wide my cheeks hurt. It feels like we're a couple... a real couple in every sense of the word. His grip on me is firm, his large hand encompassing mine, our fingers entwined. I love the feel of it—something so simple but means so much to me, to us.

As we walk toward the clinic, I can't stop the nagging sensation in the pit of my stomach that reminds me I need to talk to Oscar and soon, before things get out of hand and the secret I hold threatens to destroy us both.

"Fucking finally!" Con rolls his eyes in a big childlike huff. "Jesus, how fucking long do you need?"

Oscar tenses beside me. I stroke his hand. He takes in the movement and squeezes mine reassuringly.

"Not everyone's a two-pump chump, Con," he clips back, making me bite my lip on a giggle.

B J Alpha

Con's mouth drops open in shock at Oscar's response before he darts his eyes over to Will, who chokes on the water she's sipping.

"Daddy, I want to see the babies." Keen tugs on Con's shirt. Keen's blue eyes, so similar to his daddy's, find mine. "Paige, can you take me to the baby dogs, please?"

Con bends down. "They're called puppies, dude."

"Yeah, them."

Both their eyes meet mine, and the thought of how much they look like cute little puppy dog eyes right now makes me chuckle. I hold out my hand for Keen. "Come on, buddy, let's go."

Oscar tightens his grip on mine as I move to leave, pulling me in. He whispers in my ear, "Where will you be?" His eyes dart around the hectic parking lot, and I don't know if it's concern for me or his anxieties that have him acting irrational.

"I'll just be in those double doors." I point over toward the clinic. "Do you want to come?" Keen gives my other hand a frustrated tug as I wait for Oscar to respond.

Oscar's eyes lock on someone in the distance, and I turn my head to see what has caught his attention. It's Carl.

"I'll stay here and watch the doors," he responds without looking at me. I almost want to scoff. Watch the doors? As though something is going to happen to me.

Oscar brushes the hair beside my neck off my shoulder before sinking his teeth sharply into my skin, making me wince. I pull back to look at him questionably, taken aback at his sudden action, only to find his eyes still

294

locked on to Carl's, both of them in some sort of silent standoff. I pull my hand away from Oscar's, already missing the contact. I walk away from him and his obvious display of ownership.

His action both annoys and excites me.

Chapter Thirty-Four

Oscar

Con watches me closely as I stare at Paige's ass swaying in the floaty white summer dress she wears. "Security will follow them. They're fine."

"Mmm," I mumble back at him, unprepared to take my eyes off her for even a second. I watch as she giggles at something Keen has said. A sharp emotion hits me in the chest, a realization that she'll make an incredible mother one day. I quickly banish those thoughts, unwilling to even go there.

Ever.

I glance down at my tablet and watch Paige point out various dogs housed in the facility. I watch over my lashes as Con kicks off of the wall. "You watching her now?"

I don't answer him.

He chuckles. "You got it bad, brother, real fucking bad. You need to marry her, knock her up and make sure some other dude doesn't come and steal her right from under you."

I give him my attention now, his words hitting deep. A feeling of unease ripples through me, and I shuffle under his scrutiny, feeling as though he can see right inside me, all my flaws, all my shattered, crumbled walls, open and exposed. My fists tense, and I breathe my four, four, four.

He throws his head back on a laugh. "Shit, man, I didn't mean to scare you. But fuck, she's hot, clever, and clearly, she's something special to put up with your brooding ass."

I grunt a nonchalant response, attempting to down-play my reaction. But inside? Inside, I'm struggling to rein in my feelings. I want her back here with me. I want her by my side and in my fucking bed. With me.

The softness of the smile she holds toward my nephew should warm my heart, but all it does is annoy the fuck out of me. She should only smile like that for me. Do I make her smile like that? I feel like my lungs are caving in as I suck in a breath. I need her.

I close my eyes and control my breathing, unsure how many times I go through the process, but when I smell her familiar scent and a soft hand brushes soothingly up and down my arm, my eyes snap open. "I missed you," I choke the words out.

She scans over my face, her own etched with worry. "Maybe we shouldn't have come?" Her words sound disappointed, and I hate it. I fucking hate that I'm ruining her day.

"I'm fine," I snap back at her, and she takes a step back.

Will and Con begin asking Keen questions about the

animals, and Paige stands watching me as I pretend to work on my tablet.

"Paige, it's so good to see you."

My spine straightens at the pompous prick's words as my eyes take him in. He's wearing jeans and a white t-shirt that stretches over his broad shoulders. His messy blond hair makes him look youthful, and he has a golden tan, like he belongs in California and not New Jersey. Is this what she likes? I glance down at my own clothes of a shirt and pants, unease and jealousy filling me. I sneer in his direction.

She spins on her heel to face him. "Hi, Carl."

"And you're Oscar. Right?" He holds his hand out for me to shake. Not a hope in hell, punk. He knows who the hell I am. He's seen me before. I use my free hand to wrap it around Paige's waist, drawing her against me.

I glare at him, my eyes drilling into him dangerously. "You saw her last night. Before she came home to me." The energy around us is tense, almost standoffish, as the douche drops his hand but widens his stance as if for battle.

I take note of Paige's eyes darting back and forth between us, her mouth opening and closing as if not knowing what to say to either of us.

"My Pussy is very hairy and soft. Not like that one. That one looks old, and it has gray hair." Keen's voice plays out in the background, and Paige giggles uncomfortably at both his words and the tension between her boss and me.

Will claps her hands together. "Did you show Oscar the extension plans, Paige?" She stands between Carl and me as though defusing the situation, whereas Con moves to stand beside me, staring the asshole down, clueless why he's actually doing it. I recognize his solidarity toward me.

Paige clears her throat and replies, "No, I didn't. Come on, Os. I'd like to show you." She pulls away from me and tilts her head toward the clinic. "I'll see you at work, Carl." She smiles politely at him as I follow her, pulling her back to take my hand in hers. I glare over my shoulder at the prick watching me walk away. I give him a sly smirk equivalent to a wink and follow my woman.

A need to prove she's mine ebbs at the cusp of bare restraint.

"Carl keeps them in his office. This way." I follow her down the corridor, my teeth grinding to the point of pain when she says his name. My body is coiled tight, my knuckles white at the pressure of my balled-up fists.

Paige opens a door and walks inside. I step into his office, his scent lingering in the air. And I fucking hate it!

A sudden need to make a point, a clear point to remind her who owns her, takes over me. I need the control. I need her.

At the realization, I snap. Rushing her from behind, grabbing her hair in my hand and another on her hip, I slam her face down onto his desk. "Shit, Os." Her words come out shocked and breathy. I kick her feet apart and stand between her legs, forcing my hard cock against her ass. I take my hand off her hip and use it to free my belt, using it to wrap her hands tightly behind her back as she whimpers against me.

"Oscar, you need to calm down." She tries to shrug me off, but I hold firm.

I ignore her as I unbutton my pants and pull my leaking cock out. A hiss travels through my teeth at the thought of emptying inside her pussy again. All the while using Carl's desk as a statement.

"Os..." Her words die off when she watches over her shoulder as I tug her dress over her ass. I bend down to my sock and pull out the small pocket knife. I flick it open and cut away her panties.

"Is your pussy wet, Paige?"

Her lips part to speak, but as if frozen in shock, no words come out. I chuckle at her lack of response and decide to use my own lubricant just in case. The thought sends a thrill up my spine.

I spit down the crack of her ass and again for good measure before dragging it down to her hole. My cock oozes pre-cum at the memory of this morning's session before I drag the tip of my cock down her ass and hold it against the opening of her pussy.

I use one hand to hold her head down while the other finds its way back to her hip. I rear back, and as if guided by some magnetic force, my cock slams into her so hard it shifts her up the desk.

"Oh god." She pants when I pull back and do it again.

"Scream my fucking name, Paige." *Slam*. "Fucking scream it." *Slam*. The desk moves with each slam of my hips. Each thrust going impossibly deeper. Each time, my hand holds her so forcefully she's bound to bruise.

"Please."

"Fucking scream it!"

"Oscarrrr." Her pussy clenches around my cock, but I keep going, fucking her through her orgasm, watching in ecstasy as her mouth drops open.

"Beg me for my cum." *Slam.* "Beg me to fill your pussy." *Slam.* I hold her head down harder as I fuck her, as though my life depends on it.

Just as my balls begin to draw up, I see movement at the door. The prick's face pales, and my eyes narrow on him glaringly as he takes in the scene on his desk.

My woman faces away from him as I continue to fuck her from behind while she chants, "Os, more."

"Beg for my cum." Carl's eyes meet mine, and I stare at him. I stare at his pale, panicked face as a realization takes over his body. His shoulders slump, and I revel in it.

"Please, Os, fill me with your cum."

I slam into her again. "Who fucking owns you, Paige?"

"You do. You own me, Oscar."

And at that, Carl turns and walks away, but not before I make sure he hears me roar my release deep inside her. "I fucking own you, Paige. Me."

My cock swells and my movements stutter as rope upon rope of cum coats her pussy.

In. Fucking. Credible.

Mine.

Chapter Thirty-Five

Paige

"Let me guess, he fucked you in that dude's office, right?" Will asks as I lick my ice cream.

We're sitting watching Keen in the sandbox while Con and Oscar are talking under the trees. I glance over toward Oscar, his eyes staring right back at me.

"He's intense, but he clearly cares about you." She nudges my shoulder with hers.

"His intensity doesn't bother me," I tell her truthfully.

She eyes me skeptically. "No?"

I scoff; hell no. If anything, he makes me feel safe, cared for, and guarded, as though he'd burn down the town just to keep me. Like I'm a treasure for safekeeping, for his keeping.

"It doesn't bother me. He's caring."

Now, Will scoffs. "Caring?"

I nod, thinking about how he worried about me not being able to say my safe word the first time I gave him the first blow, about the coffee machine he ordered for me, the delivery of food he sent us, and the abundance of my favorite toiletries he somehow knew about. He's caring and kind and even though he refuses to admit it, refuses to see it even, he's thoughtful.

Oscar O'Connell is so much more than he ever claims to be. He might not realize he didn't just break down his walls; he smashed them, obliterated them to dust, determined to get out and experience the world, and I couldn't be prouder.

"Oh, you're in love with him, aren't you?"

Her eyes fill with sympathy, and I feel defensive of our relationship. Of him.

I raise my chin. "What if I am?"

She swallows thickly, her eyes flicking around the ground. "You just need to be careful, Paige. This life isn't for everyone."

Annoyance bubbles in my veins. She thinks I'm weak. An innocent girl with her head in the clouds.

"Look. I'm sorry if I offended you, but"—her eyes fill with emotion and concern—"a lot has happened. The guys... they're loving and strong and protective, but they're also dangerous to be around. They have enemies, Paige. I just don't want to see you get hurt." Her eyes implore me with her truth, and I nod, relaxing slightly, although her words echo through me.

A reminder I need to speak to Oscar.

Soon.

Oscar

I watch her with Will, my brother's wife. She giggles when Keen pulls a weird face and then proceeds to wipe his hands tenderly with some sort of wipe.

"She's going to fit right in, Oscar."

I turn toward Con, who points at Paige. "She'll probably want kids right away, right?" His words cut me deep. Kids.

He sighs. "If I hadn't fucked things up with Will the first time, I'm sure she'd be knocked up by now."

"You told her to kill your baby. Paid her to do it," I remind him in a monotone voice I've perfected. He pales and stumbles back at my words, no doubt searing him deeply. Like I intended because his words hurt me too, yet I manage to hide behind mine when they use the excuse of me being different.

He drags a hand over his messy hair while I watch him selfishly, trying to grapple with his own insecurities. "Thanks for the reminder. Seriously though, man, I'm pleased for you." He moves to slap my shoulder in a brotherly way, but I manage to step out of it, always unable to understand the need for touching when you can use words to convey your thoughts.

I watch as Paige rises and opens her arms as two small children I recognize as her niece and nephew fall into her open arms. She smothers them with kisses that make my heart constrict. An invisible void starts to open inside me as I watch her kneel down and talk to them, smile at them.

I clench my teeth as she stands and takes them both by the hand, and walks toward us. Jesus, I turn my back and breathe in.

"Os, I'd like to introduce you to my niece and nephew." I turn at her hopeful voice, staring into her expectant eyes.

I stare down at the little boy I know as Adam. He grins at me, and I quirk my lip and give him a sharp nod just as Paige goes on to introduce them. "This is Adam, and the one hiding here, this little missy..." The little girl giggles at Paige's words. "... is, Casey."

I am unsure of what I'm supposed to say and do. The familiar feeling of bugs crawling over my skin makes me irrational, and a sudden need to go back to my apartment, where I'm familiar with my surroundings and away from people, overwhelms me.

"When are we leaving?" I snap at Paige.

Her eyes widen, and then her throat works as she glances down at the kids. "I was going to show them around," she mumbles so low I almost miss it.

I clench my fists, desperate to leave. I glare at her. She said we'd show our faces and we wouldn't stay long.

Will steps forward, her eyes darting from mine to Paige's. "They came with your neighbor, right? I can show them around with Keen and then take them back? What do you say, guys? Would you like to see some puppies?" Her voice becomes animated as she speaks. I prepare for a fight, and Paige's eyes fill with disappointment that only fuels my own rage.

I turn my back without so much as a goodbye and walk toward my car.

Chapter Thirty-Six

Oscar

I can't look at her, so I keep staring ahead, somehow driving home without even thinking about where I'm going.

I can't do this. I can't fucking do it.

I can't give her what she wants, needs, and deserves.

Her longing for her family is evident. The love freefalling for her niece and nephew. Something I don't want, can't have.

I wouldn't wish my life on anyone, least of all an innocent child. To have them poked and prodded, mocked, and rejected.

Even if they were normal, what have I got to offer them? Every child deserves a father who's going to love them... something I know I'm not capable of.

Hell, I can barely touch, let alone hug someone.

No, absolutely not.

She deserves more.

A sickness washes over me; I can feel my lip tremble

with the realization. No matter how much I try and how hard I fight, I'll never win.

I'll always wish I could be more, and she'll grow to hate me, resent me in a way I couldn't live with.

It's reasonable to stop this now before it goes too far. Before she utters those words, I know are on the tip of her tongue.

I close my eyes as emotion assaults me. Finally, realization dawns on me; there is no alternative. This isn't going to work.

I force my eyes back open with a new determination.

Now I know different isn't always better too.

Paige

Oscar's body was coiled so tight it was like a spring was about to go off at any minute as he drove in silence.

I'm angry and disappointed. Jesus, am I disappointed.

He moves into the kitchen, resting back on the countertop, much like last night. Last night when he gave me his all.

"You're mad." His tone is pissed, as though he's mad at me for something. I can feel something brewing in the air, and I don't like it. He's itching for a fight, and I don't want that.

I rub over my temple, a headache edging toward the forefront. "I'm disappointed."

He scoffs, mulling over my words. "Disappointed."

"I'm sorry." My voice wavers.

His eyes snap up toward mine, cold and calculated. "For what?" The clenching in his jaw gives away his angry demeanor.

I fiddle with my hands in front of me. "For saying I'm disappointed, Oscar. I didn't mean to hurt you."

His jaw tightens. "You didn't fucking hurt me." He snaps his mouth shut and glances away. His Adam's apple bobs. "I don't want kids."

His words make me jolt because where the fuck did that come from?

I lick my suddenly dry lips. "You might change your mind, Oscar."

He glares back at me. "I won't." I can see it in his eyes, the determination set in his jaw; he won't. His mind is made up that he doesn't want children.

"Is it because..."

"Because what? Autism? Is that what you think?" His voice becomes louder with each word, with a hint of mocking.

I remain calm and in control as I watch him spiraling with each second. My heart hammers in my chest. "Is it? It's not necessarily hereditary, Oscar. They can do tests."

His eyes fill with rage, blazing with hate. "Tests?" His eyes bug out. "You've no fucking idea. Don't you dare fucking go there, Paige?" He points at me as he screams across the kitchen.

I close my tear-filled eyes and nod. "I'm sorry." He's right; I've no idea, and I can't imagine what he has gone through, nor what he's going through right now.

When I snap my eyes open, he's tugging on his hair and pacing. I straighten my shoulders. "We could adopt."

He stops in his step and leans over the counter, the whites of his knuckles proving the force of his grip; his head shakes lowly. "I don't want kids. Ever." His darkened blue eyes glare into mine, penetrating his words into me. Searing them into my core. If I want him, we won't have children ever.

Maybe he's acting irrationally; maybe he needs time to adjust. Today was a lot for him and for both of us.

The fact he's talking about children is a good thing. He's thinking of our future. Together.

I steel myself and raise my chin. "Okay. No kids."

He stares at me as if I've grown three heads, but I'm not backing down. I know what I want, and what I want is Oscar.

Oscar tilts his head as though I'm a puzzle he's trying to fix. "Just like that?" He licks his lips, a tremble wracking through his body as my eyes scan over how completely unraveled he's become.

I take an uncertain step toward him. My hand reaches out and brushes the stray hair from his eyes. I stroke my hand over his cheek and down to cup his jaw. "I want you, Oscar. You. I love you." Tears stream down my face at my own admittance. His eyes soften, and a visible resolve gives way in his body.

Oscar

I know it will never work. I know it; she fucking knows it. So why keep up this pretense of us being anything other than two people wanting to expose one another for our own benefit. My chest tightens, and I want to scream at her. "I know I'll never be enough!" But what's the fucking point?

She takes a hesitant step toward me, causing my blood to boil at how she approaches, like a predator full of uncertainty.

"I want you, Oscar. You. I love you." Her words break me internally, the pain etched in her eyes and the stream of tears on her face cracking through the walls I was already rapidly reconstructing.

I put my thoughts of permanently resolving our issues on the back burner and concentrate on the here and now. The despair on Paige's face and the meaning behind her words. Her soft hand grazes over my jawline, and I close my eyes at her tenderness. The unbearable thoughts of never feeling her touch again wrack through my body.

I need her.

If only one more time.

I need her.

In one swift motion, I gather her up in my arms, bridal style. She places a kiss on my neck that sends shivers down my spine. I inhale her scent as I stride down the corridor toward my room, squeezing my eyes shut at the pain that this will be the last time I bring her to my room.

Gently placing her on the bed, I take a step back and scan over her, burning her into my memory. Her eyes reddened from her tears, her cheeks stained with them. Her hair, I once mistook for a brunette, is now so very clear to me a unique red. Paige's emerald eyes shimmer with unshed tears as she stares back at me.

"Undress." My words come out clipped. "Please." I tack on to soften the blow, but Paige appears undeterred at them, no doubt familiar now with my lack of social skills. I watch as she slowly lifts her sundress over her head and then unclips her white lacy bra. I suck in a sharp breath as her tits bounce, her rosy nipples pointed and on display for my taking. Small bite marks litter her milky skin, and my cock twitches at the sight, now straining my pants so hard I'm surprised the zipper hasn't given way. I stroke a hand down it, determined to relish in Paige's beauty without having to release myself too soon. She scoots off the bed and stands, the flush from her neck creeping up her cheeks as she lowers her panties.

I quickly hold out my hand, and she places her damp panties in my palm. I inhale our scent while keeping my eyes latched on Paige.

"Scoot up the bed, baby. Put your head on the pillow."

She follows my instructions perfectly as I take my time and, one by one, release my cufflinks and slowly unbutton my shirt. Then I unbuckle my belt and snap open my pants; I kick off my shoes and socks and lower my pants and boxers, releasing my engorged, leaking cock. I tug my length, once, twice, until a withheld hiss escapes my lips.

Paige lays on the bed, her wavy hair splayed out over the pillows, her legs open, and her hands groping and squeezing at her juicy tits.

The sight before me is being burned into my mind, leaving a scar etched on my soul. I grimace at the notion and tuck it away along with other things to deal with later.

I approach the bed, completely naked, pre-cum oozing in strings from the tip of my rock-hard cock.

I've no intention of her leaving this bed tonight

without me filling each of her holes, so not only will her memories be full of me, but her holes too.

I crawl over her, taking her nipple in my mouth when her hand offers me her tit. I suck on the peaked nub while squeezing her other one roughly. Paige holds it in place for me, and I moan into her tit with appreciation. My cock twitches, desperate to feel her tight pussy around me. I remove my hand from her breast and hold my cock at her pussy hole. "Oh god, please. Os, please."

Her slackened mouth gapes open as I gently rock into her, so unlike my usual hard, fast, and deep fucking.

"Oh shit, Os."

I rock into her teasingly slow, then out, the steady motion hard for me to maintain. Her fingers tug on my hair. "Please. I need you to kiss me."

I pull my head from her tit, releasing her nipple with a pop as I raise above her and lower myself, so my elbows are on either side of her head.

I stare into her emerald eyes; it's as close to making love as you'd get for someone incapable of it.

Her eyes water and I take the opportunity to distract myself from the whys and lower my lips to hers. She opens them instantly, allowing my tongue access. Our kiss is slow and delicate, like our current fucking. Her nails trail down my back, causing my spine to arch in pleasure. The thought of her marking my flesh as hers was an aphrodisiac. My balls tighten up, so I grind my hips into her pelvis, hitting the perfect spot. She moans into our kiss, now becoming feverish and chaotic.

I drive into her harder. "Yes! Fuck, Os."

My tether has snapped. I clamp my teeth down on

her neck and tug, groaning when the coppery taste hits my tongue, and her pussy clenches around me. She digs her fingers into my ass, pushing it into her deeper and fucking deeper. "Fuck. Take my cock, baby."

"I want to feel you come inside me, Os."

I groan as she holds me deep inside her. "Fuck, I'm going to come." Her pussy tightens, and she screams. "Oh god. Yessss."

I release my everything inside her. Every. Fucking. Thing.

A guttural wail from deep inside me rips through my lips as cum spurts out of me so violently that blackness consumes my vision, and I'm forced to squeeze my eyes closed.

She shudders below me as I slowly open my eyes, our foreheads resting on one another's and our skins coated in sweat. She stares into my eyes with such intensity my heart dips at the shit storm I know I'm about to create.

"I love you, Os." Her words astound me. They puncture into my already tattered soul; now so damaged I know for sure it will never repair.

Not without her.

I choose to ignore her sentiment, not because I don't believe it, not because I don't feel something close to what she's describing, but because I refuse to acknowledge it. I refuse to give her hope in an already hopeless situation.

"I'm going to fuck your ass now."

She clamps her teeth down on her bottom lip as a giggle bubbles up inside her, causing my own lip to quirk. I pull back from her and kneel between her legs.

"Just the declaration of love a girl wants to hear, Os." She swats at me playfully as I flip her over and encourage her onto her knees. Her ass is high in the air; I trail my hand down her tight, milky globes before raising my hand and smacking it down hard against her flesh.

"Ouch!"

I marvel at the redness flourishing on her skin before repeating the process. Each caress of her ass cheek gets my cock impossibly harder.

"More." She wiggles her ass at me playfully.

Returning to my dresser, I pick up my belt, folding it over and then snapping it tightly for effect. Her eyes meet mine from over her shoulder. I raise the belt and crack it down hard on her ass. She struggles to maintain her position with the force, and my cock weeps at the instant red stripe over her ass cheek.

If I can't keep her, I sure as fuck can mark her, leave her with a reminder of me. Anger in my veins at my own assertion, my fists clench. As if sensing a change in me, concern mars her face.

"Os?"

"Shut the fuck up." I unfold the belt, leaving the buckle exposed, and then I raise it with such force a crack sounds in the air. I slam the buckle down on her flesh.

"Fuck!" She drops her head into the pillow, her shoulders shaking.

Repeatedly, I break her skin, but I'm past caring. All I fucking care about is making sure she has a reminder of me on her.

I drop the belt, then spit on her ass. "This is what you wanted, Paige. Isn't it? You wanted me?" I'm being an ass.

I know it. I just can't stop it. If I have to force her away, then so be it.

Her voice wavers. "Y-yes. It's what I want. I want you, Os." She sniffles, and that only pushes rage to the forefront. I push two fingers into her ass aggressively with only my spittle as preparation.

"Then you'll take me however I please, right?" She has a safe word to use; she knows it. I know it. I give her a chance to contemplate this as I probe her ass roughly with my fingers.

"However you want." Her voice is distant, as though any resolve has gone. I should care. I should, but as I bring the tip of my cock to her tight asshole and withdraw my fingers, all I can think about is coming deep inside her... so deep I will never leave her. I slam into her, and she grips the pillow, stifling a sob. "More." She cries into the pillow, and I withdraw and slam into her again. Again and again, I fuck her with wild abandonment before bringing my palm to her pussy and smacking it so hard she doesn't have a choice but to come. Her legs almost give way, but I hold her hips tight and throw my head back in ecstasy as I flood her ass with my cum. "Fucking incredible," I pant.

Paige

Something has changed. I know it; I can feel it.

I felt him make love to me. As much as he refuses to accept it, that's what it was. It was slow and passionate, loving and tender. It was beautiful.

Then when I told him I loved him, something snapped. I pushed too far, too soon. He thought he could scare me; he thought his needs, his aggression would make me take back my words? Never.

I see Oscar for who and what he is. His raw emotions teetering on the edge of insanity; his loyalty and dedication to those he loves. His inability to recognize he's capable of love. When I feel like we've broken down walls, he tries constructing another. It's draining and disheartening, but I don't care. I'll bulldoze through them and make him realize he's my everything too.

His hands shake as he gently strokes over my raw skin with soothing lotion. His eyes full of sympathy, but I refuse to let him acknowledge; instead, I tell him what he needs to hear, the truth. It's hot. I like the bite of pain. I can take anything he can give me. I always will. He glances away at that and tells me I'll be taking his cock when he's showered. Another deflection of my words, but I grin and bite back with a reminder of how much I like the taste of his cum.

His hand draws circles on my shoulders, and my eyes grow heavy at the hypnotic movement. "You should go to sleep, Paige. Busy day tomorrow." His words are ominous and riddled, but I ignore his ramblings and close my eyes.

As I drift slowly into a sleepy abyss, I swear I hear him mutter the hazy words, "I wish I felt it, too."

Chapter Thirty-Seven

Paige

A shrill alarm startles me awake. My heart pounds rapidly in shock against my chest. It takes me a few moments to figure out where the hell I am. The bed feels smaller, the sheets soft but nowhere near as silky as Oscar's. The room is light and airy—my room in his apartment.

I whack the alarm with a slam of my hand, annoyance grumbling through me. Six-thirty am. What the hell is happening?

I definitely didn't dream last night; my ass is a raging testament to it. I place my feet on the floor and decide to freshen up before I confront him.

In the bathroom, I pee and wash my hands. My eyes scan over the countertop. My personal items are missing and now replaced with what appears to be the standard items he provides for everyone else. Is he for real?

Walking back into the bedroom, I tug on the gown

and throw open the door. Marching down the corridor, I go over what this can mean. Maybe he's moving me into his room permanently? Maybe this is his plan. The thought softens the raging storm inside me.

But as I lock eyes with Oscar, my footing stumbles at the intensity of his coldness, his jaw locked tight, his demeanor unresponsive, a calculated show, a mask. A pit of dreads swirls low in my stomach. He's detaching himself.

He's detaching from me.

My heart aches, my eyes already brimming with tears, and my pulse races with anxiety, knowing what's going to come. "Os?"

He stares through me. "It's time you left, Paige." His monotone voice slices through my heart. He points toward the clock showing seven am before returning to cut into his melon like he isn't cutting into my heart.

A tremble escapes me, and I shake my head, refusing his words. "What are you doing?"

"Payment will be in your account today. Your services are rendered..." He lifts his head, his eyes boring into mine as though making a point. "Finalized."

"Finalized?" I repeat his words, dumbstruck.

He sighs heavily, placing his napkin on the plate as though annoyed with me. "Paige, if you don't leave within the next two minutes, you will be forcibly removed."

Panic creeps up my throat, drying instantly. "Oscar, please don't do this." I swallow hard, but my throat clogs with emotion, making me choke. My legs wobble with anguish. "Please." My eyes gloss over with the tears flowing freely down my face.

His jaw ticks and he closes his eyes, doing his breathing technique.

"Os," I implore again but louder this time, determined to get his attention, determined to make him see me and not through me.

He snaps his eyes open, a steely conviction behind them. "Very well." My shoulders sag in relief at his words, but as his fingers work over his tablet, it's short-lived.

The door to his apartment opens, and the same two beef heads that manhandled me out of the club the night Oscar decided to give me his everything appear.

Oscar nods toward one of them, and the moron approaches me. I take a step back, then another. "Oscar, please." My words cripple me, my aching heart beating so rapidly my whole body shakes in denial. "Please." I implore once again. He refuses to look at me, instead staring at the wall opposite the table. My heart shatters at his rejection.

"Oscar, I love you. Please don't do this." My legs give way as one takes ahold of my arm. My vision blurs through streams of uncontrollable tears. "I love you. Do you hear me? I love you more than anything." They lift me by the arms. I struggle and tug at them, helplessly trying to get his attention, to fight them off and make him hear how I feel, make him understand. "Please, Os. Please just fucking look at me!" I catch a glimpse of him as I get lifted over the shoulder of one of them. I've lost him; I know it.

I've lost him, and I'll never be the same again.

My voice comes out broken and destroyed because that's what I am.

"I'm your different, Oscar O'Connell, and you're mine. You're mine."

Oscar

"I'm your different, Oscar O'Connell, and you're mine. You're mine." Her words echo around in my head.

The door closes behind them, but I can still hear the scuffle in the hall, and her voice, screaming out to me.

I cover my ears; my heart beating so loud I can hear it, the pounding so profuse it hurts. It. Fucking. Hurts!

I swipe at the breakfast contents on the table, sending them shattering to the floor. All for fucking show anyway, all there to mask how I truly feel. How I was so sick with nervousness and trepidation that I couldn't stomach a single fucking thing. All placed there to make me appear calm and collected when I was anything but. Every movement I made was calculated, including purposely breaking the heart of the only person who has only ever made me feel.

My breathing techniques are fucking useless. I'm spiraling, and I've no means or method to stop it. I hate it. I hate myself. Hate what I've had to do.

A bubbling tsunami of emotions surges to an excruciating peak, forcing me to push myself out of my chair, desperate to feel something more. I need to let this rage out. I need to fucking expel it from my body.

Picking up the latest coffee machine, I launch it at the hallway mirror. The glass splinters in slow motion, reflecting my unraveling state. My tight fists clench at my side, and my cold blue eyes pierce through the glass as it finally disintegrates into fragments of my own fragile state.

I ignore the shards of glass cutting through my feet, my rampage not dispersing in the slightest. I upturn the furniture, thrashing through the living area like a cyclone leaving destruction in its wake. I scream. I fucking scream until my lungs hurt and my throat dries, but still, I fucking feel it there—the ache, the hate. It's there.

I attempt to rip the television from the wall, tugging and fucking tugging, but the damn thing won't shift. "I fucking hate you too!" I never wanted a goddamn tv. Never. I had one to be fucking normal. "I'm not normal."

With both hands on one side, I pull and pull, and with one final yank, I scream the words that haunt me the most, finally admitting them out loud, "I'm fucking different!" I roar.

The tv gives way. I step back, the tension in my shoulders giving way also, but as I turn to walk away with satisfaction ebbing into my veins, a painful realization hits me before it hits the glass.

"Please, fuck no."

The smash is loud, so fucking loud it seems to send shockwaves through my body. The tank doesn't shatter as gracefully as the mirror; it fucking obliterates, sending gallons of marine water cascading through my living room along with each and every form of life in it.

Obliterated.

I crumble to my knees in devastation.

Obliterated like my fucking heart.

Chapter Thirty-Eight

Paige

"Here, you look like you need this." A coffee is thrust into my hand as I stare down at my bedsheets. It's been a week, and I'm still trying to make sense of what went wrong in our last twenty-four hours together.

I know he'd done a lot so soon, and I look back on that with guilt, but he seemed to be handling it all well, with determination, a steely strength, and a vision of hope for us both. A glimmer into our potential future.

"I pushed him too much." I meet my sister's concerned eyes as she sits on my bed.

"Paige, he pushed himself. That's not on you."

I meet her eyes with a shake of my head. Her own eyes reflect sympathy, once again forcing tears to fall that I thought were all dried up. "You can't keep doing this to yourself, honey."

I choke on my tears. "I-I love him, Ebony. I didn't mean to."

She nods. "Are you sure he blocked your phone?"

I choke on a sarcastic laugh. "Definitely blocked me."

"Maybe he'll come to you?"

I shake my head again, ignoring the overpowering scent of freshly ground coffee. The gift I returned home to, I wanted to smash it, but Ebony stood in front of it as though it needed protection from me. She was right; of course, it did.

I mean, a fucking coffee machine?

I give him my heart, and he gives me a coffee machine?

I scoff at the analogy.

Ebony blows into her own drink. "How about showing up at one of his brother's houses? You know where they live, right?"

I shake my head. "The security is ridiculous, Ebony."

She grimaces and then meets my eyes. "You said they're businessmen, right?" I want to laugh at her naivety, but there's no way I'd tell my sister the type of business the O'Connell family is truly involved in. "Then why don't you go to one of their businesses?"

I muse over her words.

Small feet in the corridor pause my thoughts. "Mommy, there's a man at the door. I didn't let him in, but he's wearing a suit and asked for Aunty Paige." Adam bursts into the bedroom.

Hope blossoms in my chest at Adam's description as Ebony and I rise and place our drinks on my dresser. I virtually push past her in my haste. My bare feet thunder down the hallway toward the front door. I briefly flick my fingers through my hair with a pinch of nervousness pulsating in my veins.

He's here.

Where he should be.

The figure at the door is too small to be Oscar; his shoulders wide, and his waist wider. My lip trembles in disappointment as I open the door.

"Paige Summers?"

"Yes."

"Sign here."

I do as he asks on impulse, confusion rippling through me, but I can't think quickly or clearly enough to ask any questions.

He holds out a thick envelope for me to take before turning on his shiny heels and retreating down the steps.

Taking all hope with him.

I pull the door closed. Ebony's confused eyes meet my own. "What is that?"

I shrug before ripping into the sealed envelope. Anger fills my veins so much that I can hear my pulse beating in my ears when I go through it. "That son of a bitch!"

"What is it? What'd he do?"

"He paid my debts off. He paid my fucking debts off." I storm toward my bedroom; Ebony quick on my heels.

"He paid your debts off?"

"Yes. And bought the house!"

I swing my door open and frantically begin undressing.

"He bought the house?"

"Yes, and he paid my college fees."

I scoop my hair into a messy bun, fury making my hands shake.

"He paid your college fees?"

"Yes. And he bought me a fucking veterinary clinic."

I stare at Ebony over my shoulder, her eyes bugging out in confusion at my words. "A veterinary clinic?"

"Yes. The fucking bastard."

"He bought all that?"

I nod firmly as I gather my shit into my purse. I swear to god Oscar O'Connell is going to wonder what the hell has hit him when I get to him.

"Paige, that's huge." I turn my head around to face Ebony's bewildered-looking face, her eyes full of unshed tears. "And you say he's a businessman?"

I straighten my spine, about to dispel any awestruck illusion she's currently feeling toward Oscar right now. "He owns brothels." I glare at her, awaiting a reaction. Also failing to mention any other businesses he owns. Her eyes widen in shock, and her mouth opens, but she doesn't utter a single word, and being the bitch that I am, I go in for the kill. "And he just treated me like one of his whores." I nod toward the discarded paperwork on the bed.

Again, I fail to mention that I started out as one of his whores. I grimace at the thought, raise my chin, and stare at my sister head-on.

Her eyes lock with mine, her lips tighten, and the once broken sister's eyes now shine with a sense of pride, a strength behind them encouraging my own. She gives me a firm nod of confidence.

I grab my car keys from my dresser and head toward Club 11. If I can't see Oscar, I'm going straight to the top. To the Don. Bren.

I take a deep breath as I enter the club. It's early evening, and I know Bren likes to be home early to put his family to bed. Sky told me what a hands-on father he is and how much he enjoys the family role as much as being the don.

The security guard eyes me up and down. The glare I give him makes him shrink back, and no doubt, his balls shrivel. He doesn't want to mess with me, not tonight. I head toward the spiral staircase before I get stopped by someone stretching their arm across the handrail to halt my step. "No access." His robotic voice grates on my fraught patience.

My searing scowl blazes through him, forcing him to hold his hands up in jest. "Sweetheart, I don't make the rules."

I curl my lip. "I want to speak to Bren. Now."

He laughs, then throws out an arm toward the dance floor. "You and everyone else here." He crosses his arms over his chest with a chuckle.

I hold up the envelope in my hand. "Tell him I want to speak with him now; otherwise, the copy of this envelope goes straight to Flemming." I lean forward for only him to hear. "It has a photo of Oscar and an axe." Of course, I'm bluffing. The only thing this envelope holds is my motherfucking pay-off.

I wonder how many other sluts he's bought items for. Houses, for Christ's sake. Businesses.

As if deciding my threat is worthy, the dude motions for another goon to come over.

"Watch her. Don't let her leave." The guy nods back at him and stands in front of me, blocking the path to the exit. A glimmer of uncertainty snakes through me before I shake it out.

Hell no, Oscar O'Connell will see me.

Talk to me.

One way or another.

Bren

I stare down at the contract for the land beside our current shipping warehouse. Kozlov is allowing us to purchase it in return for a reduction on our quarterly firearms agreement. It may only be a small portion of sales, but it was an agreement I wasn't keen on in the first place. We normally separate our business from theirs, but I bought into the agreement at a high price and now will be reaping the benefits of that with the reduction. It's almost as if the crafty fucker was in it for the long haul, knowing we'd need the land to expand our distribution.

I've had Sergio De-Luco go over the paperwork. If the lawyer is good enough for the Varros family, then he's good enough for us.

I sign on the dotted line with a heavy sigh, feeling like there's more to this agreement than meets the eye. It feels like Kozlov is gearing up for a war. I just can't figure out with whom. As long as we're not in the firing line, I guess it's not our problem.

I shove the paperwork back into the folder, desperate to get home to Sky and our newborn son, Samuel. I promised I would be back in time to bathe Seb tonight. We're desperate to get him back into a routine instead of the late nights he's been having since Sam's birth.

A heavy thud up the metal staircase makes my eyes scan the security monitor. Paul's pissed-off face comes into view, his fist rising to knock on my door, but I press the release button under my desk before he makes contact. His lips break out into a knowing chuckle, aware I'm always on high alert.

He steps into the room. "Boss, got a girl downstairs causing shit."

He's agitated, unlike his normal self, and it causes my eyebrows to furrow because what he just told me isn't anything out of the ordinary. There's always some drama or other in this club. If it isn't a bunch of hens having too much drink and needing a good dicking, it's a pissed-off wife hitting her man around the head with her purse when he pays more attention to the strip show than her.

"She's saying shit about the business, boss. Oscar, too, all legit." My spine straightens at the mention of my brother's name. He continues on, "She mentioned shit about an axe?" His eyebrow raises knowingly. Although I never told anyone about the axe incident, Con runs his mouth too much when joking around. I trust Paul not to breathe a word, but the fact she knows about it proves that I need to take this girl seriously.

"She has a name?"

He winces; clearly, the fuckwit forgot to ask. I turn

toward the monitor and flick the screen to the camera at the bottom of the metal stairs. My shoulders relax slightly when I see Paige standing there, staring down one of my men. Her hands are on her hips, and her head is tilted up high. It's clear as fuck she's on some tirade.

I drag a hand down my tired face, knowing this is going to get messy. I have all on dealing with my own woman's attitude, let alone someone else's.

"Let her fucking up." I wave toward the door, and he leaves.

I sag back in my chair as I hear the click of her shoes entering my room. Paige's distraught face comes into view. Her puffy, red, vulnerable-looking eyes cause my heart to sink a little. I'm no good with this shit, no good at all. I rub a hand over the back of my neck.

"I want to speak to Oscar." She stomps her foot a little like a petulant child, and the thought makes me grin. She's a firecracker, that's for sure. Oscar called her a spitfire, and he wasn't fucking wrong. I don't know many women walking into a club and demanding to speak to a mafia don like this. "Now, Bren." She literally clicks her fingers and motions toward my phone, making my eyebrows jump up in shock. What. The. Fuck?

My spine snaps bolt upright. "Darlin', Oscar doesn't want to speak to you. He doesn't want us to speak to you either." I try to keep my voice low like I do when I talk to the other women in our family. "Now, just accept the fucking payment Oscar made and go live your life." I wave toward the door, but the look on her face tells me something I said was wrong, very fucking wrong, considering her face is turning red, and the vein in her forehead is protruding. "Payment?" Her body jolts, and her face transforms into utter disgust. "Live my fucking life? Are you serious right now, Bren?"

I open my mouth to speak but don't get the chance. "Get him on the fucking phone and tell him to come here right fucking now!" She punctuates each word, her finger aimed at my phone, her eyes burning with fire that makes my balls almost want to shrivel up.

My hand glides over the top of my head as I exhale. "Paige, he ain't going to come here. Haven't seen him in a week," I admit with a shake of my head.

The tension leaves her shoulders as her body visibly sags. All her hate seems to have dissipated. "A week?"

I meet her concerned eyes, mine mirroring hers. If truth be told, I've been worried about Oscar. But both he and my brothers insisted on giving him some time. It's his first relationship, and I know how bad it hurt me when Sky and I split; it's fucking heartbreaking, and you just want to wallow in self-pity away from the world. For Oscar, it must be so much worse. Not only does he not know how to deal with his feelings, but he won't want to admit them either, definitely not to us if he can't admit them to himself.

"He hasn't been to your Ma's?" Her soft voice sounds vulnerable. I notice her nibbling her lip as though trying to force the tears pooling in her eyes to remain right where they are.

"No."

Paige swallows thickly. "I don't like this, Bren. He

wouldn't not go to your Ma's." She clearly knows a lot about Oscar, and I can't help but wonder, not for the first time, that he's making a huge mistake letting her go. We can deal with the shit that's going to go down in the future as a family.

"We need to check on him." Her steely eyes drill into mine, leaving no room for argument.

My jaw ticks in annoyance. "Paige," I warn her, giving back as much fire right now as she's giving me.

She lifts her chin and appears to widen her stance, the action making me want to both throttle her and laugh. "I refuse to take no for an answer. Take me there right now, or so help me God, I will scream bloody murder and spill every secret I've learned about this goddamn family." Her words make my fists clench. If she thinks she can blackmail me, she can think fucking again. I stand to my full height, rage blinding my vision. No fucker threatens my family.

She swallows hard, holding up her hand, her whole body shaking in clear fear. "I'm sorry. I shouldn't have said that. Please, I just want to see that he's okay, Bren. Please, I'm..." Her words trail off as she composes herself. "I'm worried, really worried. Can you imagine his state of mind right now?"

The sheer look of concern in her eyes is enough for me to make my decision. I grab my phone and tap out a message to Cal, instructing him to meet us there.

A ball of anxiety wraps around my throat, forcing my voice to clog. "Then you'll leave him alone. I mean it, Paige."

She whimpers at my words, no doubt shattering any illusion of her reconnecting with Oscar.

"Then I'll leave him alone." Her words come out broken.

I give her a firm nod. "Let's go."

Chapter Thirty-Nine

Paige

Bren takes out his phone and types in the code to the door that Reece sent Cal.

The door doesn't click open quick enough. I force my teeth into my bottom lip, nervousness rippling through me at the sound of the door opening. I push past Bren straight into his apartment. The sheer destruction makes my knees buckle, but he catches me by my elbow, his firm grip holding me up.

Our eyes latch on to one another's, both of us in utter disbelief. His apartment is destroyed. I take a hesitant step forward, my body vibrating with terror at what we might find.

Oscar told me about Con trying to take his own life, and a pit of dread fills me, forcing bile into my mouth. He wouldn't. Would he?

Glass crunches underneath my feet, making our eyes dart toward the floor. Blood. The sight extorts an involuntary sob to lodge in my throat and our bodies to freeze at the realization Oscar is injured.

Bren's eyes snap to mine. "I got ya, darlin'. You stay here." His voice is firm, but I shake my head, refusing not to be there for Os. He clearly has the same thought as me right now.

Bren's gaze works over the carnage, and he walks down the corridor toward Oscar's room while mine scan over the living area. The furniture is upturned, and the television is ripped from the wall, but what has my heart plummeting is the sight of where the fish tank once was. My feet work before my mind does as I move toward the area. All the while, my broken heart tries to hammer hopelessly in my chest, and my body trembles with anxiety. A small bowl sits on the floor housing two fish. Our fish.

I stifle a sob, tears down my face, and I have to swipe them away.

A low mumble makes me dart my head toward the overturned couch.

The sight is soul-destroying.

Oscar lies curled into a fetal position, naked, apart from his boxers. His feet are cut to shreds, his hair a ruffled mess, but it's the empty look in his eyes that makes me fall to my knees next to him.

One of my tears hits his face, but I ignore it, instead choosing to push the hair from his eyes, but he doesn't react to my touch or even flinch. Nothing.

"Bren!"

I hear Bren's heavy footfalls, his shadow over my

body as I stroke Oscar tenderly. He barks orders into his phone.

I stroke my hand over his face, desperate to make him feel.

The apartment door swings open. "What happened? Where is he?" Reece's voice makes my eyes close in preparation for what's to come.

He lets out a wail that hits my stomach. "Help him. Fucking help him, then."

Cal tries to comfort him, but he rips away from his arms. Tugging on his hair, the sight so heartbreaking to witness. "P-Paige? You can fix him, right?" Reece lowers down to my face, his eyes flicking back and forth between mine and Oscar's, desperation oozing from his begging eyes. "Ple... please."

I swallow the lump wedged in my throat and say the only thing I can. "Yes. I'll fix him."

Cal sucks in a sharp breath at my words. No doubt pissed, I'm practically promising something I shouldn't. I don't care. I will fix him.

Me.

Reece's shoulders relax slightly.

"Maybe we should take him straight to the hospital. You know Doctor Yates is going to want to do that anyway, right?" He's speaking to Bren, but rage fills me. My blood boils. How fucking dare they?

I get to my feet and spin around to face them as they're conspiring. Holding up my palm to stop their conversations. "Absolutely. Fucking. Not."

Cal's eyes soften on mine, and he sighs before he goes

to open his mouth. I hold up my palm. "I said no, Cal. No!"

I glance over my shoulder at Oscar's state. "That's not what he'd want."

"Sometimes we have to do what's best. Not necessarily what people want." Cal speaks softly, but his words are cutthroat.

I widen my legs and puff out my chest as though ready to fight. "Bren, he wouldn't want that. You know that, right?" I plead with him to see sense, to see me.

Bren's gaze flits from mine to Cal's before landing on Oscar. His throat bobs. "Yeah."

Cal throws his arms up in defeat. "He needs treatment, Bren. Fucking help. Look at him!" He points toward Oscar, and I can't help but stand in front of him, covering their view. They're not taking him; they're not going to put him in a hospital where all his fears lie. Absolutely not.

Bren must see something in my protective demeanor because he turns toward Cal. "Take Reece and go home. I'll keep you updated."

Cal's eyes bug out. "What?"

Bren tilts his head toward Reece, who's now rocking back and forth on the floor, his state of panic obvious. Cal's eyes soften instantly. "Do you want me to call Finn or Con?" he asks as he brushes a hand over his hair.

Bren turns toward me, realizing he wants me to answer Cal, not him. The fact he's letting me control the situation tampers my raging storm because, with sheer determination alone, I'll get Oscar back.

"No, just keep them updated."

Bren nods, and Cal feigns a smile, clearly unhappy with the whole change in dynamic.

———

Doctor Yates assessed Oscar and confirmed my suspicion that he was not taking his medications, and it led to a breakdown in his mental health. He also made it clear he was not happy with our decision not to have him hospitalized.

I finally get into bed beside him, his heart beating against my cheek. When I rest on him, the motion reminds me he's still very much here with us. I squeeze him tighter, determined to never let him go.

I'm not sure what the time is when the door creaks open, and Bren pops his head inside. "My brothers and I are going to try and sort shit out in here." He tilts his head toward the living area. "Sky and the kids are coming over; we're gonna take the spare room."

I pull my head from Oscar's chest. Oh, hell no. "Take the one on the opposite side of the kitchen."

Bren's eyebrows knit together before he seems to grasp my panic. With a sickening grimace, he simply nods and leaves the room.

I resume my position, basking in his warmth. "I love you, Os." A lone tear falls down my face at my own words. His hand flinches and presses on my hair as though he's trying to stroke it, but it's too much effort.

"Don't leave me." His words are a whisper.

I swallow back the emotion overwhelming me and reply, "Never."

Chapter Forty

Oscar

A shrill phone ringing stirs me from my sleep. My pounding, fuzzy head feels heavy and dense.

I close my eyes and inhale the scent of Paige on my pillow. I know she's been here. Not only do I smell her, I can sense her too.

The bed dips, causing me to force my eyes open. Bren's broad shoulders block the light from the window.

"You awake?" His voice is so deep that if I wasn't awake, I would be by now.

"Yeah," I respond. I move to sit up but feel woozy. Then I jolt at the awareness of someone in my room. "I don't like you in my room."

Bren chuckles and replies, "What else is new? Tough fucking shit."

My lips tighten into a firm line. He was the only one of my brothers who pushed and protected me all at once. As though he knew my true capabilities and he needed to allow me to prove to both myself and him what I was actually capable of doing.

"What the fuck happened?" His eyes penetrate into mine, a mix of hurt and disappointment causing my stomach to swirl like never before.

I shrug, trying to feign indifference. "I ended it."

"Why?"

So many reasons why, but I choose to go with the easiest. "I couldn't deal with the expectations."

"Expectations? From us?" He raises an eyebrow.

I throw myself back on the bed and instantly regret it, my head now pounding at the impact.

"All of it."

"You said you had it handled. Assured me." He grinds his jaw.

I tilt my head to the side so I can get a clear view of him. "I was wrong."

Bren's body tightens, now on alert. "Not that," I snap at him. "I was wrong about her." I swallow, pissed that I'm not making myself clear. I wince at the foreign word on the tip of my tongue. "Our relationship."

Bren's muscles visibly relax. He drags a hand over the scruff on his jaw. "What's the fucking problem? She fucking loves you, clear as day." He stares back at me as though I'm an idiot. "Heard her tell you enough times over the past few days. Bathes attention on you like a fucking sap."

"Like you do on Sky?" I deadpan back at him.

His eyes drill into mine. "Exactly like that, Oscar. Like someone prepared to give who they love their whole fucking world."

"It's not enough." I snap at him and sit up. "I'm not enough!"

My heart begins to hammer at my truth.

"Says fucking who?"

"Says me, Bren. She deserves everything." My head drops down, shame and embarrassment coursing through me. "She wants kids."

Bren's calculated eyes scan over my face. "And?"

"I don't even fucking like kids," I spit out and glare at him in rage.

Bren throws his head back, laughing. "Bull fucking shit. You're all fussy over Chloe; you watch Prince like a hawk. You even crack a fucking smirk at Seb and Sam."

I throw off the sheets and stand, my head swirling slightly, making my balance a little off, but I stare down at my brother. "For the fucking record, I have earplugs in around Chloe because I can't bear her fucking shrill noise. Prince is an accident waiting to happen, Finn is so fucking nonchalant it's not even funny, and Seb and Sam are the most mollycoddled babies. Nobody has a chance to look at them, let alone pay them attention, so how the fuck you've come to that conclusion is beyond me."

Bren stares at me as though I've grown three heads before he palms a hand down his buzz-cut head. "Yeah, I feel like snapping Chloe's neck, too, when she has one of those temper tantrums." He chuckles like a deranged loon who didn't just admit to wanting to snap his little niece's neck.

"Anyway, I ain't got time for all your bitching. Get your shit together and get over to Ma's. She's cooking dinner, and I expect your ass there."

Is he for fucking real? I've just had a mental break-down, and he expects me to go and play happy family? I'm in the middle of a relationship crisis, and he shrugs it off?

"Agh, fucking Jesus, Oscar. We all have relationship shit. Sky wants to stop breastfeeding, but I like her tits big and them feeding my mouth. She ain't spoke to me all fucking day. Cal hasn't seen Reece in two days, convinced he's left home. Finn says Prince is being a little shite, and Angel won't have another kid coz of it. Point is we all have shit to deal with, Oscar, so fucking deal with it. You ain't any different to any of us, brother, and that woman... She's been by your side every damn day. Any fucking doubts I ever had about her, hell, any doubts any of us ever had about her, are gone." His words whirl around in my mind. "You ain't any different to any of us, brother."

My throat clogs, and I struggle to respond.

"And take a fucking shower. Paige washed you down, but you fucking stink. Dunno how the poor girl puts up with your wretched ass. Probably something to do with that kinky room, huh?" He wriggles his eyebrows before heading toward the door.

"Where is she?" I ask. My body tenses when my heart skips a beat.

Bren stops at the door and glances over his shoulder. "Had an emergency call about an hour ago. Told her to meet us at Ma's." I nod at him as he leaves.

Time to get my shit together.

Time to get my girl.

Chapter Forty-One

Oscar

I block out Da's tirade about Bren's decision to buy the land beside the warehouse, instead choosing to adjust my glasses and stare down at my tablet.

The fact I'm early hasn't gone unnoticed by the old prick. He also hasn't failed to notice the bags under my eyes. Clearly, he takes more notice of things than I originally anticipated. I shuffle in my chair, uncomfortable with his scrutiny solely on me.

"Doesn't look like you've eaten for weeks. Where were you last week? Your Ma missed ya."

I glance at Ma, her back to us as she works on the casserole. I refuse to make eye contact with him or even gift him any attention. He huffs loudly. "Feckin' deaf as well now?"

I ignore his rants until my phone buzzes annoyingly across the table. *Reece.* "Oscar, you at the family estate?" His voice is rushed and panicked, a bite of urgency behind his normal tone. I register Da's spine straighten, too, very aware of the difference in Reece.

"Yes."

"It's Paige. She's been taken." His words should cripple me, but all they do is fuel an anger deep inside me. Someone dared to touch what was mine. This is all my fault. I didn't have security on her today. Since my breakdown, I've lost grasp of everything. They've waited for the perfect opportunity, and, like the idiot I am, I provided them with one.

What the fuck have I done?

I push back in my chair, sending it flying.

All before I can fucking tell her how I feel.

If anything happens to her... my knuckles hurt at the tightness.

"Where was she taken from?" I insist. I grab my tablet, ready to open my app.

"The clinic. She took a call this morning for an emergency." I nod along to what Reece is explaining while simultaneously opening the app, allowing me to view the camera feed outside her clinic. Another reason I visited the clinic that day. I needed a distraction so Reece could plant cameras in and around the clinic.

I watch two men dressed in black grab her from behind while dragging her kicking into a black SUV.

There's only one person that could have done this, and while I've been wallowing in self-pity, I've given him the perfect opportunity to take what belongs to me, including my heart. I'll fucking make him pay. Fury, like no other, fills my veins, my temple pounding with the tension, threatening to break through my skin.

"I've called Bren. He asked to wait for him to get there. They're fifteen minutes out, Oscar."

I scoff. Fifteen fucking minutes? Like fuck I'll wait.

"You know what to do," I clip back and end the call.

I move toward the door with Da on my heel like a yapping chihuahua. "You best wait for Bren."

"Thanks for the advice," I grunt as I march out the door.

"You're going to get yourself feckin killed." He follows me.

"Possibly."

"Ya feckin' insane."

"Yep. So you've told me countless times." I keep marching toward my car.

"She's a feckin' woman."

I stop in my tracks and turn on him. "That's right. She's a woman. My woman. My fucking everything. Now fuck off, old man."

This is the most I've spoken to him in years. His lip curls up, no doubt to hurl abuse right back at me, but I don't have time for this shit, not when Paige needs me.

"You're not equipped for this shit, Oscar. You don't know what the feck you're doing!"

He's wrong. So fucking wrong.

I know exactly what I'm doing.

I'm stepping out of the shadows.

Chapter Forty-Two

Oscar

I glance down at the tablet once more, waiting for the tracker to pinpoint her location.

When I injected her with it, I never intended to use it for this. It was simply to know where she was at every waking moment, to protect her. Never once anticipating I might need it to save her because I couldn't protect her.

It pings, and I swallow back the bile when my hands flick over the cameras surrounding her location. Knowing I'm going to be walking into a trap with little to defend myself with doesn't phase me. I've already alerted Reece of my location, and he knows me well enough to know each and every move I'm about to make. However insane my father claims I am, he might actually have a point because what I'm about to do is equivalent to suicide. I'm going to hand myself over in exchange for her.

I pull up to the abandoned restaurant; the irony is not lost on me that the property was closed down after a feud between two prominent mafia families quite literally wiped out an entire restaurant, owners, and customers.

I'm well aware of the two snipers on the roof, the two heavies on the inside of the main room, four more in the back, and their boss in the office. I'm also aware of the four SUVs parked one street away, no doubt on standby, waiting for my brothers.

What they won't expect is me walking in there.

Alone.

No, they expect us to come in all guns blazing with armored vehicles, but I'm not about to call more destruction than absolutely necessary. It's me he wants, so it's me he'll get.

I double-check the app on my watch, the one that will allow access to the cameras in the surrounding areas, the same one I encouraged Reece to use when he was kidnapped along with his mother.

I throw open the car door. The gravel crunches under my shiny black shoes, causing me to grimace at the dust coating them.

I breathe out my four, four, four, raise my head, and stride toward the derelict building, keeping my mind on the task at hand.

It doesn't surprise me that there are locks on the door that appear untampered with. They're clearly using access around the back, but I'm not dumb enough to deal with those pricks just yet. I go around the side of the property, pick up one of the many bricks and smash a window. Unlatching the flimsy clasp, I push my way through the window into a dusty room. I try my best to ignore the dirt already attached to me, the hairs on my body standing on edge.

I take out my phone and locate Paige's ping. She's in the next room. As much as I want to run to her, I need to take my time. Be calculated and concise. I don't hear movement, but that doesn't mean there isn't any. I check my phone to see a thumbs-up from Reece. He's managed to locate my location and has access to my phone, watch, and any surrounding cameras. I just need to distract them long enough so I can keep her safe and figure out how to get her out of there.

I hear a scuffle on the floor in the next room, so I draw my back against the wall to listen. It sounds like feet being dragged. I peer through the crack in the door and what I see almost brings me to my knees.

Paige is tied to a chair in the center of the room, her feet tied to each leg, and her mouth gagged. My fists clench. Nobody gags my woman but me.

I carelessly throw open the door, step out of the shadows, and storm toward her. Her eyes shoot up to meet mine, widening first before panic takes over. Her face is stained with dirt and tears, and I want to scoop her into my arms and never release her, but first, I have to get her out of here.

I kneel in front of her and tug down the gag.

My eyes lock on to her bloody lip, and if I didn't feel like a raging inferno was taking place inside me before, I sure as hell do now.

My teeth ache from clamping my jaw shut, and my muscles tighten to the point of pain.

"Oscar, it's a trap. You have to get out of here. It's a trap." Her words come out frantic while her eyes dart around the room.

I bring my finger to her lips, the ones not so long ago I had problems touching, but not anymore. Never again.

"Shh, I know, baby. It's okay. I'm going to get you out of here."

She shakes her head. "No, Oscar. You don't understand. They want you."

I ignore her and begin to untie her hands.

Her chest rises and falls rapidly, no doubt through both terror and frustration in getting me to comply.

"Oscar, I betrayed you," she whimpers.

I close my eyes at her words, feeling the same gut-wrenching feeling the day Reece brought Paige's betrayal to the forefront.

"I know you only wanted the basic checks, but..." *Annoying the hell out of me, he fidgets on his feet. When all I want is to work in silence. I have shit to do, and Con's wedding is another nightmare I have to deal with. Bringing in outside help, such as STORM Enterprise, is a no-brainer at this point. There's no way I can continue to do all this shit on my own.*

"I'm not interested," I reply nonchalantly. Of course, it's a lie. I'd like nothing more than to figure out my little spitfire, but I want it to develop organically. Normally, instead of having to do everything so damn different.

"You can't ignore this shit, Oscar. It's about the security of the family."

That gets my attention. My back straightens, and I spin around to face him on my chair. "Go on."

He grimaces. "I'm sorry."

I swallow thickly, knowing whatever he's about to say, I'm not going to like. Hell, it's probably about to destroy me.

After the weekend I just had with Paige, my head and heart are all in. Giving myself to her like I never thought I was capable of doing is not something I treat lightly. She's broken down walls that have taken a lifetime to construct, and in doing so, I've not only given her my body, but I've given her my heart too.

I just don't know how to make her aware of it.

Annoyance rumbles inside me, especially with the puppy dog sympathy face Reece is currently wearing.

He exhales heavily. "So I did some digging."

"When I asked you not to," I snap, unable to resist.

He continues on, "Right. So it turns out Paige was placed in Indulgence."

"Placed? By who?" My fists tighten. Has all of this been a game to her? Am I a game to her? My heart rate escalates. I want to vomit, but I hate vomiting. I force the bile down and close my eyes. Breathe, Oscar, fucking breathe.

"Flemming." My eyes snap open at his name. When I cut off his daughter's head, I should have sent it to him in a fucking box.

I swallow harshly. "You're sure?"

"Positive." He drags a hand through his hair. It's a family trait; we all do it. "There's more."

I nod because, of course, there's fucking more.

"Her sister, Ebony's kids' dad, is Deacon Jessop. The guy you took out as an informant. Looks like Flemming

359

must be paying Paige to get close to you for information."

My heart feels like it has a knife piercing it. Why does it fucking hurt so much right now? I rub a hand over it.

"Oscar, are you okay?"

I meet my nephew's concerned eyes and answer him honestly, "No."

"What are we gonna do?"

I reflect on the thought for a minute. I have cameras watching her every move. They might have been put there for my own fascination with her, but now? Now they're going to be there for so much more. "We have all her angles covered. I'm going to feed her the information she needs and see what she does with it. Let it bring Flemming out of his shell."

"Are you sure? You liked her, right?"

I nod.

As soon as Reece leaves the room, I swipe the contents of my desk onto the floor with a roar. I scrub a hand down my face at the fucking irony of the situation. The only woman I want enough to try for doesn't want me back. No, she's a fucking traitor.

She used me.

Why the fuck would she want me anyway? The weirdo. The different one.

Why? When she can have so much more?

Tears fill my eyes, and I fucking hate it. I hate her.

Hate how she's making me feel.

But at the same time, I'm already craving her. I was right. She is my addiction, but she's also going to be my damnation. She's my drug, set to destroy me.

I think she already has.

"I know, Paige. I know everything."

Her body stills at my words. "You do?"

"I do. I've known for a long time."

I pull back for her to see the truth in my eyes. Her free hand caresses my jaw gently. Her touch alone forces my eyes to close and lean into her cold hand. "I'm so sorry. I love you, Oscar. I swear, I do." Tears flow down her face.

I rest my forehead against hers. "I know you do."

Then a loud clap tears us apart.

Paige

My heart is lodged in my throat as Detective Flemming approaches us. I tug on the restraints desperately. I need to help him; I don't want them to hurt or touch him.

Flemming first approached me months ago with a proposition I couldn't refuse. He was going to wipe my debts clear, including the property that Ebony and the kids live in. All I had to do was get close enough to Oscar O'Connell and relay any information I might see or hear regarding his daughter, Marianne Flemming. It didn't take me long to realize that Flemming had a vendetta against the O'Connell family. Before long, my heart was in so deep with Oscar that he could have slaughtered this man's whole family, and I'd have still been loyal to him.

I was all in, so much so when Oscar admitted to killing Marianne after her attempts at hurting his family, I stopped responding to Flemming's calls. I threw away the phone. When Oscar and I agreed on a relationship, a real one. It was exactly that to me. He is my everything. What I didn't anticipate was my naivety. Just because I'd broken one agreement didn't necessarily mean I'd break another.

So when I got the call this morning to say a dog was being rushed in for surgery and I was needed, I didn't hesitate to help. I didn't even consider the fact that no other cars were in the parking lot when I approached. Nor did I consider the fact that it wasn't Carl calling me like he normally did. What happened next was so fast I didn't have time to think. Two men dressed in black came out of nowhere, leaving me no time to consider what to do. One grabbed me from behind while the other took ahold of my legs, and they quite literally threw me into the trunk of a blacked-out SUV.

I didn't stop fighting until I was hit in the face and tied to the chair, and I've tried everything since to get the hell out of here.

The loud clapping behind Oscar makes his lips thin into a straight line. He knew it was coming, but even with my warning and pleas, I'm not sure he realizes how much danger he's actually in. He's outnumbered, and the things I've heard them discuss... my stomach drops at the thought, and bile rises in my mouth. I strain against the ropes. Oscar managed to get as far as loosening one on my hand, but it's no good since it's still too tight.

"Ah, here is the man in the background. The shadow. The brains of the operations." Flemming mocks with a wide, menacing grin on his face that makes me want to shrink back.

Oscar slowly stands and turns; I don't miss the fact he's purposely standing in front of me as though to shield me from Flemming's view, but I crane my neck to see around him, knowing somewhere in the darkened room are two of his men.

"Did you know she was fucking you for money, Oscar? Not just yours, mine too." He smiles slyly, but Oscar doesn't so much as flinch, his only giveaway being his bunched muscles and fists clenching and unclenching.

Flemming's smile drops. "Ah, so you did know? Mmm, has my little rat deceived me?" He raises an eyebrow and glares in my direction. Oscar moves to the side, blocking me once again.

"Of course, I knew. It was you that covered up the murder of my daughter. It could only be you, and so it will be you that pays."

Oscar dips his head in agreement. Just what the hell is he doing?

"Tell me, Oscar, how far are you willing to go for the girl that has taken your heart, hm?" I feel a strong arm reach around my neck, tugging it back forcefully. I hiss in response. Oscar spins round and goes for the man, his hand getting as far as the man's throat. "Get your fucking hands off her!" Two huge men dressed in black drag him away, kicking. He's roaring and fighting against them, but they're solid muscles. They hold his arms behind his back, and the other guy kicks his legs from under him. When he falls to his knees, the guy in front of him punches his jaw so hard I hear a crack. I whimper in response because the sharp end of a knife is being held at my jugular, and even swallowing makes me wince in pain. I can see they're tying his hands with rope. Taking away his control. I squeeze my eyes closed, knowing how much this is going to be hurting Oscar inside.

Oscar's feral eyes snap open and flare in defiance, not an ounce of fear in them.

"Take his fucking shirt off. The weirdo doesn't like the feeling of being touched. He's about to feel every fucking thing," Flemming spits out.

Oscar's Adam's apple bobs as his eyes latch on to mine. Strength seeps into me. My strong, fearless man might have been brought to his knees, but he's going to show them it'll take more than being touched to break him.

The guy in front of Oscar brandishes a knife, not unlike the one being held against my throat. He slashes at Oscar's shirt, then bends to rip it from his body, but as he does, Oscar headbutts the guy's nose, causing blood to spray out. "Fuck, you busted my nose."

Oscar's lip quirks in response, but it slowly disappears when a cattle prod is brought forward. Flemming raises his hand to someone, and the prod springs to life with a buzzing noise. Terror wracks through me. I try to shuffle and move. I try to tug, but the knife digs into my skin.

Oscar's calming voice halts me. "Paige, it's okay. Breathe, just breathe."

I whimper in response to his voice, his words. Where the hell are his brothers?

"Ahhhhh, fuck," Oscar roars. His body stiffens at the force of the shock that Flemming assaults him with.

His head drops forward, he pants, and then Flemming repeats the process. Tears flow down my face as I have to sit back and watch in horror and disbelief as they torture Oscar time after time.

"P-p-pleas—" I can't finish my sentence because I can feel the blood trickling down my neck as I try each time to speak, to beg them to stop. My head feels woozy, but just as I want to close my eyes, a whooshing noise pierces the air, and a heavy object hits the concrete floor with a thump.

Oscar

I wish she'd stop fighting. I wish she'd stop fighting for me. For us.

The pain is unbearable, but I refuse to give in. The moment I do, I will lose sight of her, and I need to know my brothers have saved her.

Last time I calculated, there were four minutes out. I hope I'm fucking wrong.

Paige stops whimpering, and when I can focus again, I see blood trickling down her neck. Is this it? Is she gone?

I try to stabilize myself once again, my hand searching behind my back for the knife in my sock, but I'm too dizzy to find it.

A smooth, whooshing noise pierces the room, bringing with it a newfound strength and determination. Hope.

The prick behind Paige drops to the floor, and suddenly, all I want is to reach her once again.

My fingers scramble to find my knife, and when they finally latch on to it, I make quick work of cutting off the rope. My eyes latch onto Flemming at the same time his latch onto mine. He's taken cover behind a table, but as soon as he realizes I'm free, he lifts his gun to face me.

His finger presses the trigger almost in slow motion. I suck in a breath. My last breath.

But it doesn't matter because she's free.

Someone throws themselves in front of me before falling to the floor with the impact of the bullet meant for me.

I don't have time to register anything but taking my savior's gun and lifting it, putting two bullets in Flemming's head.

I try to get to my feet but fail. The door bursts open and carnage between my brothers and Flemming's remaining men ensues. "Oscar, stay down."

I duck my head down, still cloudy from the shocks. My eyes latch on to the figure on the floor—my da. I crawl toward him, a hole in his chest and blood flowing out of the open wound. I turn and grab the remains of my shirt before pressing it tightly against his wound.

"Oscar." His voice is wheezy and low, giving me no choice but to duck to hear him better. He licks his lips, his chest rising slowly. He's going to die; I know it. He knows it. Da raises a hand and places it on mine. His touch makes me flinch, but he tightens his grip, the tremble in him giving away his struggle in doing so, but he's determined to hold on to me. I can't ever remember his touch being so purposeful and not out of anger, not out of hate. His voice is a wheeze, weak and vulnerable. Everything he is not. "I'm sorry." His breath comes out sharp, desperate to disperse his words. "I'm proud of you, son. Your Ma was right, you know. Different doesn't mean less. You stepped out of the shadows, son, and into the light." I swear there's water in his eyes. My heart skips a beat at the thought he's showing me emotion. "You're an O'Connell, and I'm sorry I never told you before." His voice chokes at the end, and he leaves me with a sad smile, his eyes empty and one single lone tear trailing down his face.

My heart pounds in my chest as I follow the tear, feeling my own welling behind my eyes. All because the man I loathed my entire life finally sees me, finally accepts me, and he's not even here anymore for me to revel in it.

Gone.

A hand slaps me on the back, forcing the only connection I ever felt with my da to evaporate. "Old fucker dead, then?" Reece stares at him emotionlessly.

"What the hell are you doing here?" I snap.

"Pft, you think I was going to let these fuckers orchestrate saving you? Fuck that." He smirks.

I stand to my feet and stare down at Da's lifeless body.

"Old bastard had to take the credit, huh?" Bren quips a brow at me, then nods toward da.

I swallow thickly, unsure of what this new emotion I'm feeling is.

Sympathy toward my father? Pride at his words? Closure?

"Your woman passed out, but I don't think you should let Finn stand over her too much longer. You don't want her opening her eyes to see him brandishing his knife like Rambo on crack." Bren chuckles.

My head spins, and my balance wobbles as I make my way over toward Paige, relieving Finn of his protective duties.

I kneel and tuck a stray lock of her hair behind her ear, my breath stuttering at her beauty. Her eyes flutter open as though sensing I'm here.

"Are you okay?"

I smirk at her words, her concern for me always at the forefront. "I am."

She swallows, and tears fill her eyes. "I love you, Os."

I stare down at her vulnerable face. "Yeah, I love you too."

Her eyebrows knit together. "You do?"

"Don't fucking ask me to say it again because I won't. I admitted it once." I quirk my lip at my own words.

Her soft hand touches my jaw, sending a shiver down my spine.

"I won't."

I narrow my eyes on her. Women like that sappy shit, and she's saying she won't ask for it. "Promise?"

She breaks out into a grin that would bring me to my knees if I wasn't already on them. "No."

I roll my own eyes. "Of course, you will."

I scoop her into my unsteady arms.

"And I'll ask you to say it back."

Standing tall, I hold her close to me.

"That's not fucking happening," I snap back.

When I step outside into the light, the sun almost

blinds me, but not nearly as much as the fiery spitfire in my arms.

I have everything I never knew I was able to achieve. I've finally stepped out of the shadows and into the light.

Finally, I see myself as the man I've always dreamed of becoming.

Oscar

Four months later

"Ma, pass the sauce, would ya?" My eyes snap up toward Finn's voice. He bounces Prince up and down on his knee while shoveling another forkful of meatloaf.

Prince turns his deep blue eyes onto me, scowling at me.

"Where did you say Reece was again?" Angel asks Lily.

"Studying." Lily smiles back, unaware. Angel catches my eyes and smirks knowingly. It's not even fucking funny how obvious it is that Reece isn't studying. The only thing he'll be studying is the girl he's currently obsessed with.

"He's so well-behaved." Sky sighs in her own innocent little world. All our eyes turn to hers; a mixture of shock and disbelief marring our faces. Is she fucking serious?

I sometimes wonder if they injected her with something at the compound she was brought up in... something that makes her see rainbows and unicorns and other fantasy shit that nobody believes in but her.

"Baby, I think Seb shit." Bren sniffs the air like a bloodhound.

Sky flicks her blonde locks over her shoulder. "Go change him, then."

Bren jolts. "Baby?"

Sky's eyes bug out, and she nods toward Seb's highchair. She tilts her head toward Seb, mimicking Bren to deal with him. He starts a tirade of mumbling. "Fucking Jesus. Wish I'd not said a damn thing now."

"Bren?"

Bren lifts Seb from his highchair, then turns toward Sky. "Mmm?"

"Can you do Sam, too?"

His shoulders sag. "I gotta?"

Sky nods and smiles up at him as though he's some kind of king. "Yes, please." His eyes flare, and I have to glance away because my brother looks two seconds away from taking Sky on the table.

"Can you believe I had to change the wedding date again, all because that old bastard died? It's so fucking close now I cannot fucking wait!" Con beams, virtually bouncing in his chair with excitement. The number of date changes for this wedding has been ridiculous, not to mention the amount of planning that goes into it. Of course, it all has to go through me too. It's a good thing I've decided to outsource some of the security this time to STORM Enterprises. It takes some of the pressure off of me.

"Uncle Con, you owe the swear jar." Charlie springs up from beside Finn.

"That's my girl." He grins at her as she goes to fetch the overflowing jar from the kitchen counter. The kid carries it everywhere with her. I swear she'll have a college fund before she reaches her teens in a few years.

"Daddy, I want a rollercoaster at the wedding." Keen's soft voice makes the table break out in laughter.

Con leans forward toward his son, who is perched on the table stroking Pussy.

"Yeah? What kind of rollercoaster?"

"Jesus!" Cal pinches the bridge of his nose and stares up at the ceiling.

"Like a big, fast one? Or a small one?" Con prompts Keen.

"One I get to ride on with Pussy and Peppa." Keen strokes his hands softly down both pets. I push my plate closer to me; the thought of pet hair landing in my dinner is not an option.

"Con, we're not having a rollercoaster at the wedding." Will chastises her soon-to-be husband.

Con scoffs. "I'm in charge of the wedding. If I have to have that douche ex of yours at the wedding, I can have a fucking rollercoaster."

"You're impossible," she snaps.

Bren walks back into the room shirtless, his broad muscles and tattoos on full display, making Con roll his eyes when his fiancée, Will, takes a little too long checking him out. He carries Seb in one arm and cradles Sam in the other.

"Bren, where'd your shirt go?" Sky asks innocently, as

though someone stole it from his back and he didn't take it off himself. I almost want to scream at her naivety.

"They shit on it."

"Again?"

Bren grimaces. "Yep." He pops the p. "Ma, it's on your bed. Can you clean it for me?"

Is he for real? He left a shitty shirt on Ma's bed? Dirty fucking bastard. I tighten my hand on my fork. My family members are fucking pigs. Thank God it's just Paige and me. Ma nods at Bren's words like the good housekeeper she's been trained to be.

"How are you coping, Ma?" Cal asks in a soft voice.

Ma smiles and gives us a shrug. "I guess I've always been preparing myself for the day it would happen. I just never expected it to end as it did, that's all, but I'm proud of him and you, Oscar. Very proud of you." She pats my hand tenderly like she always has.

The quietness of the room makes me uncomfortable, so I spring to my feet. "I've got to go. Paige should be home by now."

"She knocked up yet?" Finn chuckles.

"Absolutely fucking not!" I snap back and head toward the door.

Leaving behind a chorus of mumbles and giggles.

Epilogue

Oscar

I adjust the chain a little more, stretching her out into the perfect star. Jerking my cock in my hand, I tighten my fist around it while spreading the pre-cum over the engorged head. It's ready, so fucking ready to come in her it hurts.

Paige licks her lips, making me hiss in anticipation. "Are you ready for me, Paige?"

"Yes." Her voice is breathy, and she's panting with need. After fucking her mouth as soon as I walked in from dinner, I wasted no time in bringing her to her old room and stripping her down.

"You want my cock hard and fast?"

I climb between her legs and position the head of my cock at the entrance of her tight little hole. Flicking my finger over her clit, down her slit, and back again, I push into her tight muscled wall.

I moan in pleasure at her body sucking me in.

"Os... Os, please." I gaze up to find her lips parted

and her eyes filled with need. I grip her throat, loving the feeling of her pulse under the tips of my fingers. I press firmer when her pussy clenches on me, moving rhythmically in and out of her. The sensation of her slickness coating my cock makes my eyes roll into the back of my head.

I bend down to take her nipple in my mouth, but she winces slightly. I stop moving. "What's wrong?"

She licks her lips again, making my cock twitch at the action.

"I'm tender. I used to be like this before I was on the contraceptive injection."

I smirk at her.

"What's that look for, Oscar?"

I stare into her emerald eyes, the ones that hold so much love, loyalty, and forgiveness in them, I know I can share my truths with her, and she'll love me no matter what.

"I asked the doctor not to update your contraception at your last appointment."

"What?" Confusion coats her face. "I had an injection, Oscar." She shakes her head as though I have it wrong. I balk at her audacity.

"It was a fertility enhancer."

Her facial expression is blank. "A what?" I can feel her heart racing beneath me, pumping hard against my chest.

I sit back on my knees to look down at her, my cock still firmly in place. "Fertility enhancer."

"Why?" Her lip trembles.

"Because you wanted a baby, and I decided to give you one."

Her eyes widen. I roll my hips, eager to change the subject of having to explain the gift I'm giving her in more detail.

She tries to move her hand, no doubt to stop me from moving, but the chain restrains her, making my lip curl sadistically.

"You want a baby?" She scoffs.

"I want you to have the baby you want, and I want it to be mine," I clarify because, in all honesty, I don't like babies, but the idea of a small Paige or Oscar that I can mold into another genius is growing on me.

Her eyes fill with tears that make my heart constrict.

"I love you, Oscar."

"Mmm," I grind my hips and move. "I know," I smirk, knowing the words she wants me to whisper.

"A lot, just so you know." She raises an eyebrow at me. "Now fuck me hard and fill me with your baby."

I take ahold of her throat. "I'm going to fuck a baby into you, Paige." I slam into her hard, pull out, and slam into her again. Her tits bounce at the force of my thrusts. "Seeing your stomach swell, knowing I filled your pussy and gave you our baby, is going to drive me in. Fucking. Sane." I pump harder and faster, her walls pulling me in.

"More. I need more."

I tighten my grip on her pulse point. "Take my cum. Fuck, Paige, you want my baby so bad, don't you?"

"Yes. Yes, Oscar. Give me everything. Give me your cum. I want your baby."

And just like that, I thrust into her. Harder, faster,

and more powerful than ever before. My orgasm is ripped from me, so strong, so intense; I fall on top of her as blackness consumes my vision.

The only thing I can see is a light.

A glimmer of what's to come...

THE END

Oscar

Groaning, I roll over onto my side when my phone vibrates beside me. Glancing at the clock, I realize it's too fucking early for calls. Two thirty-six, to be precise. Reece's name lights up the screen.

"Go on."

"Oscar? It's Reece." He's panting like he's been running or something. Reece never runs...

"Of course, it's you. I don't need telling whose name came up on my damn phone," I snap, annoyed he's woken me up.

"I... I need help."

This gets my attention. I jump; my body curled tight at his words.

"I just killed a man."

Want a little more?

Would you like **more of Oscar and Paige?**

Come and sign up to BJ Alpha's newsletter for an exclusive extra scene and be the first to hear about the up-and-coming events and book news.

Use the link to get your copy of Oscar and Paige's extended epilogue now:

Oscar and Paige Extended Epilogue

COMING SOON!!!

Don't miss **CON'S Wedding Novella**
The Final Vow
Available for pre-order now:
The Final Vow

Acknowledgments

1 year on and six books later!
Tee the lady that started it all for me.
Thank you forever!

I must start with where it all began, TL Swan. When I started reading your books, I never realized I was in a place I needed pulling out of. Your stories brought me back to myself.

With your constant support and the network created as 'Cygnet Inkers' I was able to create something I never realized was possible, I genuinely thought I'd had my day. You made me realize tomorrow is just the beginning.

To some special friends.
Kate, I don't know where to start, words quite literally do not seem enough to thank you. I feel incredibly honored to be having this journey with you by my side.
Thank you for everything.

Emma and Heather. Thank you for being there for me, daily.

To Sadie Kincaid, thank you once again for everything.

You're a true inspiration hun and I wish you every bit of success coming your way.

Martina Dale, AK Landow and Jade Dollston thank you for the support and messages each day. You make me laugh when I need it the most.

Jenn and Tash, I look forward to our messages (for multiple reasons). You girls have such beautiful souls and are so supportive, thank you.

To the ladies in **Cygnets**, thank you for your constant support.

Swan Squad

This group of ladies that Tee has brought together is amazing for so many reasons.

I'm not sure I can do this thank you justice. But just know I appreciate your support more and in many cases friendships. Thank you ladies.

Bren, Sharon H, Patricia, Caroline, Claire, Anita, Sue and Mary-Anne a special thank ladies.

Beta Readers

Thank you to my Beta Readers for your continual support.

Jaclyn, Kate, Heather, Rhi and Savannah.

A special mention to Libby, who gets my manuscript in a complete mess but goes above and beyond to help me. Thank you Libs.

ARC Team

To my ARC readers thank you. I have such an amazing team and I need you to know I appreciate every message, share, graphic and review. Thank you so much.

To my world.

To my boys, I'm incredibly proud of you both.
You're first and foremost my greatest creation.
When you eventually read these acknowledgements, I want you both to know whatever dream you have I believe in you and I'm proud of you. Just be happy.

To my hubby, the J in my BJ.
You're a good en. Thank you for learning how to cook while I work.
One year on and look at what you've helped me create.
Without you I wouldn't be BJ Alpha.
Love you trillions!

And finally...

Thank you of my readers, I appreciate each and every page you turn.

About the Author

BJ Alpha lives in the UK with her hubby, two teenage sons and three fur babies.

She loves to write and read about hot, alpha males and feisty females.

Follow me on my social media pages:

Facebook: BJ Alpha

My readers group: BJ's Reckless Readers

Instagram: BJ Alpha

Also by B J Alpha

Secrets and Lies Series

Born Series

Printed in Great Britain
by Amazon

22648910R00225